William Sharp, John Parker Anderson

Life of Percy Bysshe Shelley

William Sharp, John Parker Anderson

Life of Percy Bysshe Shelley

ISBN/EAN: 9783337415532

Printed in Europe, USA, Canada, Australia, Japan

Cover: Foto ©Raphael Reischuk / pixelio.de

More available books at **www.hansebooks.com**

LIFE

OF

PERCY BYSSHE SHELLEY

BY

WILLIAM SHARP

———— ————

LONDON

WALTER SCOTT

24 WARWICK LANE, PATERNOSTER ROW

1887

CONTENTS.

CHAPTER IV.

CHAPTER V.

CHAPTER VI.

NOTE.

I T is unnecessary, in a note to a biography which
naturally is based upon all prior records of the poet
with whom it deals, to mention the authorities whose
writings have been read or consulted. But a special
acknowledgment of indebtedness is due to Professor
Edward Dowden, whose two comprehensive volumes on
Shelley form the completest and most reliable record
extant, and at the same time constitute the worthiest
monument wherewith the poet's memory has yet been
honoured.

LIFE OF SHELLEY.

CHAPTER I.

THERE are certain luminaries in whose flames
critics delight to singe their wings. Goethe and
Heine, Shelley and Rossetti have been and will remain
stars to fascinate, perplex, and overcome many a critic-
moth. And of all good poets, perhaps, nay assuredly,
there is none who in his genius and personality is at once
so perplexing and fascinating as Shelley. He is worshipped,
and he is not less ardently abhorred ; he is upheld as a
demi-god, and abjured as a sweet-voiced demon ; his
teachings are preached with fervour from the house-tops,
and are denounced with equal vehemence from neigh-
bouring summits. One admirer gives us a picture
of the poet which is so affecting as to make it seem
sacrilege to look with critical eyes upon aught which the
latter did or said ; another gives us a Real Shelley, the
caricature of an apparition. There are among us many
who look upon all admirers of the poet as the only true
children of redemption ; there are others who regard the
author of " The Revolt of Islam " as one of the most
potent latter-day vicars of the devil. To the immense
majority of people all this is mere empty clamour.

They know that they love certain poems, certain wonderful lyrics, but they do not expect to find the author thereof either an incarnation of the principle of evil, or a new Son of God. The people are so much wiser than those who would instruct them. "We know the 'Skylark,' the 'Cloud,' the 'Sensitive Plant' by heart, and we admire and revere the beauty and noble thought enshrined in 'Prometheus Unbound' and 'Alastor,' and what we want to know about the author are those facts which are beyond dispute. As for the colouring of the latter, we can do that for ourselves." This is what the popular sentiment amounts to in the instance of Shelley. So much has been written about him that his real personality threatens to vanish completely from the view of the present and of coming generations. What also is feared by some, at least, who have the fame of the poet deeply at heart, is that the rare bloom of his genius will altogether disappear in the mists of conjecture and dispute which now prevail; the poet will fade, and the socialist-philosopher will arise; the singer will become the political or sectarian stalking-horse. Instead of "Adonais," and an unparalleled lyric voice, there will be the Vegetarian and Irish pamphlets and much wearisome bluster and counter-fury.

Only sixty-five years have elapsed since, with all its extraordinary power and promise, a brilliant life ceased suddenly amid a brief turmoil of wind and sea. Yet already is there a Shelley myth, which, perhaps, even the efforts of the most intelligent students have not wholly made clear; it is certain that if the poet had lived in remote days, the transmitted records of

his life would have been so overclouded with fabulous
and conjectural statements that we should have had
little real knowledge of him.   Notwithstanding (perhaps
because of) all that has been written concerning Shelley,
it is difficult to encounter unanimity of opinion ; wheresoever two or three are gathered together, there of a
surety is the poet alternately black and white.   There is
no more noteworthy evidence of the extraordinary place
Shelley holds in men's minds than this endless ebb and
flow of opinion concerning him, this confused admiration
and distraught hatred, this instinctive love, and this per-
suasive antagonism.

The moment we seek to identify a poet with his poetry
we are in danger of illusion.   A man is not the less a
man because he sings more subtly sweet than a syren.
There is a distinction between a Voice and a Soul.   A
nightingale's twilight plaint in the beechwood is not the
less wonderful if we learn that a happy family of glow-
worms has known ruin in order to sustain the musician
in his high conceit of song.   What then can it really
matter to those of a later generation if this poet occasionally imbibed more than was good for him, if that
poet infringed a majority of the commandments ?   Marlowe's " mighty line " has not the less sonorous music
because he was addicted to loose company, and died in
a tavern brawl.

It seems advisable to preface any new life of Shelley
with some such remarks as these, for so prevalent is
the tendency to condemn or admire the man in exact
ratio to our condemnation or admiration of his poetry,
that a biographer must be prepared to find many readers

with an undue bias in one or other direction. The present writer yields to none in his reverence for the finest work of Shelley the poet, while Shelley the man has ever attracted his affectionate sympathy and admiration. At the same time, he neither feels called upon to admire all that Shelley wrote and did, nor to omit recognition of the fact that the poet and the man acted often antagonistically to each other, as if, indeed, each were a distinct identity, united by no other bond than a literary partnership.

It is my main endeavour in this short life of Shelley to avoid all misstatement and exaggeration ; to give as real a narrative of his life, from the most reliable sources, as lies within my power; to recount without detailed criticism and as simply and concisely as practicable, the record of his poetic achievements. To this end I shall chiefly rely on anecdote and explanatory detail, on poems and passages noteworthy for their autobiographical or idiosyncratic value, and on indisputable facts. I have no ambition to do otherwise than follow in the footsteps of prior biographers of the poet; in a book of such limited dimensions as this it would be unreasonable to expect more than a condensation of all really important material. Indeed, since the recent publication of Professor Dowden's memorable work, there is no possibility of room for another biography on a more ample scale. The present monograph is little more than a precipitate of that and other invaluable works which have preceded it.

There were strange rumours perturbing the minds and consciences of men at the season of the birth of Percy

Bysshe Shelley. The French nation was in a ferment
with vague prognostications, fears, and hopes, and all
Europe vibrated with the electric breath of revolution
which emanated from the human volcano of Paris. Even
in England, guarded by the sea from the immediate influx
of a more ungovernable tide than that of Ocean, men spoke
with bated breath of what had happened and what was
yet on the forefront of the time. Those who trace in
mortal lives the conjunction of starry influences will find
food for suggestion in the fact that Shelley, the poet of
rebellion, was born at a moment when all the stars of
tumult and revolt fought in their courses against the
established order of things spiritual and temporal.

At the manor of Field Place, near Horsham, in Sussex,
Percy Bysshe Shelley was born on Saturday, the 4th of
August, in the year 1792. Those curious in such matters
can see the bedroom in which he first saw the light of
what he was to find so troublous a world. Over the
fireplace there is an engraved plate bearing the inscription of his name in full, his date of birth, and the
following appropriate and eloquent lines by Mr. Richard
Garnett—

> " Shrine of the dawning speech and thought
>   Of Shelley, sacred be
> To all who bow where Time has brought
>   Gifts to Eternity."

A few weeks later, on the 7th of September, the eldest
child of Timothy and Elizabeth Shelley was christened
with the two names now so familiar to all lovers of
English poetry. The parents selected the name "Percy,"

it would seem, as one which had been borne by various
Shelleys of previous generations, while Bysshe was the
name of the boy's grandfather. A detailed account of
the Shelley ancestry would be out of place here.   In the
genesis of genius what is interesting is the immediate
ancestry—the four or five preceding generations—of the
poet or writer under consideration.   Beyond the fifth
generation there are almost certain to be links missing
in the chain of transmitted faculties and tendencies :
generally, indeed, there is no possibility of discovering the
pominant or modifying qualities gained from the maternal
side—in itself a cause quite sufficient to render the
tracing of hereditary characteristics the merest speculation.   If the lineal descent of a great poet could be
traced paternally and maternally for several centuries, no
doubt the result would be of great psychological interest
and value ; but as it is against all the laws of nature that
the blood of the male stock can remain invariably dominant through successive generations, the value of ordinary
genealogical disquisitions must be considerably discounted.   What is worthy of note is that, as Professor
Dowden has remarked, these elder Shelleys were "conspicuous by their devotion to falling or desperate
causes"; an assertion which immediately becomes significant when we remember how strenuous the poet ever
was in his defiance of tyranny, and in his adherence to
unpopular sides of national questions.

Bysshe Shelley, the grandfather of the poet, was noted
for his comely face and figure, his fascinating demeanour,
his reckless disregard of the proprieties, and (in his later
years) for his miserly avarice.   Some thirty-eight years

before his elder brother's death he won the heart of a
pretty heiress, a Miss Mary Catherine Michell, daughter
of a clergyman. The union which succeeded their elopement (for Miss Michell was only eighteen, and her
friends were antagonistic to the marriage—hence Bysshe's
having taken the decision into his own hands) lasted
eight years ; three children were the result of it, of whom
one was a boy. This son was christened Timothy, and,
in due time, became the father of the poet. After the
death of his wife, and when close upon his fortieth year,
Bysshe Shelley cavalierly wooed and (perhaps even to his
own surprise) won the affections of an heiress of noble
lineage, with whom he lived in marriage till he reached his
fiftieth year: of this union were born seven children. With
the money brought to him by marriage, and by his succession in 1790 to the Fen Place and Field Place properties,
Bysshe Shelley was fairly to be considered a wealthy
man. In 1806 he began to build, at great expense, that
Castle Goring which he never finished ; and contempo-
raneously he received the honour of a baronetcy, on
account of electioneering and other political services.
With his new dignities, however, Sir Bysshe Shelley of
Castle Goring did not the more surround himself with
the amenities of life. Although to the last a gentleman
of refinement both in appearance and manner, his
avariciousness increased yearly, and he was wont to
spend much of his time in Horsham taverns, there
not drinking, but arguing with domineering emphasis.
Latterly he lived in a small house in most undignified
state. When he was created a baronet his grandson,
Percy Bysshe, was just about to begin his Eton ex-

periences. The boy had a certain measure of awe for his grandfather, though that his respect for him could only have been superficial is evident from the fact that he was wont to overhear—and on occasion to startle or shock strangers by imitating—the old man's unseemly vehemence of speech.

Sir Bysshe's son Timothy married, in 1791, Elizabeth Pilfold, a woman, by all accounts, of rare beauty; and, so far as can be ascertained amid many prejudiced narratives, of well-balanced mind and temper. After the birth of Percy there succeeded five children; four girls, named respectively Elizabeth, Mary, Hellen, and Margaret; and a boy, christened John. It was natural that of such a union the offspring should be pleasant of aspect, but the eldest child was something more than merely comely. Of exceptionally fair complexion, the beauty of his face lay mainly in the sensitive mouth and the large blue eyes; long locks of dull-gold hair curled to his neck; and he seems to have had that peculiar poise of the head which partly is due to refinement of race, and is partly, it would seem, a characteristic of very sensitive natures. Though in youth and manhood the features were somewhat irregular, the expression which animated them became of such rare sweetness and refinement that a famous painter declared it was simply impossible to paint the poet's portrait, as he was " too beautiful."

From very early childhood Shelley was an imaginative and mentally restless child. Trifles unnoticed by most children seem to have made keen and permanent impression upon him—the sound of wind, the leafy whisper of trees, running water. The imaginative faculties came so early into play that the unconscious desire to create resulted in the invention of weird tales of legendary creatures, tales sometimes based on remote fact; in attempted delusion of neighbours; and in the experience of more or less positive hallucinations. We owe much of our scanty knowledge of this period of the poet's life to the fragmentary information in the letters of his sister Hellen; information, however, the value of which has occasionally to be somewhat discounted as not being directly reminiscent. It is clear that he was invariably a kind and gentle brother, displaying a consideration for his younger sisters which contrasts favourably with the conduct of most lads during the early years of the schoolboy stage. Great days were these for the little girls at Field Place when Bysshe was at home for the holidays; he would walk about with them, and tell them many wonderful things; he would take one of them on his knees, and thrill the soul of his listener with awful tales of wizards, hobgoblins, and secret passages. The "Great Tortoise" was long a theme of endless fascination. This strange creature, unseen of any, abode in Warnham Pond; many a romance concerning it was told by the inventive Bysshe, and if a bull roared in some distant meadow, if a tree fell in the woodland, if midsummer thunder rumbled mysteriously in skiey spaces, the sounds were always accounted to the "Great Tortoise." In later years the "Great Old Snake" usurped its predecessor's place—an interesting circumstance to close students of Shelley's poetry, where serpents are frequently and most effectively introduced. The "snake" in question had a genuine existence, and met an accidental death through

the scythe of a gardener. The boy was generally beloved,
though from his early childhood he seems to have
puzzled his worthy father, a choleric, narrow-minded, but
excellent-hearted squire, who has been absurdly abused
because he had the misfortune to hold radically different
views from those of his son, and because that son went
contrary to his desires in many things. It is suggestive
that most of Bysshe's in-door tales, narrated in the grim
hours of shadow, were grotesque or terrifying ; and hardly
less so (to them) were the games in which he induced
Elizabeth, Mary, or Hellen to take part. The children
would be robbers, led by a daring chief; discoverers in
some terrible land where awful revelations lurked in store
for them ; they would even personate spirits or fiends,
the illusion being intensified by the blue flame which
Bysshe would light and carry about in a small fire-stove.
Even as a very young boy he took the keenest interest in
chemical and electrical experiments ; and while—as his
sister Hellen has recorded—his sisters would sometimes
tremble with apprehension when he called upon them to
assist him, he never persisted in any experiment if he
saw that he was causing pain or real fear. There was
nothing of the cold-blooded experimentalist in Shelley at
any time of his life, and it was in all sincerity that, in the
beautiful opening of " Alastor," he wrote—

> " If no bright bird, insect, or gentle beast
> I consciously have injured, but still loved
> And cherished these my kindred—"

The poet's faculty of remembrance was wont to
surprise many of his friends, and even as a little boy his

memory was remarkable. Hellen Shelley records, on the authority of her and Bysshe's mother, that, when a small child, Gray's lines on the Cat and the Goldfish were repeated by him word for word after a single reading. Shelley's earliest regular instruction commenced when he was six years old. Till his tenth year he remained under the educational guidance of the Rev. Mr. Edwards, of Warnham; though these four intervening years were mainly spent in gaining bodily vigour. It is a common mistake to suppose that the poet was an ethereal being from his infancy onward; at no period (as his most discerning admirers will emphatically agree in insisting) was he too far removed from common humanity to be other than a genuine creature of flesh and blood. At a time when the author of the "Prometheus Unbound" and "The Cenci" was intensely mentally occupied with dreams of splendid poetic achievement, we find him following with vivid interest and practical good sense the public affairs which were then perturbing the whole nation, and even writing to a friend to be cautious about investments in home funds at a season of such universal disturbance and political uncertainty. Shelley seems to have naturally been of a vigorous constitution, though he had always more or less of that appearance of delicacy which is so far from rare among emotional and imaginative young folk of either sex. That he suffered considerably in his later years is undeniable, but certainly the mysterious pains which affected him in Italy were for the most part the penalties incurred by his habitual neglect of the body, by his occasional use of narcotics, and by a fitful asceticism which was undoubtedly the

shadow of the spiritual and intellectual light in which he
habitually lived.

Every student of Shelley's poetry must recollect his love
of making fragile craft out of paper or iris-flags, and
setting them a-sail on stream or pond.   How early this
sport, for a sport of irresistible fascination it always was
with him, was habitually indulged in is uncertain ; but
the poet certainly had himself as a very young child in
view when, in "Rosalind and Helen," he wrote—

> "He was a gentle boy,
> And in all gentle sports took joy ;
> Oft in a dry leaf for a boat,
> With a small feather for a sail,
> His fancy on that spring would float,
> If some invisible breeze would stir
> Its marble calm : "

When Bysshe—the name invariably used by his home
circle, probably out of deference to "Uncle Bysshe"
—was ten years old he was promoted from Mr. Edwards'
care to that of a Dr. Greenlaw, who presided over
some three score youngsters at Sion House, Brentford.   Although with the commencement of his second
decade Shelley began to experience the inequalities
and petty bitternesses of life, the time spent at Sion
House was by no means a wretched one, though the boy
certainly was not happy.   One of his biographers, who
was also a second cousin to the poet, was contempo-
raneously at Sion House, and it is to Captain Medwin's
published reminiscences that we owe the most interesting facts concerning this period of Shelley's early

life. Young as he was, that mental fever, that splendid intellectual delirium as it might more adequately
be termed when referred to in connection with his
maturer years, which is the common heritage of genius,
had filled him with the spirit of unrest, dissatisfaction,
and inquiry. For one thing, the mental stimulus too
strongly dominated the physical energies for him to care
much for the ordinary sports of boyhood, sports habitually indulged in by his companions whether in the mood
for them or not, and taken almost equally as matters of
routine as the less congenial lessons. Again, Sion House
Academy was frequented by the sons of tradesmen,
between whom and Shelley there was the shadow of a
mutual, if never very clearly defined or very militant
antagonism—a half-suspicious, half-jealous resentment on
the one hand, and on the other a quick scorn for certain
trifling, though none the less real, vulgarities. While
Shelley was still a youth he lost all perception of class
distinctions, and gladly took for granted the essential
equality of all men who could meet on common
intellectual ground. But that even genius cannot
always free itself of conventional bonds is evident from
the fact that Keats undoubtedly resented Shelley's
superior birth, when circumstances brought them together, and never felt quite at his ease with one
whom he was ever prone to suspect of condescen
sion. Keats must have been one of the most lovable,
and, in general, one of the most sociable of men, but
his somewhat arrogant and patronizing way of speaking
of Shelley is not to his credit. In fairness, however,
it must be added that the elder poet's declamatory

emphasis on political and social rights and wrongs alienated Keats' sympathies more than any real or fancied implication of social superiority on Shelley's part.

The latter's almost feminine beauty, his look of natural gentleness and innocence, tempted the boys of Sion House to affront and torment one whom they at first considered a milksop. The poor lad, well-bred, sensitive, already a dreamer of dreams, an alien among his fellows, experienced many unhappy hours during his stay at Dr. Greenlaw's academy. The majority of the boys considered him as fair prey : fagging was then an institution in full force, and all the petty tyrannies which that evil system permits were exercised upon the unfortunate youngster.

Shelley's faculty for the acquirement of knowledge, more especially knowledge of foreign languages, was quite exceptional. He was in this way all the more a cause of astonishment to his comrades from the fact that he never seemed to study, but to pass most of his time in reverie and watching the clouds, in scribbling sketches of cedars and other trees, and in "mooning." Books, especially fiction, and more particularly Mrs. Radcliffe's and other weird and sombre tales of the supernatural and the horrible, were his chief delight. This morbid literature sowed seeds in Shelley's mind which at first resulted in a sterile and valueless harvest, but which later on became fruitful indeed. Every spare moment he could secure for himself was spent in solitary reading or musing.

I might have laid more stress on Shelley's unhappiness at Sion House Academy, for undoubtedly

his early days at Brentford and Eton had a great
effect upon his character, emphasizing what was noble
in his nature, and developing certain traits which,
without being either good or evil in themselves, were
later in his life to cause both him and his friends real
distress. He was not, however, invariably unhappy.
His delight in the humblest aspects of nature, his
romances and favourite books, his day-dreams, brought
him much relief and pleasure; and it was with real joy
he received letters from home, especially from the little
sisters whom he so loved. Still, the memory of those
early days was always for him full of painful reminiscence.
A touching record of his boyish sufferings is to be found
in the dedicatory prelude to "Laon and Cythna" (more
widely known as "The Revolt of Islam"), written years
later when the poet was smarting under cruel suffering
inflicted upon him by Governmental interference with his
rights as a father. Lady Shelley and one or two other
biographers have supposed that the famous stanzas in
question were written by Shelley reminiscently of his
life at Eton, but it seems almost certain that they have
reference to his first bitter experiences at Sion House.

" Thoughts of great deeds were mine, dear friend, when first
  The clouds which wrap this world from youth did pass.
  I do remember well the hour which burst
  My spirit's sleep : a fresh May dawn it was,
  When I walked forth upon the glittering grass,
  And wept, I knew not why ; until there rose
  From the near schoolroom voices that, alas !
  Were but one echo from a world of woes—
The harsh and grating strife of tyrants and of foes.

And then I clasped my hands and looked around
But none was near to mock my streaming eyes,
Which poured their warm drops on the sunny ground :
So, without shame, I spake : " I will be wise,
And just, and free, and mild, if in me lies
Such power ; for I grow weary to behold
The selfish and the strong still tyrannize
Without reproach or check." I then controlled
My tears ; my heart grew calm ; and I was meek and bold.

And from that hour did I, with earnest thought,
Heap knowledge from forbidden mines of lore ;
Yet nothing that my tyrants knew or taught
I cared to learn ; but from that secret store
Wrought linkèd armour for my soul, before
It might walk forth, to war among mankind.
Thus, power and hope were strengthened more and more
Within me, till there came upon my mind
A sense of loneliness, a thirst with which I pined."

In the main the self-account given in these stanzas is
genuine, though as Shelley was so apt a pupil he can
hardly be said to have learnt nothing from what his
" tyrants knew or taught ": probably what he meant to
convey was that his most vital mental development was
due more to the indirect knowledge which he voluntarily
acquired.

The narrative of Shelley's early boyhood may be
closed with Medwin's description of his cousin's personal appearance at this time. " He was tall for his
age," says Medwin, "slightly and delicately built, and
rather narrow-chested, with a complexion fair and ruddy,
a face rather long than oval. His features, not regularly
handsome, were set off by a profusion of silky brown
hair, that curled naturally. The expression of his coun-

tenance was one of exceeding sweetness and innocence. His blue eyes were very large and prominent. They were at times, when he was abstracted, as he often was in contemplation, dull, and as it were, insensible to external objects; at others they flashed with the fire of intelligence. His voice was soft and low, but broken in its tones,—when anything much interested him, harsh and unmodulated; and this peculiarity he never lost. He was naturally calm, but when he heard of or read of some flagrant act of injustice, oppression, or cruelty, then indeed the sharpest marks of horror and indignation were visible in his countenance."

CHAPTER II.

AT the age of twelve[1] Shelley was removed from Sion House to more aristocratic Eton ; possibly a course resolved upon by his parents from the first, but not improbably, at least, confirmed by the desire of Sir Bysshe, who, having been honoured by his baronetcy in his seventy-fifth year, was naturally anxious that the future head of the house which it was his intention to establish should have every educational and social advantage. The change was not one that at once brought happier days to the thoughtful, imaginative, overwrought boy, who had passed so many bitter hours since he had first left Field Place. Instead of some three-score lads he found himself in a company of several hundred, and amidst a system of petty tyranny which was prone to extend to a most evil excess.

Having been well grounded, Shelley was placed at once in the upper fourth form, and as a student he seems to have made very satisfactory progress. He first

[1] This point has been set at rest by Professor Dowden, who adduces evidence to prove that on July 29, 1804, Percy Bysshe Shelley's name was entered in his own writing in the head-master's entrance book.

resided with a Mr. Hexter, a teacher of writing, and
apparently found that gentleman kindly and sympathetic; but ere long he was transferred to the house of a
Mr. Bethell, a pompous and oppressively dull assistant-
master. This tutor was the butt of the whole school, and
apparently deserved the ridicule which was freely be-
stowed upon him. It was this same Bethell who was
an involuntary actor in an often-described scene in
Shelley's room. Entering the latter one day he found
the boy occupied in the production of a blue flame,
and on angrily inquiring what was taking place, was
jocularly answered that his pupil was raising the devil.
A volcanic battery was on the table, but the master was
unaware of its properties; seizing hold of it he was suddenly hurled back against the wall by the unexpected
force of the electric shock. A severe thrashing was the
penalty for this misdemeanour, but probably Shelley felt
that the suffering inflicted by the head-master's rod was
fully discounted by the reputation he gained among his
admiring fellows. This head-master was a Dr. Keate,
distinguished among his compeers for pugnacity,
vigour, and self-assertion, and among Etonians for
his brutality. The latter has been called justifiable
severity, but a man who can leave his guests in order to
flog a batch of youngsters, and return with intensified
gaiety and appetite, or who can gleefully thrash eighty
delinquents successively, can hardly claim to be considered as nothing more than severe. Shelley received
many floggings, besides the innumerable fag-thrashings
from older schoolfellows, but to corporal chastisement
he finally became indifferent, and even endured it with

courageous defiance. The lad's life was undoubtedly rendered miserable to him for a long time. Records of this period have been left by several of his schoolfellows, all markedly consistent. He was baited, worried, jeered at, and tormented till he gave way to paroxysms of rage, which " made his eyes flash like a tiger's, his cheeks grow pale as death, his limbs quiver." By the time he had reached the upper-fifth form, however, he had not only won a few devoted friends, but had made himself feared and respected. His fury when roused to extremes of anger and indignation, his reckless denunciations of those in authority, his wild language, his love of reading and solitude, his experimental antics, and his often eccentric demeanour, earned him the name of " Mad Shelley." Even then, however, his great moral courage and nobility of instinct impressed themselves upon some of his comrades.

Shelley's happiest hours during his residence at Eton were those in the late afternoon of each day and at night. In the afternoons, he would roam the beautiful country around with a sympathetic friend, or seek a remote spot where he could uninterruptedly pore over some thrilling romance or mystic dissertation (for poetry does not appear to have really enthralled his mind until the last year or so of his schoolboy life) ; in the evenings, he would indulge in his forbidden chemical pursuits, now sending off fire-balloons, now playing at spirit-raising by means of mystically compounded flames—or in reading some scarce tome of wondrous lore which he could not well have smuggled out-of-doors. The pleasant hours spent in the summer afternoons were remembered in later years, when gliding on the Serchio, near Pisa, with his friend Williams; in the complete version of his "Boat on the Serchio" (Buxton Forman's edition, vol. iv.), there is a pleasant autobiographical reminiscence :

> " Those bottles of warm tea—
> Give me some straw—must be stowed tenderly ;
> Such as we used, in summer after six,
> To cram in great-coat pockets, and to mix
> Hard eggs and radishes and rolls at Eton,
> And, couched on stolen hay in those green harbours
> Farmers call gaps, and we schoolboys call arbours,
> Would feast till eight."

Often at Eton, and when home at Field Place, Shelley would steal out into the night ; and especially when the moon was full the temptation to these nocturnal ramblings was almost irresistible. Moonlight always had a supreme fascination for the poet. Its transforming power, its faculty for rendering weird and mournful that which ordinarily is commonplace, and its association in his mind with the revelations of the spirit-world, caused "the perilous moonshine" to exercise a powerful influence over him. In his eagerness to encounter the supernatural he would frequent haunted spots, graveyards, and any place or locality which held out any promise of satisfaction to his longing ; nor is there any reason to suppose that if a spirit had answered his summons the lad would have been grossly terrified. This would-be communication with what lies beyond mortal ken is a common desire among imaginative youths, and its main interest in connection with Shelley is the manifest colouring which it gave to all his early productions in prose and verse. In his beautiful "Hymn to Intellectual Beauty" he refers, while describing how the first conception of intellectual beauty suddenly came upon him, to these nocturnal experiences.

> " While yet a boy I sought for ghosts, and sped
>> Through many a listening chamber, cave, and ruin,
>> And starlight wood, with fearful steps pursuing
> Hopes of high talk with the departed dead.
> I called on poisonous names with which our youth is fed,
>> I was not heard, I saw them not—
>> When, musing deeply on the lot
> Of life, at that sweet time when minds are wooing
>> All vital things that wake to bring
>> News of birds and blossoming—
>> Sudden, thy shadow fell on me ;
> I shrieked, and clasped my hands in ecstasy."

Of all the friends of his own or of much older age, whom Shelley won during his stay at Eton, none was more valued or exercised a more important influence than an elderly physician named Dr. Lind, between whom and Shelley the first link was the common love of chemical experiments and philosophical disquisitions. The friendship between the old man and the fervent schoolboy was one peculiarly touching. Dr. Lind seems to have been a man of benevolence of temper and nobility of mind ; in his youth he had been a great traveller, was always an ardent student of life and knowledge, and had exceptional personal charm. Shelley loved and revered him, and gained constant comfort and refreshment from what he described as his " kindly toleration and purest wisdom."

This fine friendship between the boy of sixteen and the grey-haired old doctor has been commemorated by the poet in two of his poems. In " Laon and Cythna " ("The Revolt of Islam") the physician is introduced as the old hermit who liberates Laon from prison, and thereafter ministers to his needs—

> " That hoary man had spent his livelong age
> In converse with the dead, who leave the stamp
> Of ever-burning thoughts on many a page
> When they are gone into the senseless damp
> Of graves. His spirit thus became a lamp
> Of splendour, like to those on which it fed.
> Through peopled haunts, the city and the camp,
> Deep thirst for knowledge had his footsteps led,
> And all the ways of man among mankind he read."

Dr. Lind, again, is Zonoras in "Prince Athanase": the following extract therefrom is doubly interesting, as the record of this friendship, and for its autobiographical hint as to Shelley's remarkably rapid intellectual development—

> " Prince Athanase had one belovèd friend,
> An old, old man with hair of silver white,
> And lips where heavenly smiles would hang and blend
>
> With his wise words; and eyes whose arrowy light
> Shone like the reflex of a thousand minds.
>
> *   *   *   *   *   *
>
> Such was Zonoras; and as daylight finds
> An amaranth glittering on the path of frost,
> When autumn nights have nipt all weaker kinds,

3

Thus had his age, dark, cold, and tempest-tost,
Shone truth upon Zonoras ; and he filled
From fountains pure, nigh overgrown and lost,

The spirit of Prince Athanase, a child,
With soul-sustaining songs of ancient lore
And philosophic wisdom, clear and mild.

And sweet and subtle talk they evermore,
The pupil and master, shared ; until,
Sharing the undiminishable store,

The youth, as shadows on a grassy hill
Outrun the winds that chase then, soon outran
His teacher, and did teach with native skill

Strange truths and new to that experienced man ;
Still they were friends, as few have ever been
Who mark the extremes of life's discordant span.

Shelley's literary life may fairly be said to have at least
budded at Eton. It was before his departure therefrom
that he began, in tentative fragments, the poem of
"Queen Mab," though its composition, as we now know
it, must be set down to the writer of 1812–13 ; that he
wrote some of the short poems afterwards published in
the long-sought, but not yet discovered, volume, "Poems
by Victor and Cazire," and also (according to Medwin) a
portion of a poem on the subject of the Wandering Jew ;
that, in collaboration with Medwin, he wrote a romance
entitled "Nightmare," and that he finished his much-
discussed boyish effort in fiction, "Zastrozzi."

The year commencing with the early summer of 1809
was for Shelley a period full of feverish production and
keen intellectual stimulus. He left Eton abruptly, for

what reason has never yet been made clear, though
most probably his full expression of his views, his per-
sistent studies in branches of knowledge tabooed at
school, and his defiant attitude against what he considered
oppression—together with a natural, but none the less
unpleasing, arrogance—invited the ill-will of Dr. Keate
and others in authority. When he left, it was with the
goodwill of his comrades, and he seems to have received
quite an exceptional number of parting presents from
friends and admirers. What is still more significant is
the fact that he was frequently visited in Oxford by those
who had been attracted to him during the turbulent years
of his schoolboy life. Before passing to the account of
the new and vivid life beginning for Shelley with the
autumn of 1809, I am tempted to quote a passage from
Professor Dowden's record. Shelley was an apt scholar,
and undoubtedly gained a great amount of classical
and miscellaneous knowledge while at Eton ; but, as
Mr. Dowden says, he may have learned more indirectly
than through the official channels of information. " Perhaps his most important studies at Eton," says Mr.
Dowden, "were those of his own choice, and not of
compulsion. The grandeur of the verse of Lucretius
and his daring conceptions held him as with a potent
spell. Among writers in English, Franklin delighted him
with his announcement of the victories of mind over
matter ; already he felt the strong compulsion of Godwin's
doctrines in the " Political Justice." With Condorcet,
he dreamed of the endless progress of the race, and of
human perfectibility. He translated in his leisure hours
several books of Pliny's " Natural History," being

especially impressed by the chapter "De Deo," in which the Roman philosopher censures superstitious myths of the loves and wars of anthropomorphic deities."

After his matriculation at Oxford in April, 1810, Shelley returned to Eton for a short time, and on July 30th, made his school-speech, the subject being the declamation of Cicero against Catiline. It was probably before his final departure that he entertained a number of his friends at a sumptuous banquet, nominally with the proceeds of "Zastrozzi," which was published about the beginning of June. That the young author received £40 for his romance is almost inconceivable ; that he fully expected to receive at least that amount is a different matter. Probably Medwin confused the information he had obtained ; in any case, it is much more likely that the supper was paid for out of funds supplied by Sir Bysshe Shelley, than out of any honorarium forwarded by the publishers of "Zastrozzi."

Before this event Shelley's liking for a girl-cousin, Harriet Grove, had ripened into real sympathy and affection. Miss Grove was exceedingly pretty, was of an ardent temperament, and flirted with orthodox religious and social opinions in a way that wholly charmed her unconventional cousin. According to Medwin, she wrote some chapters of " Zastrozzi "—an assertion that has been derided by some writers, admitted by others, and allowed to pass without emphatic comment by Professor Dowden. It seems to me more probable, considering the uniformity of the style of this romance, that Harriet had at most nothing more to do with it than the composition of certain passages, suggestions as to character and incident, and hints as to the development of the plot.

When Bysshe took up residence in Oxford he continued to correspond at great length with Harriet, and gradually the young girl and her friends became uneasy and alarmed at the advanced and often extravagant opinions expressed in the young undergraduate's epistles. There was at this time no definite engagement, but the elder Groves and Shelleys, as well as the young people themselves, looked upon an ultimate union as a foregone conclusion. Shelley undoubtedly loved his beautiful cousin in all sincerity, not merely, as some have supposed, regarding her with the boyish affection born of sympathy, community of tastes, and mutual admiration.

Shelley's love of nature, always keen, became intensified during the season he spent at Field Place before he went to Oxford. Long walks in the early morning, rambles by night, and solitary musings in lonely places at once soothed and stimulated his imagination. During the Christmas holidays of 1809 and throughout 1810 he was busy writing prose and verse with one or more collaborators. "Zastrozzi," as we have seen, was finished at Eton; "The Nightmare" never saw the light of day; in the autumn of 1810 was published "Original Poetry by Victor and Cazire," and in December of the same year his second romance, "St. Irvyne; or, The Rosicrucian" left the printer's hands, while the windows of a bookseller's shop in Oxford exhibited "The Posthumous Fragments of Margaret Nicholson."

When in the Michaelmas Term of 1810 Shelley took

up residence in Oxford, he had the right to consider himself an author of more or less repute. In introducing
him to the intending partner of a bookseller and printer,
well-known in Oxford, Mr. Timothy Shelley added that
his son had a literary turn, and graciously invited his
acquaintance to indulge Bysshe in his printing freaks
"Zastrozzi" had readers, no doubt, though it is not easy to
imagine any one being vitally interested in this story of
the romantic adventures of a desperate outlaw and in his
high-flown sentiments. It is unjust, however, from the
comparative point of view, to speak of it as a ridiculous
failure. It was written in imitation of the "Monk" Lewis
and Mrs. Radcliffe style of authorship, and appealed to the
crude, mawkish, and sentimental taste in the literature of
fiction then prevalent; and that it did successfully appeal
to numerous readers is evident from the fact that many
years after its appearance it came to be included in the
once popular series known as the "Romancists' and
Novelists' Library," where it figures as No. 10. Any
reader of this monograph will find no difficulty in becoming acquainted with Shelley's prose works, which a
few years ago were issued in a handy volume. So it will
be enough to add here that "Zastrozzi" is a puerile and
morbid story, sufficiently excellent in its degree to deserve
to rank just below Lewis' and Mrs. Radcliffe's romances
in point of interest and truth to life, and interesting to
the student of Shelley only because of its authorship.

The young novelist-poet entered University College as
a Leicester scholar. "University" was fixed upon by
Mr. Timothy Shelley as the college where he himself
had been trained in the ways of wisdom and unwisdom,

and the nomination to the Leicester exhibition was due to an influential family connection. According to Hogg —the friend whose record of Shelley's Oxford life is at once more interesting and valuable than any other, and one of the most vivid biographical sketches in our literature—Bysshe during his first term was more occupied with chemical and scientific pursuits than with literature ; yet it is clear from what we know of his productions at this time that he dabbled considerably both in prose and verse.

Few visitors to Oxford, with any interest in literature, fail to see the rooms in " University " which Shelley occupied, rooms on the first floor in the corner next the hall of the principal quadrangle. Of all universities in the world Oxford was about the least attractive for a youth like Shelley. His training, his bent of mind, his rapidly maturing revolutionary ideas, along with his inherent indifference to what was clothed with the veneration of age and even of romance, wrought against his perception of what was lovely and of good report in the ancient city and its still more ancient institutions ; he was conscious only of its intellectual stagnation, its spiritual torpor, its bondage to the most wearisome conventionalities.

Before Shelley left Field Place to take up residence in Oxford, he went to London and introduced himself to Mr. Stockdale, the publisher. The object of his visit was to arrange for the publication of a small volume of poems by himself and a friend, " Poems by Victor and Cazire." No copy of this production is known to be extant ; if ever one is discovered it will almost certainly be found to be devoid of any poetic merit. Later on

Shelley submitted to the same quarter the " epic poem"
"The Wandering Jew," a production in the composition
of which Medwin claimed a large share. In any case,
however, it is of little or no poetic value.

Soon after the freshman had settled down to the
routine of college life, he sent to Stockdale the manuscript of his second romance, " St. Irvyne ; or, The
Rosicrucian." By a letter from University College, of
the 19th of November, we learn that Shelley had over-
estimated the length of " St. Irvyne "; that the romance
was evidently inspired by Godwin's " St. Leon"; and
that its issue was imminent. From a previous letter we
learn that he accepted the responsibility of its publication ;
and in one of December 18th, he asks that copies may be
sent to one or two friends. It was put forth anonymously
—" By a Gentleman of the University of Oxford." "St.
Irvyne " is in some ways an improvement upon "Zastrozzi,"
but it is equally morbid, unreal, grotesque, and inflated.
Students will find it in the same series as its predecessor,
as No. 60.

Before " St. Irvyne " solaced or astonished its not very
numerous readers, Shelley indulged in a printing escapade
at Oxford. He had written a number of verses, most of
them mere rhodomontade, but had not the critical
faculty to realize their worthlessness. He showed them
to his friend Hogg, who first condemned them and then
suggested their being altered here and there so that
they should read as burlesques. A Mr. Munday (whose
partner, Mr. Slatter, was the gentleman to whom Mr.
Timothy Shelley introduced his son when the latter first
went to Oxford) produced the verses at his own expense,

under the absurd title which Shelley and Hogg had decided upon—"The Posthumous Fragments of Mrs. Margaret Nicholson, Edited by John Fitzvictor." The lady whose " posthumous fragments " were thus honoured was one Peg Nicholson, a maniac washerwoman who, some few years before Shelley was born, had attempted the assassination of King George III. The secret of the real authorship was well kept, but even if it had been discovered by the Oxford authorities it is improbable that Shelley would have incurred anything further than a reprimand and a warning. The booklet seems to have had a fairly good sale among the undergraduates, who were taken with its exaggerated vehemence and general foolishness. About this period also—according to Mr. Henry Slatter—Shelley wrote a third novel, in conjunction with Hogg, and gave it the title " Leonora," probably the name of the heroine. The printers who began to set it up refused to proceed on account of the " free notions " which were interwoven with the narrative, and Shelley took it to a printer at Abingdon named King ; the latter had nearly completed the printing of it, when the premature extinction of " Leonora " occurred owing to the abrupt expulsion of both its authors from Oxford on account of Shelley's famous tractate on the Necessity of Atheism.

It is time that the reader should be more adequately introduced to Shelley's great friend and associate during the short period of his college life.

Thomas Jefferson Hogg was the son of a gentleman of good family, a staunch Tory who transmitted his proclivities to his son, who in his mature years, however, held all his opinions more as a matter of convenience

than of conviction.   In temperament and nature, Hogg
had nothing in common with Shelley ; but he had a
taking presence, was clever, and even intellectual, and
had a general vitality that charmed the younger of the
two.   The chief intellectual bond which united them
was their common love of the great Greek and Latin
poets and philosophers ; but, from the outset, Hogg
sincerely admired while he never quite understood his
brilliant friend.   In his invaluable record of his and
Shelley's life at Oxford, he has occasionally allowed his
imagination to fill up the blanks of memory, but in the
main his account is accurate.   A real friendship united
the two young men ; even where Hogg laughed at the
enthusiastic poet, he admired the noble, ardent, and refined character of the youth, and where Shelley differed
materially from his elder companion he was never blind
to his mental powers, his kindly worldliness, his genial
cynicism.   So closely linked are the Oxford experiences
of Hogg and Shelley that it is impossible to dissociate
them whenever we think of this period of the poet's
life.

It is impracticable to give Hogg's narrative in all its
vivid detail, but as his is the only authentic record of
this time, I shall endeavour to adequately condense
from those ever-fascinating pages dealing with " Shelley
at Oxford."   Hogg the Oxonian was a very different individual from the egotistical and soured Hogg, "the
man of the world," who in 1858 so markedly betrayed
his incapacity to appropriately continue his story of the
greatest of English lyrical poets.

It was at the commencement of the Michaelmas term

(that is, about the end of October) that Hogg made the acquaintance of Shelley. Had he known that a few months later their acquaintanceship would lead to his expulsion from Oxford, he would not have invited the newcomer to his rooms, as he frankly did. "I happened one day to sit next to a freshman at dinner; it was his first appearance in hall. His figure was slight, and his aspect remarkably youthful, even at our table, where all were very young. He seemed thoughtful and absent. He ate little, and had no acquaintance with any one." One or other broke the ice, and the conversation turned upon German and Italian poetry, the boyish freshman impetuously maintaining his admiration of the former. Both were so interested, that the clearing of the tables found them still in animated discussion. Hogg invited his new friend to his rooms; and while Shelley discoursed with wonderful facility and enthusiasm, his host gradually lost interest in the subject of argument, and paid more and more attention to his vivacious companion.

" I had leisure to examine, and I may add, to admire, the appearance of my very extraordinary guest. It was a sum of many contradictions. His figure was slight and fragile, and yet his bones and joints were large and strong. He was tall, but he stooped so much, that he seemed of a low stature. His clothes were expensive, and made according to the most approved mode of the day; but they were tumbled, rumpled, unbrushed. His gestures were abrupt, and sometimes violent, occasionally even awkward, yet more frequently gentle and graceful. His complexion was delicate, and almost feminine, of the purest red and white; yet he was tanned and freckled by exposure to the sun, having passed the autumn, as he said, in shooting. His features, his whole face, and particularly his head, were, in fact, unusually small; yet the last *appeared* of remarkable bulk, for his hair was long and bushy, and in fits of absence, and in the agonies (if I may use the word) of anxious thought, he often rubbed it fiercely with his hands, or passed his fingers quickly through his locks unconsciously, so that it was singularly wild and rough. In times when it was the mode to imitate stage-coachmen as closely as possible in costume, and when the hair was invariably cropped, like that of our soldiers, this eccentricity was very striking. His features were not symmetrical (the mouth, perhaps, excepted), yet was the effect of the whole extremely powerful. They breathed an animation, a fire, an enthusiasm, a vivid and preternatural intelligence, that I never met with in any other countenance. Nor was the moral expression less beautiful than the intellectual; for there was a softness, a delicacy, a gentleness, and especially (though this will surprise many) that air of profound religious veneration, that characterizes the best works, and chiefly the frescoes (and into these they infused their whole souls), of the great masters of Florence and of Rome. I recognized the very peculiar expression in these wonderful productions long afterwards, and with a satisfaction mingled with much sorrow, for it was after the decease of him in whose countenance I had first observed it. I admired the enthusiasm of my new acquaintance, his ardour in the cause of science and his thirst for knowledge. I seemed to have found in him all those intellectual qualities which I had vainly expected to meet with in a university. But there was one physical blemish that threatened to neutralize all his excellence. 'This is a fine, clever fellow!' I said to myself, 'but I can never bear his society; I shall never be able to endure his voice; it would kill me. What a pity it is!' I am very sensible of imperfections, and especially of painful sounds—and the voice of the stranger was excruciating; it was intolerably shrill, harsh, and discordant; of the most cruel intension—it was perpetual, and without any remission—it excoriated the ears.[1] He continued to discourse of

---

[1] From the various accounts wherein reference is made to Shelley's voice, it is evident that Hogg's remarks are not wholly exaggerated. The poet's voice was described by Medwin as a " cracked soprano," by Peacock as " discordant," by Thornton Hunt as " a

chemistry, sometimes sitting, sometimes standing before the fire, and sometimes pacing about the room."

Next day Hogg paid a visit to Shelley's rooms. He found his new acquaintance quite unaware of the lapse of time, but glad to see his late host. Shelley appeared unwell, and troubled at his scout's presence, but brightened up after Hogg had stirred the fire and made the room look more comfortable. Hogg, who had imagined the young undergraduate to be purely of a literary turn, was amazed at the " scientific chaos" he perceived around him.

" Books, boots, papers, shoes, philosophical instruments, clothes, pistols, linen, crockery, ammunition, and phials innumerable, with money, stockings, prints, crucibles, bags, and boxes, were scattered on the floor and in every place ; as if the young chemist, in order to analyze the mystery of creation, had endeavoured first to reconstruct the primeval chaos. The tables, and especially the carpet, were already stained with large spots of various hues, which frequently proclaimed the agency of fire. An electrical machine, an air-pump, the galvanic trough, a solar microscope, and large glass jars and receivers, were conspicuous amidst the mass of matter. Upon the table by his side were some books lying open, several letters, a bundle of new pens, and a bottle of Japan ink, that served as an inkstand ; a piece of deal, lately part of the lid of a box, with many chips, and a handsome razor that had been used as a knife. There were bottles of soda water, sugar, pieces of lemon,

---

high natural counter-tenor." On the other hand, there are equally authentic statements witnessing to its sensitive *timbre* and delicate modulations—especially pleasant when employed in the reading of poetry. The truth seems to be that Shelley's voice was an agreeable one, save when argumentative emotion or any mental excitement raised it to a high pitch, when it became strident and painfully shrill.

and the traces of an effervescent beverage. Two piles of books supported the tongs, and these upheld a small glass retort above an argand lamp. I had not been seated many minutes before the liquor in the vessel boiled over, adding fresh stains to the table, and rising in fumes with a most disagreeable odour. Shelley snatched the glass quickly, and dashing it in pieces among the ashes under the grate, increased the unpleasant and penetrating effluvium."

A little further on Hogg relates how it was he was often able to go on with his studies even while in Shelley's company, for the poet was wont to be overcome during the evening by extreme drowsiness for some three or four hours. Some delightful pages follow describing their intellectual excursions, and also their wanderings in the neighbourhood of Oxford; Shelley's fondness for pistol-practice; and his passion for making paper boats and setting them a-sail on any stream or pool he encountered. Valueless papers, envelopes, mere notes, and at last cherished epistles would go to the formation of these paper navies, while Hogg would look on with impatience, and not without occasional resentment when cold and hunger induced him to regard his companion as some-what feather-brained. Anecdote after anecdote follows, each illustrative of the many-sided character of the poet, and all enabling us to realize the simplicity and beauty of his nature. He was a voracious reader, and his reading was not of the kind which young men as a rule indulge in very assiduously : Plato, Plutarch, Euripides, Lucretius, and Lucan were among the authors whose books he was wont to peruse with the same eagerness as when at Brentford and Eton he devoured " Monk " Lewis' romances.

While at Oxford Shelley kept up a varied correspon-

dence, chiefly on speculative philosophy and religion,
and among his most favoured epistolary disputants were
impressionable young ladies, including pretty Harriet
Grove. Partly as the immediate outcome of this correspondence, partly from his earnest study of Locke's
treatise on the Understanding and of Hume's Essays,
notes began to accumulate : a precipitate of these was
made, and the result was the famous tractate on the
Necessity of Atheism.

In this dissertation Shelley sets forth the statement
that all belief rests on the conviction of—(1) the senses,
(2) the reason, (3) testimony. The argument proceeds
that in the case of the Deity none of these proofs are
available, and the tractate concludes with that favourite
device of the not very clear as well as of the clear of
mind—a *Q. E. D.* The essay was afterwards incorpo-
rated in the "Notes to Queen Mab." The tract was
printed at Worthing, and the author managed to persuade
Munday, of Oxford, to allow it to be sold at his shop.
It was even advertised in *The Oxford University and
City Herald* as about to be published. It was sown broadcast, the author himself acting as the main distributor.
This method of proselytizing was continued when Shelley
produced his Irish pamphlets. Enclosed in envelopes to
dignities and persons of repute, it brought discussion to
the obscure author, to whom discussion was as manna
to one an-hungered. Messrs. Munday and Slatter were
at last put on their guard ; Shelley was remonstrated
with, but remained obdurate ; and finally all the copies
of the obnoxious tract which were readily procurable
were destroyed. The authorities, however, took the

matter up, with the result that the college-life of Percy Bysshe Shelley and Thomas Jefferson Hogg came to an abrupt conclusion. It is not quite certain whether or not the initiatory suspicion that Shelley was the author was due to indirect hints or suggestions, or to specific information. In any case, a meeting of the authorities was convened, and Mr. Percy Bysshe Shelley, of University College, was summoned to answer certain questions. Shelley refused to give either affirmation or denial, but the evidence of his handwriting was in itself sufficient for condemnation. When Hogg heard what had occurred, he generously insisted on facing the tribunal, and endeavoured to clear his friend. Thereafter he demanded that his and Shelley's case should be considered as one, and that if any penalty were to be incurred it should be shared in common. While the council were endeavouring to reach a decision it unfortunately happened that they caught sight of the two delinquents marching arm-in-arm to and fro in the quadrangle; and though the young men were only trying to possess their souls in patience until the fateful moment should arrive, their action was taken as a contumacious flaunting of their indifference in the face of their august superiors. The upshot was that on the same afternoon (March 25, 1811) a document, bearing the college seal and signed by the master and dean, was affixed to the hall door, declaring unto all readers that Percy Bysshe Shelley and Thomas Jefferson Hogg were publicly expelled for contumacy in refusing to answer certain questions put to them.

Hogg's account of the incident and Shelley's own

statement are full of interest, but there is not space here for reproduction of details concerning this unfortunate event. Shelley felt his expulsion keenly, was almost prostrated by the sentence when he found it irrevocable, and was only saved from utter wretchedness by his growing anger and indignation at what he considered gross injustice on the part of the authorities. There is no question but that the latter acted foolishly as well as uncharitably in their extreme procedure—some milder punishment, even a sentence of rustication, would have been ample, and much more just. That they were wholly reprehensible, as some Shelleyan enthusiasts would have us consider, it is absurd to assert. The young men had distinctly brought themselves within the sphere of insubordination; and for insubordination, whether morally justifiable or not, there is naturally punishment. Many Shelleyans speak as if Shelley and Hogg had been entitled to the full privileges of manhood: a great mistake, for while no official dicta can interfere with independence of judgment on the part of undergraduates, they can very materially affect any public expression thereof. In the majority of cases an undergraduate is not a man, though college youths are always "men": he is simply in a pleasant limbo between manhood and schoolboyhood. Generally, undergraduates are boys in years, tastes, and manners; and as "superior boys" it is on the whole as well that they should be ruled over. Hence, while we may reprobate the severity of the college council which expelled Shelley and Hogg, we must in justice admit that it acted quite within its rights. In the matter of infliction of *some* penalty it would have failed in its duty had it waived such altogether; and here most unbiassed persons will agree, whether, intellectually, their sympathies be with Shelley or with his judges.

On both sides there was great heat; otherwise the issue would have been different. Had the undergraduates been given a week, or even a few days, to consider their position, some compromise would indubitably have been arrived at. That the council regretted having dispensed such summary justice is evident from the fact that at the last moment the delinquents were informed they need not actually leave on the morrow of their sentence—information which fell on ears stubborn through scornful wrath. Probably, even, if an appeal had been made, the council's decision would have been negatived so far as concerned the sentence of expulsion. It is useless to speculate on what did not happen, yet one cannot but wonder how very different Shelley's life might have been had he remained at Oxford for the usual period. He would almost certainly not have married Harriet Westbrook, an event which was the beginning of much sorrow and suffering, transitory happiness, and intransient pain—one which also ushered in years of splendid, and in some ways of unparalleled, achievement in literature.

On the morning of March 26th, after a gloomy breakfast, relieved in part, no doubt, by Hogg's unflagging good spirits, the two "martyrs" (as it was a consolation to them to consider themselves) departed by coach for London. That evening they put up for the night at a coffee-house near Piccadilly, and ultimately slept the

·divine sleep of youth whereof no council could defraud them.

With this incident the record of Shelley's boyhood and youth terminates : henceforth he is to be considered as having entered upon the troublous state of manhood. I have dwelt at some length upon these early years of the great poet, for they are full of interest and significance for all students of his life and work. In the ·case of many men of letters the biographer could dismiss the years of adolescence in a chapter, and would ·even do well sometimes to content himself with a few introductory passages ; but there are certain authors whose lives require to be considered from childhood, whose early formative experiences it would be unwise not to recount with as ample detail as practicable.

It was a great sorrow to Shelley to leave Oxford. Although not in sympathy with its institutions, nor, as ·already stated, appreciative of certain aspects of its mental and spiritual life, he loved it for its beauty, its natural environment, its facilities for culture, its easy ·possibilities of seclusion. The brief period he spent in the ancient city was one of the happiest seasons in a life that was ever too emotional and high-strung to withstand the discords and perpetual jars which beset even mortals whom the stars of fortune have marked out as children ·of eternity.

CHAPTER III

THE age of eighteen and a half years is an early period at which to withstand assaults against both one's dignity and one's heart. In his expulsion from Oxford, Shelley's pride was sorely wounded, though there was something soothing to him in the thought that he had endured disgrace in a righteous cause. What was a more keenly felt blow was the final upbreak of the definite or understood engagement between himself and his pretty cousin, Harriet Grove. In his desire to emancipate her (Shelley was always desirous of emancipating somebody, and would probably prove an intolerable nuisance among either the saints or the damned of the "Paradiso" or the "Inferno" of the orthodox) from the fetters of conventionality and an obsolete faith, the young enthusiast not only alarmed Miss Grove herself, but also her worthy parents. The result was the conclusion of the hopes which both or either entertained of the closer union of marriage. Shelley was greatly affected by this blow to his intentions, but his sufferings were transient. Some of his admirers would have it that he endured a lifelong hurt from this early mischance, but without the slightest basis for their sentimental belief. Nine out of ten lads fall in love ere they emerge from their teens, some much more passionately than Shelley did at any time of his life. When Shelley loved, his affections centred on two individuals—the person whom he regarded with the bodily eye, and the glorified or idealized " double " who dominated his imagination—and as a rule the passion of his nature expended itself upon the "double." Unlike Keats, he had no cause to dread the approach of Love : he had no premonition of consuming fires which would waste and destroy if they were not quenched. He would gladly have married his cousin, but when the union was tabooed he sorrowed, sulked, pulled himself together had one or two slight relapses, and then thought about it seriously no more. It was not long after " the crush ing blow " that he was taken by the pretty face of another Harriet, in the autumn succeeding his marriage with whom Miss Grove was happily joined in matrimony to a wealthy squire, who, if not so young and handsome as " Bysshe," was "a very tolerable gentleman," and held no obnoxious Radical opinions.

The reader will remember that Shelley and Hogg spent the night of their arrival in London at a coffee-house near Piccadilly. Before they went to bed they made a call on the Groves, and spent a very dull evening ; thereafter, about two in the morning, they called upon the naturally astonished Medwin. Next morning the search for lodgings was commenced, and rooms were at last found in Poland Street. Here the two friends worked, read, slept, and were moderately happy. But Bysshe suddenly discovered that parental was no more to be dared with impunity than collegiate authority. To his proposal to return to Field Place, and bring with him his companion in misfortune, he was informed by his father that his reception into the family circle again depended entirely on his agreeing to dissociate himself from Hogg, and even cease all correspondence with him. Hogg at this time came in for the greater blame, with some reason perhaps, owing to his superiority in age. Percy indignantly declined to agree to what he considered would be an act of gross ingratitude and disloyalty, and' the consequence was that his irate father told him to provide for himself. Shelley therefore found himself on his own resources, and if it had not been for the kindness of friends, including his unselfish young sisters and their schoolmate, Harriet Westbrook, he would have fared ill indeed for a time.

A great deal of abuse has been lavished upon Mr. Timothy Shelley, afterwards Sir Timothy, for his so-called rigour to his son. From all accounts it is easy to gather that Shelley's father was a kindly-natured, choleric English gentleman, a country squire, and with his full share of the prejudices and narrow views which country gentry are commonly supposed to display. If fate had dealt somewhat unkindly with Percy Bysshe Shelley in making him the child of an unsympathising father, it was no less disagreeable to Mr. Timothy in giving him a poet and an enthusiast for his son and heir. The worthy squire did not understand or care anything about humanity and its rights. What was the use of a private individual making himself miserable and a nuisance to quiet folk when there were the Board

of Guardians and the House of Commons to set all possible discords into a delightful harmony ? Justice for all,
freedom of thought and expression, equality of laws,
rectification of long-standing abuses, adjustment of the
principles dominating the relationship between capital
and labour, the alteration of the marriage and divorce
laws — in a word, the people *versus* the privileged
minority—all this was wearisome rhodomontade to the
squire of Field Place. When we consider his training,
position, and views, we must in common fairness admit
that, under very trying circumstances, Timothy Shelley
at the worst behaved blunderingly and hot headedly.   It
is beyond question that he was a well-intentioned, kindly
gentleman, of a class which fortunately is becoming
more and more restricted every decade. There is not
much gain if, in the attainment of true liberalism, of true
radicalism, we cannot sympathise with conservatism and
prejudice. An illiberal radical (type of a tribe which
unfortunately is at present innumerable and influential)
is not only a much more objectionable individual, but a
more potent enemy of free thought, of national and personal freedom, than the most thoroughgoing Tory of the
Timothy Shelley type. Undeniably the squire of Field
Place was often very foolish, and his foolishness was of a
kind that must have been specially objectionable to a
young man like his son Bysshe; but Shelley, on the other
hand, had no sense of the necessity of that spirit of
kindly compromise without which the friction of domestic
and social life is apt to become intolerable. It is possible
to be unflinchingly true to one's opinions or to avoid
open acquiescence in contrary views, and yet to dispense

with argumentative excitement on every occasion of dispute or disrelished assertion. Shelley, however, never
could compromise in the trifling any more than in
the really important things of life. Theoretically, one
admires courageous consistency : practically, even the
most patient of relatives and friends come to resent that
temper which will be as uncompromising in an affair of
domestic etiquette as in a matter of vital importance.
As so often happens between two radically different
natures, even when each is anxious to meet the other
half-way, Mr. Timothy Shelley and his son found themselves in constant disagreement. The squire was anxious
to do what he could for the strange youth, whom he
wholly failed to understand, and in the main he acted
not heartlessly if undeniably foolishly and with unnecessary bluster. The most entertaining account of him is
to be found in the brilliant narrative of Hogg, though
naturally he is not represented there in his best aspects.
Mrs. Shelley has always remained a somewhat shadowy
figure. Percy seems to have had a real affection for her,
but to have been chilled by the fact that in the distur-
bances which his ways of life and thought, even as a boy,
caused at Field Place she sided with her husband. In
the first place, it was natural for her to do so; in the
next, she as naturally feared that his influence over his
sisters might be permanently prejudicial. She seems to
have affected his life, for good or evil, in an exceptionally
slight degree.

Notwithstanding Mr. Shelley's favourable opinion of
Hogg, formed at the dinner at Miller's Hotel (so amus-
ingly described by Shelley's friend)—where he had

been persuaded to attend and meet the delinquents—a repeated and even more emphatic sentence of exclusion from Field Place was shortly pronounced against the two friends, save on conditions to which Bysshe absolutely declined to agree. The choleric member for New Shoreham (a dignity of which he seems to have been inordinately proud) endeavoured by various means to bring about a separation between Hogg and his son, with the result, finally, that the former received a parental notice to leave London and begin his legal experiences in the north.

On Shelley's distinct refusal to meet his father's wishes he received a message to the effect that he was forbidden Field Place, that monetary supplies would be stopped, and that he would thenceforth have to provide for himself. On the face of it, this seems a hard doom to be pronounced by a wealthy gentleman against a son whose main offence was a consistency (or stubbornness—either term equally appropriate, according to point of view) on a par with that parentally displayed. But though the young poet was certainly wrathful, and probably taken aback at the turn of affairs, he did not in consequence endure any hardship. The loyal companion who had left Oxford with him lent him money; small sums of cash were sent to him by his sisters; and his Uncle Pilfold gave him both an affectionate welcome and material assistance. Possibly, also, Shelley knew his father well enough to be assured that the latter would not remain for many months in his stubborn mood, if even many weeks. Before Hogg's departure for York the two friends went much about together; sometimes to Hamp-

stead, sometimes to Kensington Gardens, occasionally to
Clapham Common, in order to see the Misses Shelley at
Mrs. Fenning's boarding-school in that district.   At this
time Percy's favourite sister was Elizabeth, and he was
very eager that she and Hogg should fall in love with
each other.   Already the youthful philosopher-poet had
resented the existent marriage laws, as hurtful to the
true well-being of society, and was prepared to go to
almost any extremes in order to emphasize his aversion
from an unjust and evil state of things, and to help on
the much-needed reformation.   He would thus have
gladly seen his sister and Hogg live together by private
contract, that is, without either civil or ecclesiastical
sanction, and even those who condemn his principles
must admit that Shelley was here, as at all times, prepared to act up to his convictions.   He would willingly
himself have lived in an union unsanctioned by any
marriage ceremony ; though he came to recognize that,
as long as an undue proportion of discomfort and suffering of mind and body has to be borne by women, it
would be unkind, unjust, and unwise to demand of them
a sacrifice so completely beyond anything required of men.
In his statement of his views on the marriage question,
Shelley, in his early years, allowed himself to be carried
away by indignation and the zeal of reformation.   Blinded
by the combined light of what he saw and detested and
what his imaginative mind pictured forth for his solace
and delight, he seemed oblivious to all the wrong and
suffering which would inevitably succeed any abrupt and
arbitrary change in the laws regulating the marital relationship of men and women.   He was disheartened at

the slow progress made towards what he believed to be
the higher civilization ; he would fain have lived to see
the laws against which he was wont so vehemently to
protest, speedily disappear. He believed in the ultimate
national realisation of a truer conception of marriage ;
and he foresaw that divorce and other allied subjects
would soon or late come to be discussed with at least
comparative freedom from prejudice. It must ever be
remembered to his credit that at a time when to utter
a word against the still unreformed institution of
marriage was perhaps considered a more heinous offence
than to express a disbelief in the Deity, he had the
courage to protest with all his power against what he
considered to be an evil and a tyrannical state of
things.

It has been supposed that it was about this time
Shelley wrote a " Poetical Essay on the Existing State of
Things," for the purpose of assisting a certain patriot of
the name of Finnerty, who had been imprisoned for libel.
It is really doubtful if the authorship can be attributed
to him, but, except for Shelleyan specialists, it really is a
matter of no moment whether or not Shelley wrote the
" Poetical Essay "; what is of interest is the undeniable
fact that in his practical sympathy with the patriot-
journalist, Finnerty, we have another instance of
Shelley's habit of letting hand and heart act in
unison.

Some time before his expulsion from Oxford Shelley
had made the acquaintance (as the bearer of a message
and also of a letter of introduction from his sister
Elizabeth) of one of his sister's schoolmates, a Miss

Harriet Westbrook.[1] That even after a slight knowledge of this young girl Shelley thought highly of her
is fairly clear from the fact that, in a letter to Stockdale the publisher (January 11, 1811), he particularly
requests that a copy of the just-issued " St. Irvyne " be
sent to her at a specified address. After Mr. Timothy
Shelley's exclusion of his son from Field Place, Percy's
sisters vented their sympathetic emotion upon the not
unwilling ears of the romantically-inclined Harriet. When
the latter went home for a time she became the medium
for the transmission of the small sums which his sisters
managed to save for their martyr brother ; to her Shelley
appeared an altogether superior being, shamefully ill-
treated—and to the poet she came almost as a minister-
ing angel. Harriet was a really pretty, according to some
accounts a lovely, girl, with beautiful hair, brilliant complexion, a pleasant voice, and a bright and cheerful
manner. When she yielded her affections to Shelley she
was only sixteen. The Westbrooks were not a family
with which either Sir Bysshe or Mr. Timothy Shelley
would naturally like the future head of " the house " to
be closely connected. Mr., commonly called Jew,
Westbrook, was a well-to-do coffee-house keeper ; in
addition to his functions as a tavern host he was wont to
add those of a money-lender, hence his sobriquet—for
there does not seem to have been any real basis for the
statement that the relatives of Shelley's first wife were of
the Jewish race. The family lived in Chapel Street, near

[1] The younger Miss Westbrook was christened Harriett, but
most of her friends, and Shelley himself, spelt the name with only
one *l*.

Grosvenor Square, and besides Mr. and Mrs. Westbrook
consisted of Miss Elizabeth (the " Eliza " of the Shelley
letters and biographies) and of Miss Harriet—the elder
sister (older by a good many years) a sour, affected, in-
terfering, and troublesome woman ; the younger full of
spirit, and at once charming and comely.   Partly from
romantic sentiment, partly from genuine affection, Harriet
Westbrook discovered that she "cared for" Mr. Percy
Shelley, poet and reformer.   Her elder sister would fain
have won that young gentleman for herself, but when she
realized that he was insensible to her physical and mental
attractions, she did her best to ensure a union between
him and her sister.   The Westbrooks would not have
tolerated Shelley had it not been for the circumstances
of his birth and prospects ; and it was only when Mr.
Westbrook ultimately discovered that the heir to the
baronetcy in succession to the squire of Field Place was
perverting (Shelley considered it *converting*) his daughter's
views, and at the same time steering clear of any definite
engagement, that he sought to put an end to, or place
some check upon, the young man's attentions.

   When Harriet Westbrook first knew Shelley she held,
as was natural, no pronounced opinions of any kind.
Whom the poet loved he proselytized.   When she first
learned that Percy was an atheist Harriet was shocked,
but to his religious, philosophical, and social views she
ere long lent a ready ear.   She was a clever girl, more
intellectually inclined and more widely cultured than
the majority of young ladies at that period, and in
these respects she was doubtless a fitting mate for
Shelley : there were radical differences of nature, how-

ever, which were of more vital import than any simi-
larity of views upon mental problems.   The young
people saw more and more of each other, and, when
they were separated, an active correspondence was maintained.   It is tolerably clear that Shelley's interest was at
least in great part due to his desire to make the most of
the good chances afforded him by fate for the saving of
a human spirit from the thraldom of conventionality and
effete faith.   If his views had been powerfully attracted
to an opposite pole of thought, or religious conviction,
he would have looked upon Harriet as a "brand" to be
"pluckt from the burning."   The outcome of the tragi-
comedy which began with the elopement of the young
lovers was sad enough to invest any recital of their brief
married life with an ever-imminent shadow.

We can see from Shelley's letters to Hogg (who in
April left London at his father's summons) that he had
nothing either of the early reticence or the later com-
municativeness of the lover.   His friend, noticing the
frequency of Shelley's allusions to having seen Miss
Harriet Westbrook, allusions generally familiarly expressed, naturally concluded that something more ardent
than ordinary liking was entertained for the young lady
by his impressionable comrade ; but to his broad hints
and badinage on this subject Shelley only replied with
perfect *sang-froid* that his correspondent was mistaken,
and that though he liked his "little friend," there was no
likelihood of love.

It was after Hogg's departure, and in considerable
part owing to the kindly mediation of Shelley's maternal
uncle, Captain Pilfold, that father and son were so far

reconciled as to permit of the latter's paying a visit to Field Place. The result of this visit was an arrangement whereby Mr. Shelley agreed to allow his son an annuity of £200, with full permission for Bysshe to reside wheresoever he chose, and to pursue his own way of life, but on the understanding that though he might correspond he was to have no personal communication with Hogg. The terms were reluctantly accepted, but the young poet rejoiced at the comparative freedom he could now enjoy. If the annuity seems a rather small sum when we consider Mr. Shelley's means, it must be remembered that the amount in question would certainly go further in the early part of the century than now. Shelley, moreover, was only a boy in years, and probably his father thought a small annuity would, from every point of view, be better for his son than an allowance which would enable him to indulge in "freaks" which might have a baneful effect upon his after-life. Bysshe was quite aware that he was heir to a large fortune, but he also had no expectation of ever enjoying it. The fear, or rather the conviction, of early death had taken possession of him. Like many young men of an imaginative bent, he was more conscious of the shadow cast by the beauty of life than of its exceeding brightness. The most joyous music has ever somewhere, howsoever subtly indeterminate, a pathetic note ; and in the jubilant music of our youth those of us blessed or cursed with imagination are apt to be over-sensitive to the thrilling minors which escape senses less acute. With the conviction that he had but a year or two, at most but a few years, to live, Shelley naturally thought little of his possible future wealth, and was well content to have an adequate income meanwhile. He had dreams of poetic greatness, but he doubted if he would live long enough to snatch a single fadeless laurel from the ever-reluctant hand of Fame. Dominated, from his boyhood onward, by an intense ardour of enthusiasm in the cause of the suffering and the oppressed, he was more anxious to do some little measure of good in his day than to sing the fairest songs. He would fain have followed Christ, but not as the Christians do. To work for suffering humanity, to break down the barriers of caste and prejudice, to help to inaugurate the new kingdom of righteousness in strict accordance with the socialistic doctrines of the Nazarene prophet—to an aim such as this he would gladly have solely devoted himself. That he became more and more the poet, the singer, and less the practical reformer (though never less the prophet and seer) is a matter to be thankful for so far as we are concerned, though it is certain that, in his early manhood at any rate, Shelley would rather have thrown in his lot with the active iconoclasts than with those who stand aloof and sing.

From his ready and uncomplaining acceptance of his father's offer, moreover, we can draw an important inference—namely, that he had not at that time the slightest idea of marriage with Miss Westbrook. Shelley was never without a fair amount of shrewdness in the conduct of monetary affairs, and had he foreseen what was shortly so unexpectedly to happen, he would undoubtedly have stipulated for a more adequate allowance. After his reconciliatory visit in May to Field Place, he yielded to one of those attacks of nervous unrest

to which he was subject throughout life, and spent the
ensuing weeks, now at Field Place, now at his Uncle
Pilfold's house at Cuckfield, now in London, and for a
brief while at his Cousin Grove's place—Cwm Elan, near
Rhayader, in North Wales. At the time the beauty
of the Welsh mountain scenery does not seem to have
strongly affected him, though that it insensibly impressed
him is clear from the autobiographical passages in some
of his poems written within the next few years. He was
mentally too perturbed to care much for scenery at this
period of his life. It must also be remembered that
Shelley the poet was an outgrowth of Shelley the political
reformer and humanitarian enthusiast, and of Shelley
the writer of crude romances. Up to the composition of
"Queen Mab" (1812) he wrote no poetry of any value :
and his real poetic life may not inappropriately be
stated to have practically commenced with "Alastor :
and other Poems" (1815–16).

It was during Shelley's visit to Rhayader that Hogg
received a note which astonished him. He learned that
his friend would probably, ere long, be in York, *with
Harriet Westbrook;* that the latter's father had "persecuted her in a most horrible way by endeavouring to
compel her to go to school;" that Harriet had appealed
to the writer, whose advice (*of course*) was to resist such
stupendous and appalling tyranny ; that she had written
to the effect that she threw herself upon his protection,
and would fly with him ; and "that gratitude and admiration demand that I should love her for ever."

Knowing Shelley's opinions anent matrimony, Hogg
at once wrote and counselled marriage ; but it did not

require his emphatic persuasion for Shelley to throw his principles overboard and determine to repay Harriet's trust with the reward of a legal marriage. Theoretically, it would have been a higher morality for Shelley to have acted consistently with his firm convictions ; practically, none can regret his having acted as any gentleman would have done. It is not so easy to excuse him for, later on, permitting his children to be baptized—an application of the spirit of compromise which shows how weak even a great man can sometimes be.

As soon as he had returned to London he made hurried preparations for elopement. He was in a ferment of excitement, and allowed himself (probably was for the moment incapable of thinking out his position) no time for consideration. He admired and sincerely regarded Harriet Westbrook. To the social distinction between the heir to a baronetcy and great wealth and the daughter of a tavern-keeper, howsoever respectable, Shelley was naturally wholly indifferent ; to her charms of mind and body, her accomplishments as a musician, a reader, and (to Shelley —essential characteristic) a listener, he would not have been the youth he was had he not been keenly sensitive. Even her trimness and neatness, a kind of exquisite completeness which characterized her appearance, attracted one who was seldom neat and never trim, whose wild eyes and dishevelled locks startled or offended many worthy people, and whose habits and common demeanour were so unlike those of most young men. Harriet had done wisely in appealing to Percy's hatred of tyranny, for she knew that this was the dominant passion of her eccentric lover ; though where the "tyranny" was in Mr.

Westbrook's having decided to send his sixteen-year-old daughter to school for another half-year it is not easy for ordinary mortals to perceive. Keen suffering, sorrow, and remorse would have been avoided had Mr. Westbrook been able to prevent the elopement of his daughter with Percy Shelley, or had the latter behaved with somewhat less Quixotic chivalry, and insisted on Harriet's remaining in pupilage for at least the specified six months. However, as Shelley had sown for the whirlwind, he had, by the law of nature, to realize its violence when its time was come. To him the reasons for elopement seemed not only justifiable but good, and not only good, but imperative. As for Harriet Westbrook, most fair-minded persons will decide that she deserves neither praise nor blame. She had come to entertain the same opinions as those which Shelley had communicated to her, verbally and orally; and she plainly thought she was acting up to the high moral philosophy of the Shelleyan Persuasion in refusing the ignominy of a return to school, and in throwing herself upon her preceptor's charge. That the Westbrooks, or at any rate that Eliza Westbrook, schemed towards the due fulfilment of a marriage between the young people, is fairly clear; but I am convinced that Harriet was innocent of aught save a sense (with a charm of its own) of impropriety in going anywhere with Shelley until their union had been sanctioned. That she fully realized what she was doing is unlikely. Had Shelley said nothing to her, she would probably have eloped with him, vaguely taking it for granted that "it would be all right"; had he straightforwardly said that she could only go with him as his mistress, and explained what this signified, she would, in all likelihood, have rescinded her decision as to accompanying him, whatever domestic course she might have taken. She was unmistakably in love with the idolized brother of her friends Elizabeth and Hellen Shelley, but it is even more indubitable that Shelley did not return her affection as a lover. He expressly spoke in one of his letters to Hogg as being actuated more by will ("exerted action" is the exact phrase) than by "inspired passion." In a word, a romantic young girl of sixteen fell in love with an ardent and enthusiastic youth of nineteen; the latter regarded her as a probable recruit to the great army of practical reformers, and was more eager for her conversion than for any loverlike favours. In the brief space which elapsed between his return to London and his elopement with Harriet Westbrook, Shelley passed from exultation and exaltation—exultation at Harriet's surrender and trust, exaltation arising from the glow which warms the heart of the successful proselytizer who sees a disciple take on a willing martyrdom—to doubt, anxiety, and despondency.

Early one morning towards the end of August (1811), Shelley and his cousin Charles Grove met Harriet and drove to the inn in Gracechurch Street, whence the Edinburgh coach at that time departed. No adverse fate brought any Shelleyan or Westbrook authority upon the scene, and in the gathering dusk—for the north mail did not leave till the evening—the fugitives waved goodbye from the top of the coach to young Grove, who went home with probably the lightest heart of the three.

By the time the coach reached York, a night and a
day after leaving London, the bridegroom-designate had
begun to realize that this harsh and tyrannous world has
an ignoble but insatiable desire for cash. With something of that same audacity which had once prompted
him to write, under an assumed name, to the great
preacher Rowland Hill and offer to address his congregation for him, Bysshe had successfully applied to his
uncle Medwin for £25, for elopement expenses—without,
however, specifying the object of the loan. £25, however, does not go far, when coach and inn and other
incidental expenses have to be incurred for two young
people, neither of them possessed of worldly knowledge or
accustomed to carefully calculate expenditure. While
they rested to change horses, Shelley scribbled a hasty line
to Hogg, for deliverance at his friend's rooms in York
on the morrow. This message is short, but, like the
Japanese dog, unfolds tale after tale: " Harriet is with
me. We are in a slight pecuniary distress. We shall
have £75 on Sunday, until when can you send £10?"
O unanthropomorphic Deity of the Iconoclasts, is this
your reward to so ardent and unflagging a disciple?
Must this young poet-enthusiast-reformer-protester endure
the abomination of an empty purse, even as common
folk—yea, even on his elopement journey? It were
enough to make such an one accept a Government
pension and denounce all patriots!

The £25 borrowed from Mr. Medwin thus seems to
have almost entirely disappeared by the time the borrower
had reached York. " A slight pecuniary distress " is
Shelleyan for " hard up," and the modest request for

£10 shows that the extremity was real enough. As for
the larger amount, due "on Sunday," it is now known
that this was no certainty, though Shelley had good
enough reason to depend on two-thirds of it, as the
quarterly allowance from his father was about due. The
remaining third was an expectancy from Mr. Medwin—
the same friend, it will be remembered, who had already
advanced a similar amount—but this sum never came,
for Uncle Medwin was wrathful enough when he learned
for what purpose his one advance had been employed.

At last Edinburgh was reached, and with the least
delay practicable the runaways were quietly married.
This event took place on the 28th of August, when
Percy Bysshe Shelley, *ætat* 19, became the lawful husband
of Harriet Westbrook, *ætat* 16. As Professor Dowden
has pointed out, the irony of fate was not wholly absent,
for in the books of the registrar Shelley is set down as a
Sussex farmer !

Like a dutiful son, Bysshe immediately conveyed to
his father the news of his marriage. Probably he expected a letter in return characteristically full of abuse,
affection, and exaggerated vehemence ; but he was certainly not prepared to find himself once more thrown
on his own resources. Supplies were stopped, even
the quarterly allowance then due was retained, and
"all was at an end." It would have gone badly with
Shelley at this time had it not been for Hogg, and, in
a greater degree, for his Uncle Pilfold, who had taken a
fancy to his enthusiastic, wonderful, eccentric, puzzling,
lovable nephew ; and who in time of need behaved in a
way that should make us resent any sweeping aspersions

on avuncular generosity in general. When Mr. Timothy
Shelley wrote to Mr. John Hogg to announce his son's
latest escapade he did so succinctly : "My son has withdrawn from my protection," he wrote, "and has set off
for Scotland with a young female."

Here was depravity, even crime, indeed. Atheism
was nothing to it. If Shelley had wronged the girl
who trusted him, and had simply departed for a while
with his mistress, Sir Bysshe and Mr. Timothy Shelley
would have severely reprimanded, but would not have
found it very hard to forgive him. "Young blood" and
"wild oats" are convenient phrases to cover many
brutalities and meannesses. But to marry, actually to
marry, a coffee-house keeper's daughter—this was too
much.

While Field Place was in as dire confusion and dis-
may as the Tuileries on that August morning in '92 when
the tocsin of revolt sounded far and wide, the young
husband and wife were spending their days happily
enough in the Scottish capital.

Hogg was not long in joining his friends. Readers
of these pages who are unacquainted with that biographer's record of the Edinburgh experiences of the
trio are to be envied, for they have a pleasure before
them. Hogg always narrates well, and few romances
are more entertaining than the first part of his life of
Shelley. How they laughed, these young people, at all
the depressing solemnities of the worthy Presbyterian
folk ; at the awful prayers, and still more dreadful ser-
mons in " the kirk," at the penitential day called the
Sabbath, whereon, had it been possible, even the human

brain would have been prohibited from its habitual functions. Shelley would sit in one of the formal church-
pews and stare amazed, and either sink into depths of
sighing despondency, or break into a shriek of wild,
eldritch, incontrollable laughter followed by abrupt departure amidst an universal scowl from the offended
congregation.

Some weeks passed pleasantly enough, though Hogg
and even Shelley were occasionally bored by the placid
pleasure which Harriet took in reading aloud certain
highly intellectual and ethical classical works ; the poet
was wont to fall asleep, much to his young wife's dis-
approval and discontent. Even at this early period of
her matrimonial life, and when she was undoubtedly
happy, Harriet frequently spoke of suicide not only as
a justifiable act under certain circumstances, but as per-
missible in most cases—nay, further, of the possibility
that she would herself at some future date put her theory
into practice. Not only to Hogg, but to strangers, she
would refer to suicide as calmly and resolutely as if she
were merely referring to a prospective change to another
country ; even at school she had entertained the idea—
when distraught or even perturbed by any girlish unhappiness—of self-murder. If Hogg's account be credible, and
his statements bear every sign of genuineness, Harriet
even attempted suicide while at the seminary at Clapham
Common. In a most interesting letter of Shelley's
addressed to Miss Hitchener within two months from
his marriage, he describes the circumstances which led
to his elopement with Mr. Westbrook's younger daughter,
and therein incidentally refers to the fact that suicide

had always been a favourite theme with Harriet, but that
he had discountenanced it as the alternative to undesired
life save when one had become convinced of utter
uselessness and experienced unappeasable unhappiness.
It is necessary for the reader to bear these facts in
mind, as we approach the record of that catastrophe
which was the cause of so much misery to all concerned, and has ever since been the source of so
much acrimonious dispute among all sorts and conditions of men. It seems beyond reasonable doubt
to those who have really gone into the affair in all
its bearings, that Harriet Shelley was abnormally in-
sensitive to certain matters to which most men and
women are keenly alive, that, in a word, she had
either an exceptional stoicism or a bluntness of feeling germane to—if not the symptom of the condition
of—a partially diseased brain. It would be unjust to her,
however, not to concede that in the ordinary course of
life she was a cheerful, clever, and amiable person, and
that as a wife she was as sympathetic as her nature
permitted, and in all things dutiful and loyal.

Those but slightly acquainted with Shelley the poet
might easily imagine Shelley the man to have been
keenly sensitive to the beauty of ancient buildings and
the picturesque aspects of ruins, and all that was at once
venerable and lovely. But he was no lover of the by-
gone, save the intellectual past wherein his mind so often
found comfort and stimulus ; he ever looked forward,
heedless of surroundings out of sympathy, as he conceived
them, with his aspirations and dreams. Thus it was that

neither Edinburgh nor York—cities which have charmed
and enthralled many true poets as well as generation
after generation of men—at all fascinated Shelley. Even
that enchanted valley of Bethzatanai, of which he afterwards wrote, would at this period of his life have seemed
to him infinitely wearisome had the dwellers therein
yielded never to any iconoclastic frenzy, denounced no one
nor anything, made no endeavour after a more ideal state.
Neither Holyrood, facing the rugged slopes of the Craigs,
nor York Minster looking serenely along the flow of the
quiet Ouse, interested him so much as a debate upon
Irish politics, or a philosophical epistle from the divine
Miss Hitchener. The lady just named was a friend
whom Shelley idealized to the seventh heaven. At this
time the star of Miss Hitchener shone most radiantly in
his mental vision ; the hardly less splendid though
ruddier light of Hogg illumined the same imaginary
sphere, wherein shone briskly and vividly enough the
inferior brilliancy of Harriet.

Thus it was that five weeks in Edinburgh more than
sufficed for Shelley, and that a move south came to be
determined upon. In addition to his disgust at the
repellent, and to him grossly unspiritual, Presbyterianism
then rampant in the Scottish capital, his lack of sympathy
with the intellectual tastes and aims of those with whom
he came in contact, and the fever of mental and physical
disquiet which henceforth, with ever rarer and shorter
intervals, held him thrall, there was the necessity of
economy. For some time then and thereafter he lived
upon funds supplied by his Uncle Pilford, or raised on
the basis of his legal expectations.

York was decided upon, and thither one morning in October the three companions set out from their pleasant rooms in George Street. Although the expense could be ill afforded, Harriet's wish as to travelling by private post-chaise rather than by coach was acceded to. The journey, an uncomfortable one, occupied three days. To Hogg's surprise an inn was selected, but Shelley explained that he had determined to make a sudden journey south to see if he could not soothe the paternal wrath, and obtain the necessary means, the absence of which was daily becoming more serious.

Immediately after Shelley's departure Miss Eliza West-brook appeared upon the scene. Even if we considerably discount Hogg's remarks concerning Harriet's sister, it is difficult to find her in any way attractive. Shelley, however, does not seem to have then keenly disliked even if he did not actually like Eliza Westbrook, and there were excellent reasons for her stand-off attitude towards Hogg.

An amusing, a clever, a good-natured, and in some respects loyal companion, Hogg was utterly without high principle. When his desires were strong, they had to be gratified ; that was his philosophy. He was an epicurean in the mistaken sense of the term ; in his philosophy was little of the beauty and dignity of the true epicureanism. By an act of criminal folly during Shelley's absence he shattered the latter's high ideal of friendship and caused him poignant grief and suffer-ing, lowered himself irremediably in his own estimation, and forfeited the trust of the confiding girl who had come to look upon him as a brother. In a word, Hogg took advantage of his friend's absence to endeavour to seduce his wife. His action is inexcusable howsoever regarded ; but doubly so when it is certain that he had never the faintest hint of encouragement. Harriet repulsed him indignantly, and Hogg at last so far realized his shame as to offer to write to Shelley and confess all ; an offer which Mrs. Shelley, knowing her husband's nature, wisely declined, though she decided that the matter could not be kept from him on his return. It is Hogg himself who bears witness to the fact that morality was Harriet's favourite theme, and that she found most pleasure in works of a high ethical tone. Yet, notwithstanding his knowledge that her chosen mind-companions were Telemachus and Belisarius, he imagined that the young girl would listen to his passion and act shamefully and treacherously at once to her ideals and her husband.

When Shelley returned, he saw that something unpleasant had occurred. The two friends went out into the fields, and there the sin was duly confessed. Contrite and ashamed as Hogg really seems to have been, Shelley was too shocked to be at first aware of anything save the spiritual tumult of his fallen ideals and ruined hopes. Ultimately he extended a sorrowful forgiveness to his friend, though he realized that they could never again be to each other what in the past they had been. Even in his generosity, however, Shelley saw that they must part company, so without informing Hogg he gave directions for an immediate departure.

To add to his unhappiness the journey south had been unfruitful of any reconciliation between him and his father, and the question of means was becoming more and more imperative.

So, early one morning in November, Shelley, accompanied by his wife and sister-in-law, left for Keswick. For some time thereafter Hogg frequently wrote asking to be taken again into the fold, but Shelley, though almost Quixotically generous and loyal, resolutely declined to see him yet awhile. At Keswick the young people resided in a small house called Claremont Cottage, from the garden of which can be had (for it still exists) a lovely view of Derwentwater and Bassenthwaite against the heights which rise towards the lofty summits of Hindsgarth, Skiddaw, and Scawfell. Here Shelley enjoyed, as he had never hitherto done, the ever-varying loveliness and wonder of mountain beauty. Especially in mid-winter, when the skies were clear, the atmosphere radiant, and the hills garmented with snow, were his delight and enthusiasm called forth. While in the Lake country he came to know Southey. Between them there was only a superficial literary sympathy, and a very real social and political antagonism ; as a man, however, Southey had the young poet's warm regard. Wordsworth, the most ungenial of bards to brethren-in-song, paid him no attention, and Coleridge was not then in the Lake country. The other neighbours (with the exception of William Calvert) were mostly either not very cordial or were persons with whom Shelley did not wish to associate ; one of the kindest was the Duke of Norfolk, who asked Shelley and his wife to pay a visit to him at Greystoke, and who interceded with Mr. Timothy Shelley on behalf of his son. Although Mr. Shelley

for a while remained obdurate, one important outcome of
the visit was the relenting of Mr. Westbrook, who intimated his willingness to allow his daughter £200 a
year; an intimation promptly acted upon, to the relief of
the young pair, who when they went to Greystoke had
hardly a guinea between them. Southey behaved with
his characteristic kindness to his youthful friend. He
negotiated with Shelley's landlord for a lower rent, sent
linen and other household articles to the cottage, and
lent books from his voluminous library. Unfortunately
Shelley had idealized the elder poet too much, and the
inevitable reaction in due time occurred; Southey became
an apostate, a disappointing man, a renegade from the
cause of humanity, and what not. A sincere regard existed
between them, however, as men. I have not space
wherein to dwell longer on this acquaintanceship, though
tempted to do so by the remembrance of many characteristic episodes. Besides the production of a variety of
short poems, more "valuable to philosophical and reflec-
tive minds" than to those who love poetry *as* poetry
(ominous assurance!), Shelley spent part of the early
winter in the composition of a volume of essays, presumably on political and ethical subjects, and of a
romance entitled "Hubert Cauvin," which has never
been discovered in manuscript or any other state. With
a vivid recollection of "Zastrozzi" and "St. Irvyne" I
cannot believe we have lost much by the disappearance of
this romance dealing with the revolutionary period of
French history—though, doubtless, it would prove to be
superior to either of its predecessors. Under the most
favourable circumstances, Shelley never could have be-

come a great writer of fiction; his insight into ordinary humanity was slight, he had too little sense of humour, and mere abstractions were too real to him. Moreover, while in poetry he journeyed on wings—sometimes on fiery pinions, but always on wings strong and wide—in prose he too often walked on stilts; or, at least, seems to do so, so great is the contrast between his poetic music and his prose rhetoric.

In December Shelley heard through Captain Pilfold of a scheme at Field Place whereby he was to be offered at once a handsome sum in the event of his consent to entail the estates on his heir male, or, failing such, upon his younger brother. This bribe, as the poet believed it, was to amount to no less than £2,000 a year. Nothing more vividly shows Shelley's high moral resolve in a good cause, his unflinching loyalty to what he considered right, his will and power to emphasize by practical demonstration his hatred of any evil system, than his indignant refusal to entertain the proposal for a moment. Poor as he was, and with real poverty looming in the near future, he was not going to perpetuate by a selfish action the great evil of the law of primogeniture. His indignation and scorn are genuine, if expressed with Shelleyan vehemence ; the best test thereof being the fact that he refused affluence when he might have had it by appending his signature to a document drawn up, for what seemed to them a wise and good end, by his father and grandfather. That *he* could be asked to entail all this " command over labour" on a possibly altogether unworthy individual, that he should be subjected to this "insult," was more than the ardent, consistent, true-hearted young fellow could stand. Even those who still approve of a system which many of our wisest men have condemned as unjust to individuals and harmful to the national well-being, must admit that Shelley in this matter behaved with the utmost honour and rectitude. It also is to the credit of Mr. Timothy Shelley that, though hurt and disappointed by what seemed to him his son's extraordinary and almost maniacal behaviour, he agreed, early in the ensuing year, to regrant the allowance of £200 a year. Thus, in 1812, the poet and his wife had a yearly income of £400, a sum not at all increased by any literary labour on the part of Shelley, but considerably diminished by printer's bills and charitable deeds.

Early in January Shelley discovered that William Godwin—the famous author of the "Political Justice," which for over two lustra had charmed, repelled, and in one way or another influenced all thinking men in England—was alive. With characteristic impetuosity he wrote at once to the great man, who replied to his evidently very youthful and very ardent correspondent with a kindly letter, which at the same time intimated that he would prefer to enter into correspondence with a human being instead of with Abstract Enthusiasm. Upon this Shelley wrote a long and (to his biographers and students) most important letter. He refers to the influence that Godwin had exercised over him from the moment he first became acquainted with the "Political Justice," gives various details concerning himself, his circumstances, his work, and his aims, and does so with an apparent self-sophistication which has been the source of endless bewilderment. What did Shelley mean by certain extraordinary mis-

SHELLEY. 81

statements, one or two trivial, others more serious? Many say that he consciously lied; others maintain that he told the truth *plus* his own irregular way of doing so, laying more stress on sentiment than on fact (a very vague way of putting it); and others frankly state their belief that he wrote in all sincerity. This question of Shelley's veracity in small matters will perhaps never be satisfactorily settled. Professor Dowden's remarks on this subject are so much to the point that I quote a portion of them. He "was one of those men for whom the hard outline of facts in their own individual history has little fixity; whose footsteps are for ever followed and overflowed by the wave of oblivion; who remember with extraordinary tenacity the sentiment of times and of places, but lose the framework of circumstance in which the sentiment was set; and who, in reconstructing an image of the past, often unconsciously supply links and lines upon the suggestion of that sentiment or emotion which is for them the essential reality. There are not a few persons who from their own experience can vouch for the existence of such transforming powers of recollection; their lives have been for them a train of emotions and ideas rather than of events, and in recalling foregone events an involuntary artistic instinct is at work, unconsciously adapting circumstance to feelings by the aid of a winnowing wind of desire astir amid the mobile cloudland of the past." This is in every way the most satisfactory aspect of the question, and as likely as not is the most just.

If either Godwin or Shelley could have foreseen all that was to indirectly happen from this correspondence!

Shelley, at any rate, with his keen sense of uncompromising morality—a sense which was active even when it
was outraged by contrarious action—would have revolted
from what lay in waiting.

It was while at Keswick that a burglarious attempt
was made upon the Shelleyan household. The actuality
of this story has been much disputed, but I confess that it
seems to me entirely credible. In any case it is surely
going too far to discredit Shelley's version and acquiesce in
the negative assertion of an ignorant dalesman. Professor
Dowden, I am glad to see, evidently believes Shelley's
story, though he does not directly say so. Some time
ago Mr. Hall Caine published some remarks from the
opposite point of view, but instead of throwing further
doubt on Shelley's statements, his remarks only seem to
me to confirm the reasonable and just view. Too much
has been made of the real and hallucinatory episodes in
Shelley's life : at most they are merely episodes, and
in no way affect his character or his actions.

In Shelley's third letter to Godwin he abruptly
announces his intention to leave Keswick at once for
Dublin : " I do not know exactly where. . . . We go
principally *to forward as much as we can* the Catholic
Emancipation." Irish politics had always fascinated the
young enthusiast, and though in religion what was then
called an atheist and now an agnostic, his principles were
of too lofty a kind not to impel him towards temporary alliance with persons enduring a gross injustice.
In the abstract Shelley did not care a straw whether it
were Pope or Presbyter who held ecclesiastical sway in
Ireland ; but what he *did* enthusiastically, and even pas-

sionately, reprobate was the subjection of the Catholics to an insignificant Protestant minority. Before he left Keswick he had written his famous " Address to the Irish People."

On the 3rd of February Shelley and his two companions set sail from Whitehaven for the sister island. The vessel put in at the Isle of Man, and the bad weather continuing after her departure, a northern port was made for, so that it was not until the 12th the travellers reached Dublin. They found accommodation at 7, Lower Sackville Street. Here Eliza Westbrook acted as dispenser of the funds, keeping all the Shelleyan cash "in some nook or corner of her dress." On the morrow of their arrival Shelley sought out a printer, and arranged for the publication of his "Address." It was written so as to suit the simplest readers, and was announced at the small sum of a five-penny bit. In due time the printer sent round several hundred copies of the edition of 1500, and Shelley's soul was filled with ecstasy. His aim in coming to Ireland was merely "to effect a fundamental change in the constitution of the British Empire, to restore to Ireland its native Parliament, to carry the great measure of justice called Catholic Emancipation, and to establish a philanthropic association for the amelioration of human society all over the world." If we sympathetically and somewhat sadly smile at this programme, we cannot refrain from admiration of the enthusiasm and high hopes which animated the youthful reformer.

The author of the "Address" pursued a method of distribution which is more noteworthy for ingenious

eccentricity than for general applicability. The booklets
were sown broadcast : sixty public-houses rejoiced in
their possession ; humble and needy strangers were
employed to sell or bestow any number of copies.
Shelley and Harriet took up a position in the balcony
of their house ; and the Irish people literally perceived
words of wisdom raining down from heaven. No doubt
many a worthy citizen, resentful against England and
intolerant of his country's wrongs, yet felt indignant on
the sudden receipt of a book from on high upon his
portly "presence" or on the crown of his well-brushed
hat. A certain discrimination, however, was shown by the
distributor. " I stand," writes Shelley to a friend on the
eventful 27th of February, " I stand at the balcony of
our window and watch till I see a man *who looks likely.*
I throw a book to him."

The "Address" took captive the minds of many
readers, and Shelley's name passed from mouth to
mouth. At an important Catholic meeting on the 28th,
quite unknown as he was to his audience, he seems to
have attracted attention by his youthful fervour. At the
outset he incurred some slight opposition, mainly because
of some tolerant remarks concerning the Protestants.
Even then he perceived that while Catholics and Protestants alike clamoured for freedom of thought and
worship, freedom was the last thing either were capable
of conceiving : whichever side happened to be in power,
with it lay the decision as to the interpretation of that
most loved, most often uttered, most abused word in
our language. Protestants bewail Catholic intolerance
and persecution, and Catholics in turn proclaim to the

faithful the revengeful and bigoted spirit of the Protestants. There is, there can be, no spiritual freedom in faiths based on dogma, supported by dogma, preaching dogma. This Shelley realized, and for this he has never been forgiven by the "unco' guid" of either persuasion or of the innumerable sects which derive therefrom.

But Shelley, though his most frequent phrase was "for ever," had no intention of remaining "for ever" in Dublin. As a matter of fact, in less than two months' time he realized that his mission in Ireland was over. The debased and unhappy nation had not risen *en masse* on the publication of the "Address" and its pamphlet successors; the authorities had not prosecuted "the young English gentleman"; and the world went on very much as before. There was no particular diminution in smoke, but the fires flamed not and the lava-flood remained inert.

In the "Address," "Proposals for an Association of Philanthropists," and the "Declaration of Rights," the author shows a keen sympathy with the oppressed, a burning indignation against the tyrannous, and considerable mental grasp and foresight. He was much ridiculed in his lifetime, and is still subjected to mild mockery, for his wild hopes. The most fit comment thereupon is a reference to the fact that Catholic Emancipation has taken place, that reform has been brought about, and that other changes which he foresaw are either already accomplished or on the eve of fruition.

Shelley had another motive for return to England. The divine Miss Hitchener, the schoolmistress of the Sussex village of Hurstpierpoint, longed to see her

ardent correspondent and friend (as well as, out of
amiable politeness, his wife, and, out of civility, his sister),
even as that individual yearned to see the "soul of his
soul." Like Miss Westbrook, this highly intellectual
and—in correspondence—attractive woman rejoiced in
the name of Eliza. Whether for the reason of a suitable
distinction, or because she was of too noble-spirited
mould to have a name shared by numerous unintellec-
tual and unspiritual persons, the Shelleys substituted
therefor the more euphonious "Portia." In a short
space of time Shelley found it expedient to change this
Shakespearian designation to the "Brown Demon."

Ere long she was hated by Eliza Westbrook, disliked
by Harriet Shelley, and finally repelled by the "soul of
her soul." It seems she had at last to be bribed to take
her departure. Yet even after the experience of the
"Brown Demon" Shelley did not outgrow his tendency
to invest every new and sympathetic correspondent with
such hues of ideal splendour as would have made the
apparition of Gabriel a tawdry spectacle.

After leaving Ireland the trio wandered about day by
day until they temporarily settled in a cottage at Nant-
gwillt, near Rhayader, in North Wales. Thence they went
to Cwm Elan, to Chepstow, and, in June, to Lynmouth.
The manifold beauties of sea and sky at this loveliest
spot in Devon took captive, as they well might, Shelley's
imagination. The poetic impulse in him began to awake
into true life. Land and ocean, the caverned shore for
ever resonant with tidal music, the changing glories of
atmosphere and cloud, enchanted and stimulated his
sensitive nature.

The curious admixture of boyish enthusiasm and simplicity and the mature power of sedate argument and decision, which throughout his short life characterized Shelley, is exemplified in the way in which at this time he would send his "Declaration of Rights" and other revolutionary tractates on adventurous voyages in little balloons, sealed bottles, and so forth—and in his grave and weighty "Letter to Lord Ellenborough," on the latter's judgment against a printer for having issued the third part of Paine's "Age of Reason."

The late summer of this year was one of the comparatively serene periods in Shelley's life. He was happy with his wife ; he had a kindly toleration for Eliza ; and "Portia" (by this time Miss Hitchener's name was changed again to Bessy) had not yet become the "Brown Demon." And, above all, he was beginning to realize that he was indeed a poet, though even yet he had written little or nothing on which to base a claim so often unjustifiably put forth.

In September yet another change occurred, and Shelley installed himself with the three ladies at a beautiful residence called Tannyrallt, near Tremadoc, in Carnarvonshire. Here, besides delighting in his surroundings, he practically interested himself in Mr. Madocks' great scheme for the reclamation of part of the land from the sea, and by his enthusiasm, example, and advice materially assisted the fulfilment of the project. In his eagerness to be of further use he even made a sudden journey to London, in order to interest a number of people in Mr. Madocks' philanthropic quest. To the biographer the most interesting fact in connection with

this London trip is the circumstance that Shelley and
Godwin then met face to face for the first time. Each
was charmed with the other. To the budding poet the
author of " Political Justice " seemed a nineteenth-century
Socrates, a fit mortal for deification if any disruption
of the existent heavenly hierarchy should occur. To
the somewhat worn and disappointed philosopher his
new friend seemed a possible disciple who would pro-
pagate the latter-day gospel of the Godwinian cult. During the few weeks of the Shelleys' stay in town the two
friends saw much of each other. Mary Wollstonecraft
Godwin, the only daughter of Godwin by his unfortunate
wife, Mary Wollstonecraft, was at this time absent on a
visit to friends in Scotland; but it is probable—as she
returned to London on November 10th, and as Shelley
did not leave for Wales till three days later—that she
caught at least a glimpse of the man with whose future
life hers was to be so closely connected. It was during
this visit also that Shelley practically forgave Hogg, by
voluntarily resuming the intimacy which had been checked
by the latter's criminal folly at York. He called upon
his late friend (who had returned to London in the pursuit of his profession), and let him see that, so far as was
possible, all would be as of yore. Hogg was very glad
to be really friendly with Shelley again. He undoubtedly
admired and had a sincere affection for his eccentric
comrade, and probably bitterly regretted the act which
had demonstrated his untrustworthiness.

By the middle of November (1812) the Shelleys and
Miss Westbrook (for the " Brown Demon "—alas, for
ruined ideals on either side—had been got rid of) found

themselves again in Wales. It was with intense satisfaction that Shelley exchanged the griminess of London
for the freedom and beauty of the hill-country, where the
loftiest of the mountain fells were taking on their first
wintry snows. But even in the delight of being once
more out of the too crowded haunts of toiling London, the
poet found that his sympathies were more with humanity
than with nature. The latter was to be his stimulus, his
delight, his love ; but the former was to be the object of
his life's devotion.

> " Let me for ever be what I have been,
>   But not for ever at my needy door
>   Let Misery linger, speechless, pale, and lean ;
>   I am the friend of the unfriended poor."

The winter passed rapidly, for every hour was occupied. Harriet read widely, and studied Latin so per-
severingly that she projected an epistle to a friend in that
language. Plato, Lucretius, Thucydides, Xenophon,
Plutarch, and other classical writers (mainly historians),
and among the moderns Spinoza and Kant, afforded
Shelley subject for continuous thought and speculation.
Poetry he also wrote in a slight degree, and "Queen
Mab" began to grow. But most of his time was occupied
with the Tremadoc embankment labour, and in attending
to the poor and distressed. The winter of 1812–13 was
one of great severity, and the suffering among the
labouring population was keen and widespread. Medwin
relates how he had " often heard Mr. Madocks dilate on
Shelley's numerous acts of benevolence, his relieving the

distresses of the poor, visiting them in their humble
abodes, and supplying them with food and raiment and
fuel during the winter." Other witnesses have recorded
his generosity and his self-sacrificing donations of money
at a time when his own means were straitened.

With the sense of impending calamity which oppresses
every reader of the record of Shelley's early married
life, it is with a sensation of surprise that one discerns
how happy at this time were the young poet and his
girlish wife. To realize this one does not need the
evidence of the remark in one of his letters to Hogg, that
"when I come home to Harriet I am one of the happiest
of the happy."

By the close of the winter "Queen Mab" and a
number of short poetical pieces, sufficient to constitute a
small volume, were in a more or less finished state of
readiness for the press. But the poet had other dis-
turbances besides the Tremadoc affair. In February
Leigh Hunt was sentenced to fine and imprisonment on
account of his "libel" in *The Examiner* upon the Prince
Regent, and throughout the length and breadth of the
country a sound of expostulation went up—a protest
not drowned by the jubilant cackle of the Conservative
geese who rejoiced at the curtailment of any liberal-
minded man's freedom of speech. Naturally Shelley
"boiled with indignation." Though hard pressed in
money matters, and with prospective expenses anent the
advent of the child for whom Harriet had already begun
to prepare, he at once forwarded £20 wherewith to head
a subscription for the benefit of the "martyr to liberty."
Leigh Hunt also records that while in prison he received

a letter from Shelley with "a princely offer"—but both
this offer and the public subscription were, under the
circumstances rightly, declined by the genial man of
letters, who was happier even in arbitrary confinement
than ever the too sensitive Shelley was in the course of
his short life.

The stay at Tannyrallt was abruptly brought to a close
by a strange incident which is alleged to have occurred
towards the end of February. One wild night Shelley
heard the noise made by some intruder. Springing from
bed and seizing his pistols he descended to the room
which had been broken into; seeing his antagonist he
fired and was fired upon, and a minute later the burglar
or assassin had vanished. An hour or two later Harriet
and Miss Westbrook having retired to their bedrooms,
leaving Shelley and his manservant, Dan Healy, down-
stairs on watch—a second attack was made. Shots
were again interchanged, and a hand-to-hand conflict
ensued. Just as the assailant was gaining the mastery,
Dan (who had been sent to ascertain the hour) rushed
into the room, and the murderous villain suddenly fled.
Shelley's "night-gown" was pierced by a ball from his
antagonist's pistol, and he declared, not only then but
years later, that he had received permanent injury in the
hand-to-hand conflict. That Shelley absolutely and
entirely believed in the whole episode is undeniable.
Harriet did so, and her letter to Hookham shortly after
the event is full of circumstantial evidence. Both
believed that the mysterious intruder was a would-be
assassin, and a man named Leeson was the suspected
person. Without considering the assassination story as

altogether impossible, it is much more likely that the
scoundrel was a burglar more than ordinarily daring on
account of Shelley's youth and known delicacy, and also
on account of the probable ready gold of the young
philanthropist, who was almost daily wont to relieve the
poor, and who but a short time before had sent an
indigent widow a five-pound note. But eight out of ten
people then and now consider the whole affair to have
been an hallucination. The evidence in support of this,
however, is counterbalanced by that to the contrary. If
the pistol-ball presumably fired by the assailant was found
indented in the wainscot *towards* instead of *from* the
direction of the window, there was the testimony of the
ball-pierced night-gown. But, whether hallucination or
not, the Shelleys were so much alarmed (Shelley himself
was for a time entirely prostrated by the nervous shock
and constant apprehension) that an immediate move far
from Tannyrallt was decided upon. There is one thing
which is absolutely clear to all unprejudiced persons,
namely, that while the episode may have been hallucinatory, it was no figment of Shelley's. Personally I do
not hesitate, after a careful examination of all the evidence
for and against the Shelleyan account, to believe that,
substantially, the story is true. There is no real evidence
in favour of the assassin theory, but this has nothing to
do with the fundamental truth of what is alleged to have
occurred at Tannyrallt. Naturally enough the poet
never disallowed the idea of attempted assassination;
even in Italy, years later, he sometimes feared that his
adversary was on his track. We may fairly conclude that
the house was entered by a desperate burglar, and that

the encounter, pretty much as related by Harriet in her letter to Mr. Hookham, actually occurred.

Dublin was the city of refuge chosen by the alarmed young people ; thence they went to Killarney, and took a cottage on one of the lake islands, probably on either Ross or Dinas. But April found them again in London (or rather the Shelleys, for Miss Westbrook had temporarily remained in Ireland, owing to the lack of funds at the poet's command), for early in that month they were the guests of Mr. Westbrook at his house in Chapel Street, Grosvenor Square. Their stay here was brief, and after some experience of hotels they settled in apartments close to Piccadilly.

The spring passed into midsummer, and for Shelley the season was one of pleasantness and comparative quietude from mental excitement. Hogg's detailed account of the poet's life at this time should be read, or Professor Dowden's pages based thereon, setting forth the strange ways of the eccentric poet, and of his—(I had almost written " daily routine," but to couple "routine " with Shelley's name would be impossible)—varied experiences. In the spring he placed in the hands of Mr. Hookham, the publisher, the manuscript of his "Queen Mab," and arranged for its publication in a limited edition. Ere the end of June Harriet gave birth to a girl-babe, and Shelley, not yet of age, realized that he was not only a husband but a father. The baby was christened Ianthe, possibly after the violet-eyed lady of "Queen Mab," though, poor child, it was destined to bring, not happiness, but grief to its parents. That he loved the little one is beyond doubt; and though it is

by no means always safe to accept a poetic record as a
strictly veracious statement, one cannot read his touching
and beautiful sonnet to Ianthe without realizing his absolute sincerity.   In this sonnet there is unmistakably
set forth his love for wife and child :—

> " Dear art thou, O fair and fragile blossom ;
> Dearest when most thy tender traits express
> The image of thy mother's loveliness."

In the first beauty of motherhood Harriet seemed
closelier drawn to Shelley than ever.   It was not long,
however, before he noticed with pain and sorrow—what
was evident to Hogg and others as well as to himself—
that his young wife betrayed a strange and growing insen-
sibility to her child and even to him ; that she lost her interest in those matters of the heart and mind which to
him were so far above all mundane circumstances ; and
that she was no longer the Harriet whom he had known
and loved.   Maternity seemed to have been the spell
which resolved the angel into the commonplace woman.
Alas, poor Harriet ! insensible you may have been, even
commonplace, but if wood will mate with fire there can
be but one result.   To be ideally loved by a man like
Shelley is to court sorrow and disaster.   We are mortals,
and to be loved otherwise than with human imperfection
is calamitous misfortune.   None of us is adapted for en-
thronement upon a sunlit pedestal.   As Miss Hitchener,
the divine Portia, "the soul of my soul," passed away
from Shelley's life as the " Brown Demon "; as Eliza
Westbrook, once intelligent and amiable, awakened in her

brother-in-law "an inexpressible sensation of disgust and horror to see her caress Ianthe," and even "sometimes [made him] feel faint with the fatigue of checking the over-flowings of [his] unbounded abhorrence for this miser-able wretch"; so poor young Harriet was to pass out of the valley of enchantment into the highway of wearisome and even repellent common folk. That Harriet was in some ways to blame for the growing estrangement is un-questionable, but it is with almost unmixed pity we read of her life from this time forth. On the other hand, again, it must not be forgotten that Shelley married his wife out of chivalrous generosity, and not from love as commonly understood. Love, the overwhelming love of a man for a woman, was lying in wait for him, but the time was not yet come.

Not long after the birth of Ianthe (or, to give her her full title, Ianthe Elizabeth—for the second name had been added out of compliment to Shelley's well-loved eldest sister) her parents went to reside at Bracknell, in Berkshire. The deciding motive for this change was Shelley's desire to be near some new friends of the name of Boinville. The Boinvilles he had first met at the house of mutual friends and had been charmed by their emotional manners and their quick sympathies. Mrs. Boinville has a peculiar interest for the student of Shelley's life. In the course of time she descended, per-haps, from the throne of a Domination to that of a Power; but there in high state she remained, and knew not the vulgar dust which enveloped what were once equal ideals. It must, however, be added that the devotee worshipped at the Boinville shrine from afar, for after a brief period of idolatry within the actual presence, circumstances permanently separated the twain. In a letter to Peacock written some years later, Shelley curiously but unconsciously affords a clue to his own nature while describing Mrs. Boinville : "It was hardly possible for a person of the extreme subtlety and delicacy of (her) understanding and affections to be quite sincere and constant." This is a saying which shows that Shelley had more knowledge of human character than he is often credited with. It probably was true of Mrs. Boinville ; it certainly was true of himself.

From Bracknell the Shelleys went in the autumn to the Lakes, and thence with little delay to Edinburgh. Before this, however, Shelley, at his mother's desire, had paid a secret visit to Field Place, where once more he enjoyed his mother's and sisters' company. He had also gone to London on the attainment of his majority, and after unsuccessful negotiations with his father, had raised a few hundred pounds on the ruinous alternative of a post-obit. The winter of 1813 was spent in Edinburgh ; so far as Shelley was concerned, mainly in arduous and abstruse study. Beyond the prose dissertation entitled "The Refutation of Deism" he produced little literary work. Early in 1814 he renewed his visit to Bracknell, and rejoiced in the sympathetic companionship there afforded him. From there, in March, he wrote an urgent letter to his father anent his pecuniary troubles and the necessity of resorting to ruinous means of procuring money, but without any satisfactory result. By this time Harriet was again pregnant, and it occurred to Shelley (or it was suggested to him by Godwin) that if a son and heir were born to him

Sir Bysshe and Mr. Shelley might seek to bring forward a claim of illegitimacy, on account of his marriage in Scotland as a minor with a minor. To prevent any trouble in this direction he re-married Harriet at St. George's, Hanover Square, on the 24th of March. This re-marriage is, to us, the seal upon Shelley's early happiness.

Want of sympathy and other alienating influences had now set in clashing currents from either side. Harriet became hard and indifferent; her husband grew more and more disappointed and disenchanted. Ianthe was but a frail bond of union; her mother's refusal to nurse her, and Harriet's general heedlessness of her baby, still further exasperated Shelley. In April Eliza took her departure, and with her went Shelley's wife and child, while he remained in the congenial household of the Boinvilles. The well-known "Stanzas: April, 1814," were written at this time. With all their charm and significance they are yet to me more the production of a prose writer than of a poet : such a line as—

"Duty and dereliction guide thee back to solitude,"

would have been almost impossible to Shelley a few years later. In May the coming crisis had cast its shadow before it. The poet addressed to his wife some pathetic lines wherein he pleads against her alien attitude. It was while conscious of his ruined love and vanishing affection, and while suffering keenly from Harriet's indifference to his appeals, that Shelley met Mary Godwin. Love arose, nay love enveloped them both ere they were aware of their position ; like a fiery wind it consumed

7

and swept away all obstacles to their passion. Mary Godwin was then in her seventeenth year, but had the carriage and demeanour of one accustomed to womanly ways of thought and action; she was fair to look upon rather than lovely, of an intellectual type; of a calm and apparently passionless exterior, she had an ardent nature, and was, in a word, just such a child of William Godwin and Mary Wollstonecraft as the theorist might have prophesied. By training, by temperament, by imagination—in all things, she was fitted to mate with such an one as Shelley. She could be to him all that Harriet had been, and infinitely more : as he could be to her an ideal, a friend, and a husband—a triune creature beyond the conception of the girl-wife who had voluntarily left him, though without thought of definite separation.

That there were barriers to an absolutely sympathetic union between even such kindred spirits as Percy Bysshe Shelley and Mary Godwin was inevitable. Shelley had no compeer upon this earth. No fellow mortal could have satisfied the whole desire of his heart. Perhaps this almost fantastic yearning for the unattainable—this desire of the moth for the star—is the heritage of many of us. It is a longing which shall be insatiate even in death : but of necessity there can be few of us who, in the words of Mérimée, so passion for this passion as did Shelley. Like the strange phantoms in *Vathek* he was for ever conscious of a fiery heart agonizing in unquenchable flame.

Lady Shelley has sympathetically narrated the impression made by Shelley upon Mary Godwin, and how the poet won her love. And as for the extremity of

emotion which this new love—or rather this first advent
of love—excited in Shelley we have the unbiassed and
unexaggerated record of Peacock, who at this period
was closely intimate with the poet.

" Nothing that I ever read in tale or history could
present a more striking image of a sudden, violent, irresistible, uncontrollable passion, than that under which I
found him labouring when, at his request, I went up from
the country to call on him in London. Between his old
feelings towards Harriet, from whom he was not then
separated, and his new passion for Mary, he showed in
his looks, in his gestures, in his speech, the state of a
mind ' suffering, like a little kingdom, the nature of an
insurrection.' His eyes were bloodshot, his hair and
dress disordered."

But though love had come upon Shelley so over-
whelmingly, he did not surrender without a fierce struggle.
It was the constraint he put upon his emotions that produced the spiritual turmoil in which he suffered by day
and by night. It was almost accidentally—though inevitably—that heart learned the secret of heart : that
friendship stood forth revealed as love. The stanzas
addressed to " Mary Wollstonecraft Godwin: June, 1814 "
are the poetic record of this period of passionate uncertainty. As verses they are touching in sentiment, but
juvenile in expression : for so consummate an artist as
Shelley was soon to become there is an unenfranchised
lyric movement which surprises the student of his poetry.

The fourth and fifth stanzas are at once the best and the most interesting.

" Upon my heart thy accents sweet
  Of peace and pity fell like dew
On flowers half dead ; thy lips did meet
  Mine tremblingly ; thy dark eyes threw
Their soft persuasion on my brain,
Charming away its dream of pain.

We are not happy, sweet ! our state
  Is strange, and full of doubt and fear ;
More need of words that ills abate ;—
  Reserve or censure come not near
Our sacred friendship lest there be
No solace left for thee or me."

From a pathetic letter written by Harriet from Bath early in July it is manifest that she had no idea of the permanency of the separation. Four days' silence had been sufficient to break down her reserve. Not having heard from Shelley for this brief period, she feared that some misfortune had waylaid him, and therefore she wrote a letter of anxious inquiry to Hookham the bookseller, as one certain to be acquainted with Shelley's whereabouts. But by this time the latter had become convinced (on evidence very dubious even when most presentable) that his wife had been unfaithful to him : that, in a word, Harriet's as yet unborn child would not be of his parentage. Later he came to believe absolutely that in this point, at any rate, he had wronged Harriet, and that Charles Bysshe was veritably his own son. With his peculiar views on marriage—views, it must be remembered, shared by his wife—the contract between a man and a woman was one dissoluble at will, on proven incompatibility of mind and tastes : and still more imperative seemed disunion when married lealty no longer existed. From what we know of Shelley it is certain that had he believed in Harriet's love and constancy he would, at whatever cost, have refrained from the course which in fact he pursued. Harriet does seem to have given *him* (I have emphasized the pronoun, for none other believed for a moment in her disloyalty) some cause for suspicion. But while one can at most only surmise, it seems indubitable that she was guiltless of any wrong to her husband.

When Shelley realized that in no case could he again regard Harriet as his wife—by which he meant something more than a mate—and that Mary Godwin had won his love, he determined to explain his position fully to the unfortunate girl who had borne him his well-loved Ianthe and was in due time to give birth to his second child. He would offer her his friendship, and even urge her to live with him and Mary. Incredible as it may seem, he saw nothing incongruous in this extraordinary proffer.

But before it was made, and while the curious complication of Shelley's relationships was weaving its web of good and evil, the husband and wife had an interview in London at the former's request. It is not known what was agreed upon or disputed at this meeting, though it is highly probable that Shelley definitely assured Harriet of the close of their matrimonial connection. But reconciliation as understood by Mrs. Shelley was now impossible, though she did not for some time

surrender the idea of her husband's loyalty. She looked
upon his desertion of her with a philosophical tolerance
which does her credit. It was but an attack of passion,
a curable mania. Months, even a year or so might pass,.
and then this new divinity would fall from her high
estate even as had succumbed the "Brown Demon,"
once "the soul of his soul." She bitterly resented, she
gave no shadow of condonation to the part played by
Mary, but she believed in the impermanency of the new
connection. She was, fortunately or unfortunately, incapable of real passion, and so could not calculate possible
results. As for Mary Godwin, she shared her father's and
her lover's views on the marriage contract; and, what is
more to the point when we come to consider *her* responsibility, she fully believed that there was no barrier to her
union with Shelley, insomuch that Harriet (as she had
every reason to believe) had been unfaithful.

NOTE.—It will be as well to give here, as succinctly as practicable, the record of Harriet Shelley's after-life. She continued to
correspond with her husband after his departure with Mary Godwin,
and, as already stated, hoped against hope that he would tire of his
passion and return to her. Shelley had made for her the best monetary settlement within his power, so she was not dependent upon her
father or any one else. (Early in 1815 she was in receipt of an income of £400, one half of which was paid by Shelley, the other by
her father.) She returned to Bath, and there awaited her confinement. Naturally, she declined to accept her husband's proposal
that she should join him and Mary in Switzerland : for one thing
she relied on a change of his sentiments when her child should be born.
The latter event occurred on the last day of November, and the
eight-months' baby proved to be a boy. On his return to England
Shelley visited her, and they agreed to name their second child
Charles Bysshe. It is to Mary Godwin's diary that we are indebted

A fortnight later than the interview just referred to Shelley and Mary Godwin departed for the Continent.

for most of our knowledge of Shelley's life at this time. He saw Harriet on several occasions, and she became more and more convinced of the insuperableness of the breach between them. Unfortunately the portion of the diary from mid-May until the ensuing July (1816) is non-existent—so that in Mary Godwin's journals there is no further reference to Harriet Shelley until the day when a letter from Hookham brought tragic news. Shelley was pleased with his little boy, but the child brought no reconciliation between husband and wife. Charles Bysshe, it may be added, died in boyhood—some four years after the Spezzian sea had calmed for ever the passionate unrest of his father's life. When at last Harriet realized the finality of her disunion with Shelley, she gave way to bitterness of heart. If her love had been strenuous she would have yielded to despair ; that this was not so is to be inferred from the fact that disappointed, resentful, eager for pleasure to alleviate her pain, she formed a new connection. This resulted unfortunately, and then poor Harriet foresaw nothing worth living for. From her schooldays onward (as the reader will remember) she had always maintained not only the inviolable right of every human being to end at will his or her life, but had also again and again, at long intervals and before various witnesses, reiterated her intention to put her theory in practice the moment the burden of life should become insupportable, or even oppressive. In no fit of despair, but intolerant of her misery, she left her lodging near her father's house one day early in November, over two years after Shelley's departure with Mary Godwin, and found surcease of all pain in the waters of the Serpentine.

It has been my aim as far as practicable to narrate the incidents of Shelley's life impartially, and to do so it was necessary to avoid the language either of unqualified approval or of condemnation. I therefore leave readers to form their own conclusions on the painful incidents of Shelley's separation from his wife, her subsequent course of life, and her suicide. But I must warn those who wish to be in a fair position to judge that they cannot attain such a position from the perusal of a short monograph like this, not even from the

monumental work of Professor Dowden.   They must go to the
original records, to the correspondence of many persons writing
from different standpoints, and must take into consideration many
circumstances necessarily omitted from this memoir.   Without
making any dogmatic statement, I wish simply—as one who has
thoroughly studied the question in all its bearings, and who is
familiar with all that can be adduced for and against the persons
concerned—to assert my belief that Shelley was guiltless of wrong
intent, that he believed he was acting not only consistently, but
wisely and even justly, and that his sorrow and life-long regret for
the malfortunate outcome of his action were genuine.   Harriet was
unhappy, and, in accordance with her principles, she acted aright in
putting an end to her life.   We may condemn the act, but it is
absurd to speak of suicide as a cowardly or evil resort when it is due
to honest conviction of its desirability and even rectitude.   Shelley
experienced bitter grief when he heard of the death of the woman
whom he had married, and who had borne him two children, and it
is doubtful if his philosophy brought him real comfort—the philosophy that told him he could in nowise be held responsible for what
had occurred.   It is with deep regret those who revere Shelley have
to condemn him for his unjust suspicions of his wife's disloyalty,
suspicions which he afterwards admitted were baseless.   It is a sad
story, howsoever regarded : perhaps the easiest way of escape from
difficult judgment is to admit that Harriet, an unsuitable wife for
a man like Shelley, was latterly foolish and unsympathetic—that
Shelley, intoxicated with the vision of the ideal life, behaved
unwisely, and even wrongfully, in his conduct of certain realities.

CHAPTER IV

WHEN Shelley and Mary Godwin left London on the morning of the 28th of July (1814), they were accompanied by the latter's half-sister, or half-sister by courtesy. Miss Clara Mary Jane Clairmont — by her relatives called Jane, but to the Shelleys and their friends known as Clare or Claire — was the daughter, by a former marriage, of Godwin's second wife. She was like Mary Godwin in certain of her tastes, but intellectually she was her inferior. Mary was fair and suave, Claire was dark and extremely vivacious. Both were at this time young girls, and were affectionate companions if not friends. They had an elder half-sister, Fanny Imlay, the daughter of Godwin's first wife, Mary Wollstonecraft, who had lived in unlegalized marriage with a Mr. Imlay. Miss Imlay was of a less ardent and more timid disposition than either of her half-sisters, and would probably, had she been at home in this eventful July, have dissuaded Mary from elopement with Shelley. Before readers wonder why Shelley, holding the principles he did, did not openly ask Mary Godwin (with similar principles) to accompany him from the house of her father (who, again, held principles identical), it must be borne in mind (1) that Shelley had a wife living; (2) that his means were very limited, and would speedily be more so, as Mr. Westbrook would at once cease the annual allowance he made to his daughter Harriet and her husband, a course, moreover, which Mr. Timothy Shelley might also adopt; and (3) that Godwin's daughter was considerably under age.

There are all the elements of a tragi-comedy in this episode. Not very many months previously Shelley had written to Godwin a letter of boyish enthusiasm, more ambitious, apparently, of the master's reception of him as a worshipping disciple than of any other honour or glory the world could bestow. And now he elopes with the philosopher's young daughter, and, moreover, includes another of his mentor's children in the party. Yet, all the time, Shelley never seems to have realized that Godwin had any just cause of complaint against him. As a matter of fact, the blow was not one entirely without compensation. The author of the " Political Justice " was familiar with the unpleasantnesses of poverty, and there was balm to his wounded spirit in the knowledge that, for the time being at any rate, he would not need to provide for either Mary or Claire. And he foresaw, what actually occurred, ultimate valuable monetary assistance from Shelley.

There is some uncertainty as to whether or not Miss Clairmont left Godwin's house with Mary with knowledge of what was about to take place. Her own account (but she was by no means always a reliable authority concerning herself) was, that she left the house in the silent summer morning, believing that she and Mary were only going to

indulge in an exceptionally early walk; and that when they
encountered Shelley at the corner of Hatton Garden he
begged her to accompany him and Mary to France, as
she was a good French linguist, and they were unfamiliar
with the language. However, it is a matter of little importance.

The three journeyed to Paris, and thence with little
delay to Switzerland, by way of the Jura. It had been
their intention to perform the journey across France on
foot, and to this end they had hired a donkey for the
conveyance of their luggage. Mainly, however, on
account of Mary's indifferent health, a mule-drawn
vehicle was engaged, which carried them across plain
and hill till they passed the Jura, beheld the heights
beyond Neufchatel, and finally reached Brunnen on the
lake of Lucerne. Here Shelley began the last (unless we
consider the fragment styled " The Coliseum," composed
in 1819), and what promised to be much the best, of his
prose tales—the romance entitled "The Assassins." There
is nothing of the "Zastrozzi" style about this well-written
though occasionally somewhat stilted narrative. The finest
portion of it describes the beautiful valley of Bethzatanai.

Want of money caused an abrupt return to be necessary, and the homeward journey was made by way of the
Reuss and the Rhine. This trip was greatly enjoyed by
Shelley, and gave him the main part of the material where-
from he extracted the glorious lines of "Alastor." It
came to a close at Gravesend on the 13th of September,
and is faithfully recorded in Mary Godwin Shelley's
" History of a Six Weeks' Tour."

Monetary troubles, disagreeables of various kinds, including visits to Harriet, occupied the autumnal and early winter months. Early in January of 1815, Shelley's prospects very materially improved, owing to the death of his grandfather, Sir Bysshe. By an arrangement with his father, now Sir Timothy, he found himself in the possession of a yearly income of £1,000. Of this allowance a fifth part went to the sustenance of Harriet and the children, and no inconsiderable portion of the remainder was charitably and generously expended.

The months went past very happily so far as Shelley and Mary were concerned. More and more each realized that they had not been blinded by passion, but that each was genuinely suited to the other. Many hours weekly were spent by Shelley in assisting the necessitous, and it is said (though on extremely dubious authority), that he even walked a hospital, in order that he might acquire sufficient medical knowledge to be of real service to the poor whom it was his wont to visit. Perhaps these experiences insensibly increased his morbid fears concerning his own health; at any rate, at this period he became convinced that he had but a short time to live. Undoubtedly he was fragile in body and frail in constitution, but neither then nor later does he seem to have suffered from any organic complaint, although, in the spring of 1815, a transient abscess (the origin of much pain and alarm) had formed upon one of his lungs. Probably it was nephritis that attacked him at intervals; to this affection could be attributed most of his symptoms, along with the nervous disorder which had naturally ensued from his habits of fasting, from insufficient sustenance, and excessive mental excitation.

At all times, from his boyhood onward, he consciously dwelt in the shadow of early death ; a fact which must be borne in mind when we come to consider his poetic development, powers, and achievement.

On or about the 20th of February, Mary gave birth to a seven-months' girl-babe, a delicate infant, but for whom the father and mother hoped all things. Some ten or twelve days elapsed, and Mary awoke to find her little one dead. The grief experienced by both parents was poignant. There is a touching pathos in the entries of Mary's diary about this time—

"*Sunday, March 19th.*—Dream that my little baby came to life again ; that it had only been cold, and that we rubbed it before the fire, and it lived. Awake and find no baby. I think about the little thing all day.

"*Monday, March 20th.*—Dream again about my baby."

In mid-May, Claire Clairmont left her friends for a time, greatly to Mary's relief, who had tired of her constant companionship and her somewhat capricious temper. Soon after this Shelley found London again becoming intolerable, for was not "sumer y-comin in"? Therefore he hasted away to seek refuge in Devon. A little later, however, he and Mary found a suitable cottage at Bishopsgate, on the eastern borders of Windsor Park. Here Shelley was close to the lovely woodlands and the river, far from noise and disturbance, and in in this locality he passed many happy days. Here it was that "Alastor" was written, the poem wherein Shelley first rises into the realm of absolute poetry. Sometimes Peacock, then a resident at Marlow, would walk over and join the young people for a short time; and late in August a delightful water excursion was made, in which both Peacock and Charles Clairmont were of the party. Those were happy days indeed for Shelley, as the friends sailed or oared their way up the lovely river reaches, till at last, in the golden September glow, the spires of Oxford rose above the riverine alders and willows. At the ancient city they disembarked, and Shelley showed Mary his former haunts, and the rooms he and Hogg had occupied when the fiat of expulsion had gone forth against them. Thereafter they proceeded up-stream to a mile or two beyond Lechlade, fourteen miles from the source of the Thames, but finding the stream too shallow they had perforce to return. Windsor was reached again in four days, and all felt better in mind and body for the happy experience. Shelley, as Clairmont wrote to his sister Claire, had even obtained "the ruddy, healthy complexion of the autumn," and had become "twice as fat as he used to be." With pleasant companionship, freedom from trouble, joy in the beauty of earth, river, and sky (and, as Peacock records, wholesomely fed), Shelley found it easy to believe that health was no impossible dream for him. But in the midst of this transient happiness he was keenly alive to hints of melancholy and sadness. While night descended upon stream-swept Lechlade, he was touched with the pathos and mystery of the scene. The Thames near Lechlade has inspired at least two great poets since Shelley's time, one of whom was but recently in our midst; but none has written lovelier stanzas than those composed by the youth of twenty-three.

A SUMMER-EVENING CHURCHYARD, LECHLADE, GLOUCESTERSHIRE.

THE wind has swept from the wide atmosphere
Each vapour that obscured the sunset's ray ;
And pallid evening twines its beaming hair
In duskier braids around the languid eyes of day ;
Silence and twilight, unbeloved of men,
Creep hand in hand from yon obscurest glen.

They breathe their spells towards the departing day,
Encompassing the earth, air, stars, and sea ;
Light, sound, and motion own the potent sway,
Responding to the charm with its own mystery.
The winds are still, or the dry church-tower grass
Knows not their gentle motions as they pass.

Thou too, aërial Pile ! whose pinnacles
Point from one shrine like pyramids of fire,
Obey'st in silence their sweet solemn spells,
Clothing in hues of heaven thy dim and distant spire,
Around whose lessening and invisible height
Gather among the stars the clouds of night.

The dead are sleeping in their sepulchres,
And mouldering as they sleep ; a thrilling sound,
Half sense, half thought, among the darkness stirs,
Breathed from their wormy beds all living things around,
And mingling with the still night and mute sky
Its awful hush is felt inaudibly.

Thus solemnized and softened, death is mild
And terrorless as this serenest night :
Here could I hope, like some inquiring child
Sporting on graves, that death did hide from human sight
Sweet secrets, or beside its breathless sleep
That loveliest dreams perpetual watch did keep.

The Windsor woods were in all the glory of early autumn when the travellers returned. Amid the lovely foliage and in the serene air Shelley's genius expanded like a flower. A new mastery had come to him; the faculty of expression was no longer painfully inferior to the conception. That lovely poem "Alastor," the more fascinating because of its autobiographical significance, grew as the autumn waned ; and ere the last gold of the lime and elm had been mingled with the fallen amber and crimson of the oak and beech, it had reached its majestic close.

Before referring with brief detail to " Alastor," I must return to Shelley's early poem, "Queen Mab." Corrected and recast in 1812, this precocious production saw the light early in 1813. In 1821, a London bookseller named Clark issued a pirated edition, greatly to the annoyance and anger of the poet, who was then abroad. " Queen Mab " and its heterodox Notes have been frequently republished in this country and in America, and have undoubtedly had a wider circulation than any other of Shelley's writings. It is asserted that the poem, with its voluminous notes, has had a very considerable influence upon the working classes in the direction of free-thought. It is beyond question that, as an intellectual and socialistic pioneer, Shelley is still reverenced and loved by thousands who would never think of reading the " Prometheus" or the "Cenci," or who would not care for either if they did. The chief Notes are (1) "On Wealth;" (2) "On Marriage;" (3) "On Necessity;" (4) "On Deism;" (5) "On Christianity;" and (6) "On Flesh Eating"—an argument in favour of vegetarianism, republished in 1813 as a separate pamphlet, under the title "A Vindication of Natural Diet." The metre of "Queen Mab" is the unrhymed lyrical iambic.

> How wonderful is Death,
> Death and his brother Sleep !
> One, pale as yonder waning moon
> With lips of lurid blue ;
> The other, rosy as the morn
> When throned on ocean's wave
> It blushes o'er the world :
> Yet both so passing wonderful !

※ ※ ※ ※

> The Fairy's frame was slight, yon fibrous cloud,
> That catches but the palest tinge of even,
> And which the straining eye can hardly seize
> When melting into eastern twilight's shadow,
> Were scarce so thin, so slight ; but the fair star
> That gems the glittering coronet of morn,
> Sheds not a light so mild, so powerful,
> As that which, bursting from the Fairy's form,
> Spread a purpureal halo round the scene,
>   Yet with an undulating motion,
>   Swayed to her outline gracefully.
>   From her celestial car
>   The Fairy Queen descended,
>   And thrice she waved her wand
>   Circled with wreaths of amaranth :

8

Her thin and misty form
Moved with the moving air,
And the clear silver tones,
As thus she spoke, were such
As are unheard by all but gifted ear.

" Queen Mab" is the Fairy Queen, whose knowledge of things, past, present, and to come is all-embracing. The mortal whom she visits is Ianthe; the latter's soul is withdrawn from her body, and ascends in Mab's magic car. They reach the Temple of Nature, and mentally survey the ancient empires of Syria, Egypt, Judæa, Greece, Rome, and Carthage. Ianthe is taught what lessons of humility and hope to draw therefrom, and is then instructed upon the evils of the Present; the crime of kingship, the atrocity of war, the tyranny of priests and rulers, the primal evil of religion; then comes the praise of necessity, the true religion, faith in which is incompatible with a belief in a personal God or future punishment; and finally the future is foretold. The magic car redescends, Ianthe's spirit re-enters her body, and she wakes to find her lover by her side. The aim of the poem is to attack dogmatic religion and the social state, and, of course, much depends on a reader's own views whether or not he sympathizes with its revolutionary bias. Some uncritical admirers would have it that it is one of the greatest poems ever written, but assuredly such enthusiasts are misled by the glamour of the spirit of rebellion, for a poem must be adjudged *as* a poem and not as a philosophical treatise. It is in no sense a great poem. Herein all qualified judges agree.

But it has passages of considerable beauty, and is distinctly a noteworthy production, howsoever regarded.

Shelley's genius in "Queen Mab" is like a subterranean fount, which occasionally projects a stream of brilliant spray: in "Alastor" this stream rises steadily and in splendid volume. All that had impressed the young poet in Wales, the Lake country, Killarney, Devon, Switzerland, on the Rhine, and on the Thames, was given forth again in concentrated form. The name of the poem was suggested by Peacock. It is a Greek term, signifying an avenging spirit. Alastor is, as Mr. Symonds has well put it, the Nemesis of solitary souls. The narrative relates how the poet leaves his home, and wanders far abroad through the empires of the East, even unto Cashmere, where he has a vision of a veiled maid, a vision which causes the fire of deathless yearning to arise in his heart. At length, in pursuit of this phantasmal beatitude, he reaches "the lone Chorasmian shore;" here he embarks in a little shallop, and is whirled by the current past the precipitous heights of the Caucasus, through a wild and terrible mountain cavern, and is at last stranded close by the verge of a great fall of water. The poet then roams through a primeval forest, in a remote corner of which he finds death. The allegory is easy of perception, and at any rate need not be enlarged upon here, as in every edition where "Alastor" appears there is Shelley's own explanatory preface. It will be sufficient to say that "the veiled maid" is the ideal love unattainable in mortal guise. This passionate quest of ideal loveliness haunted Shelley's dreams by day and night. Again and again he has uttered something of the pain at his heart—in " Alastor," in the beautiful " Hymn to Intellectual Beauty," in " Epipsychidion," and in many of the short poems.   In " Alastor " the poet was enraptured with the dream of encountering ideal loveliness incarnate ; in the " Hymn to Intellectual Beauty," written a year later, he realizes that this ideal must ever win his passionate devotion, but that never in mortal image would he find the likeness of what is eternal.   All that Shelley had hitherto written had been defaced by many artistic flaws; but in " Alastor " he passes from apprenticeship to masterhood.   His blank verse is at once beautiful and majestic ; and even where it challenges comparison with that of Milton or with that of Wordsworth, it has a lyrical, an overwelling music of its own which few poets have equalled.   No poet has excelled Milton in felicitous use of sonorous names, but even in Milton it would be difficult to select many passages to surpass the following—

> " The awful ruins of the days of old :
>   Athens, and Tyre, and Balbec, and the waste
>   Where stood Jerusalem, and the fallen towers
>   Of Babylon, the eternal pyramids,
>   Memphis and Thebes, and whatsoe'er of strange
>   Sculptured on alabaster obelisk,
>   Or jasper tomb, or mutilated sphynx,
>   Dark Æthiopia in her desert hills
>   Conceals."

What sound and majesty in the lines describing the windings of the vast Caucasian cavern ! what dignity and beauty in the close of that invocation to Nature—

"Earth, ocean, air, beloved brotherhood"—which opens
" Alastor" !—

> " Enough from incommunicable dream,
> And twilight phantasms, and deep noonday thought,
> Has shone within me, that serenely now
> And moveless, as a long-forgotten lyre
> Suspended in the solitary dome
> Of some mysterious and deserted fane,
> I wait thy breath, Great Parent, that my strain
> May modulate with murmurs of the air,
> And motions of the forests and the sea,
> And voice of living beings, and woven hymns
> Of night and day, and the deep heart of man."

What solemn closing music in those lines which forbid
mourning for him who is at last made one with Nature—

> " Art and eloquence,
> And all the shows o' the world are frail and vain
> To weep a loss that turns their lights to shade.
> It is a woe 'too deep for tears,' when all
> Is reft at once, when some surpassing Spirit,
> Whose light adorned the world around it, leaves
> Those who remain behind, not sobs or groans,
> The passionate tumult of a clinging hope ;
> But pale despair and cold tranquillity,
> Nature's vast frame, the web of human things,
> Birth and the grave, that are not as they were."

The first quarter of 1816 was memorable to Shelley
for two events. On January 24th Mary gave birth to a son
—the child to whom the name William, in honour of
Godwin, was given, and who a few years later was buried

in that lovely Roman cemetery where lie the remains of two of England's greatest poets. In March " Alastor ; and other Poems " was published. Little notice was taken of the book, though it was so unmistakably the production of a poet as noteworthy as any then living. Many unpleasantnesses, including the exceedingly undignified and ungenerous conduct of William Godwin, who, to use a vulgarism, stole from Shelley's pockets while he hit him over the head—caused the poet to make up his mind to go to Switzerland again. The immediacy of this trip was urged by Claire Clairmont, who had again joined the Shelley household. She had another aim in view than the wish to see Geneva. In London she had become acquainted with Lord Byron, the most brilliant and romantic man of his time, as well as the most celebrated poet. She had called upon him to solicit his interest in obtaining a post for her in a certain theatre, but from the first moment she saw him she fell in love with him. Byron was conscious of her infatuation, and took advantage of it. Claire knew of his intention to go to Geneva, and aware of the fact that he had no intention of burdening himself with her company, she urged Shelley to make that Swiss town his goal, in order that she might meet her lover. The Shelleys did not even know that she was acquainted with the name, much less the person, of "Childe Harold." The lake of Geneva, encircled with endless beauty and grandeur, haunted and hallowed by the memories of Rousseau, Gibbon, and others who had dwelt by its shores, was full of fascination for Shelley. The boating, too, promised to be a source of never-ending delight.

In the warm noon-day to lie in the bottom of the *chaloupe*, to hearken to the lap-lap of the rippling water alongside, and to watch the pageant of the clouds overhead; in the twilight or starlit evenings to glide towards the flower-fragrant shore, above which rose the yellow moon, then nearly at the full—here were prospects of infinite charm ! About the same time, Byron arrived at the hotel where they had taken up their quarters, and an intimacy soon arose between the poets. Ere long they left the hotel. Byron and his travelling physician and friend, Polidori, occupied the Villa Diodati (where Milton had visited a friend on his homeward way from Italy), and Shelley, Mary, and Claire the Villa Mont Alégre. The two poets became joint owners of a boat, and many were the excursions which were made, including one round a great part of the lake, to Chillon and Lausanne. Whether or not the intrigue between Byron and Miss Clairmont was a thing of the past ere the former and the Shelleys met at Geneva is uncertain ; but it was not until the knowledge could no longer be kept from them that Claire Clairmont confessed to her friends that in her reckless passion she had given herself to Byron. In the friendly intimacy which came to exist between the two poets, the literary admiration was on the part of Shelley, the personal admiration on the part of Byron. The latter found himself refined and inspired by his spiritually-minded companion. The younger poet was fascinated by the splendid genius of the elder, but he perceived his great faults of character, and sorrowfully regretted the usurpation of such a mind by selfish, unlofty, and even base ideas. At the same time he recognized the fact that Byron made himself out much worse than he in reality was; that his evil nature was superficial; and that he had as splendid capacities for good as for poetical creation. " Count Maddalo " and many of Shelley's letters show how just and discriminating was his estimate of his brilliant friend—or rather acquaintance; for Shelley could not love a man who, in the deeper questions of life, seemed to him to fall so far short of a manly attitude. That, on the other hand, Byron recognized the fineness of Shelley's nature is clear, from his emphatic statement, made after the latter's death : " He was the most gentle, the most amiable, and least worldly-minded person I ever met ; full of delicacy, disinterested beyond all other men, and possessing a degree of genius joined to simplicity as rare as it is admirable. He had formed to himself a *beau ideal* of all that is fine, high-minded and noble, and he acted up to this ideal even to the very letter."

The " Hymn to Intellectual Beauty " was at least conceived during the lake voyage just referred to, though at this time very little poetry was actually written by Shelley. Like many ardent worshippers of nature, he often found himself mute in her presence. He wrote in the afterglow of memory, not in the full light of the moment's enjoyment. The beautiful lines to Mont Blanc were an outcome of his emotions as he lingered on the Bridge of Arve on his way through the Valley of Chamouni, whither he had gone with Mary to inhale the serene air of the greatest of the Swiss mountains. On their return to the Genevan lake-side they found another visitor in the person of " Monk " Lewis. Naturally, now, the evening chats resolved themselves into ghostly discussions.[1] At least one famous book was the outcome thereof. On Byron's suggestion each member of the party undertook to write something weird or ghastly. Shelley began a semi-autobiographical story which came to nought. Byron commenced a tale called "The Vampire," which he fully mentally cartooned, but of which he only wrote a fragmentary portion. Polidori indulged in an absurd narrative more fantastic than impressive. Mary Shelley disappointed the others by her non-production of any story; but, as it turned out, she was only waiting for an adequate motive. One evening she heard Bryon and Shelley discussing the nature of the principle of life, and the possibility of communicating the vital spark to inanimate matter. That night, as she lay sleepless, she had a waking vision of a student of mysteries creating a human monster, and of his terrible emotions when his task resulted in unexpected success. Here was a theme indeed. The result was the extraordinary romance, "Frankenstein," a book which has made a permanent mark in the literature of the West.

In the early autumn Shelley and Mary returned to England by way of Fontainebleau, Versailles, and Havre. Mid-September found them Peacock's guests at Marlow, whence they went for a short time to Bath and, at intervals, elsewhere. Early in 1817 they settled in a

[1] According to Professor Dowden, ungenial weather confined them to the house, and to pass the time they indulged in the perusal of a book of ghastly narratives, entitled "Fantasmagoriana." He says nothing about the appearance of M. G. Lewis upon the scene.

cottage-house at West Marlow, on Thames-side. But, ere this, tragic and important incidents had occurred.

The year 1816 had been and was to prove a memorable one to Shelley. Early therein his negotiations with Sir Timothy had collapsed; "Alastor" had been published; the visit to Switzerland had been made, and a friendship with Byron been formed. The late autumn was to bring forth much unhappiness. Godwin was hard pressed by poverty, and Shelley was forced to disappoint him monetarily owing to the impracticability of raising further funds. In the midst of the anxiety and worry caused by pecuniary troubles, alarming news came concerning Godwin's adopted daughter. Gentle, affectionate, unhappy Fanny—the daughter of Mary Wollstonecraft by Mr. Imlay—had long been subject to dire dejection. One day she left home, and having reached Swansea, whether *en route* or as a goal we know not, she put an end to her life by poison, and was found dead in her hotel. Shelley, who on behalf of Godwin had hastened to Bristol in pursuit of the unhappy fugitive, felt the blow so keenly that his nervous system almost gave way. He made all speed home from the west to break the sad news to Mary. The calamity aged Godwin, upon whom the burden of years had begun to press heavily. While Shelley yet sorrowed for and brooded over the death of the unfortunate girl, whom he had always regarded with affectionate brotherly sympathy and true friendliness, he received another painful shock. He and Mary had left Peacock's cottage; Mary had gone to Bath, and he had gladly undertaken a visit to Leigh Hunt, whom he had always greatly admired, and who had recently given

him some kindly words in a magazine. On the first
day of his visit he received a letter from Hookham, of
whom he had made inquiries concerning his separated
wife Harriet. This letter conveyed the tragic news that
" Harriet Smith " had drowned herself in the Serpentine.
Leigh Hunt's companionship and sympathy did more
than anything else to sustain the poet under this sudden
affliction ; this, and his own conviction that Harriet herself would have been the last to hold him responsible
for the tragedy. He had now two duties to perform
without delay ; to take his children by Harriet, Ianthe
and Charles, under his protection, and to fulfil his contract of marriage to Mary Godwin. All this meant extra
expenditure, and, moreover, Shelley was soon to find
Claire Clairmont and the child of her intrigue with
Byron practically dependent upon him. On the 30th
of December in this eventful year a nominal reconciliation took place between Godwin and Shelley, and on
the same day the latter and Mary became legally wedded
at St. Mildred's Church in London.

CHAPTER V

TO Shelley's reiterated demands for the custody of his children, their maternal grandfather, Mr. Westbrook, turned a deaf ear. This gentleman desired to deprive Shelley of his rights as a father, and he accordingly instituted a chancery suit. He laid the utmost stress on Shelley's separation from Harriet, the illegal union with Mary Godwin, the poet's atheistical and republican publications, especially "Queen Mab," and his avowed heterodox opinions. Shelley's defence was dignified, truthful, and to the point. But, as was to be expected, Lord Eldon as Lord Chancellor decided against Shelley, and on the main question judgment was given on the 27th of March (1817). The final settlement was not made till the midsummer of the following year, by which time Shelley had left England never to return. The children were placed under the care of a Dr. Hume, to be educated in principles which their father considered mistaken and harmful; and to this end he was legally bound to furnish the annual sum of £200.

Such a judgment as Lord Eldon's would now happily be impossible, but there is no doubt that it was fairly arrived at, and considered by most impartial people to be just and reasonable. To us who know Shelley, Lord Eldon's judgment seems harsh; but if we consider the case purely on its own basis we shall find that, according to the then prevalent views of morality and the right of public interference with private opinion, the decree was reasonable if not strictly justifiable. Shelley suffered much from this adverse decision. He felt not only wounded, but outraged; and his resentment was only tempered by that lofty spirit which more and more possessed him and strengthened him for noble work yet to be done, and for, mayhap, nobler work never to be accomplished in his short life.

The poet needed all the rest and soothing quietude obtainable at Marlow to enable him to bear up against his recent sorrows—the suicide of Fanny (Imlay) Godwin, the even more tragic death of Harriet, and the deprivation of his paternal rights. He even feared his own imprisonment on account of his avowed opinions. To add to his trouble, Claire Clairmont in January gave birth to her and Byron's illegitimate child. To the little girl the name of Alba (the Dawn) was at first given, but afterwards this was changed to Allegra.

While awaiting the slow decision of the law, Shelley's anxious season of probation was lightened by the sympathy and kindness of friends, especially Leigh Hunt. At the latter's cottage in Hampstead, one February evening in 1817, there was a gathering of poets. The genial host was a cultivated company in himself; there was the boyish-looking youth who had given utterance to so many extraordinary dicta in prose and verse, and undergone strange vicissitudes, the P. B. Shelley, who was by some considered an authentic emissary of Satan, by others a vapouring lunatic, and by a few a man of genius; there was a Mr. Reynolds, now well known by name to all students of English poetry; and there was a youth with vivid eyes and mobile mouth, called John Keats. Shelley liked Keats from the outset, but the younger did not at first take to the older. Keats was above all things the poet—not, like Shelley, the poet *plus* the seer, *plus* the philanthropist, *plus* the reformer. It was enough for him to live and feel, and the whisper of green leaves in the woodlands was infinitely more worthy of audience than the oratory of all the agitators in the kingdom. He was but a boy in years, moreover, and the joy of the world was too keen in him to allow him to share Shelley's raptures and agonies. It is clear, also—though this is not to his credit—that his attitude towards Shelley was suspicious, if not actually resentful, on account of the latter's superior birth and social status. He was, of course, speedily set at rest on this point, and the twain would doubtless have passed from mutual respect and admiration to assured friendship had it not been that Death, who was drawing near for both, had already projected his shadow toward the younger. In the ensuing months the two poets saw each other at intervals, but circumstances prevented their becoming really intimate. For Shelley's friendships and life at this time, the student cannot do better than turn to the delightful fourth chapter in the second volume of Prof. Dowden's " Life "—the only thoroughly complete and satisfactory biography of the poet in existence.

Shelley had now in very truth entered the sphere of poetic creation. The wings which had already borne him so nobly in " Alastor " proved able for as lofty and more prolonged flight. At all times the poet was wont to compose in the open air, by river, sea, mountain, or amid the vernal and autumnal woodlands. His last great poem was written in his boat upon the Bay of Spezzia ; the Pisan pine-woods, the heights of the Euganean hills, the Venetian lagoons, beheld the birth of some of his most famous lyrics ; fronting the sea at Livorno was the Villa Valsovano, on the windy roof of which most of " The Cenci " was written ; and the greater part of " Prometheus " was composed amid the gigantic ruins of the Baths of Caracalla, less desolate then in their lonely grandeur than now in their tourist-haunted "picturesque-ness." And amid scenes as lonely, if not so immediately impressive, Shelley's second great poem was written. " Laon and Cythna ; or, The Revolution of the Golden City "—usually known as " The Revolt of Islam "—is in splendour of poetry not inferior to " Alastor," though its length, remote allusions, digressions, and the intense, rarefied atmosphere of the whole, stand in the way of its being a popular poem. It is said that early in the year of its composition Shelley and Keats each agreed to write a long work in verse, and that the results of this under-taking were " Laon and Cythna " and " Endymion." Howsoever this may be, there is no doubt that both these poems were begun in the spring of 1817. When the blackbirds were in full song Shelley commenced the work he had set himself to do. Keats's object was to tell a beautiful legend beautifully ; Shelley's aim was to foretell, hasten, inaugurate the new reign of peace on earth and good-will to men. Stanza by stanza it grew, as day by day the poet lay in his boat while it floated on the slow stream under the beech-groves of Bisham, or as he wandered among the ferny glades and shadow-chequered alleys of the adjacent woodlands. Written in the Spenserian stanza, "Laon and Cythna" has a keener, wider, more lyrical music than the linked and long drawn sweetness of the verse of "The Faerie Queen." In it the poet speaks out of the suffering and experience of his life, and gives utterance to all the desire of his heart. His hatred of priestly and kingly oppression and intolerance, his passionate faith in humanity and its proud destiny, his principle of the equality of women with men, his doctrine of unfettered love, his aspirations towards a bloodless revolution which would bring about a confederation of all the nations of the world, his hopes for a golden age which would as immeasurably outvie that chronicled through centuries of song as the era in which he lived transcended the barbarous savagery of feudal days—all that experience had taught him, intellect assured him, faith promised him, was enshrined, was— in Mr. Symonds' words—"blent together and concentrated in the glowing cantos of this wonderful romance." The poet's own prefatory remarks should be read, wherein will be found the re-assertion of that principle which underlay all Shelley ever wrote, the principle that Love is the sole law which should govern the moral world. The motive of the poem is borne along upon a stream of narrative, but at all times the latter is subordinate to the end in view. A spiritual conflict, of mighty import, of vast issues, takes place beyond the turmoil of mere mortal struggle. "The Revolt of Islam" is an epic of the human spirit, as well as of the struggle of peoples for freedom. Laon is a young poet-prophet, whose words rouse a struggling nation (*Islam*, by which Shelley meant the nations of the Levant under Turkish rule) to a defiance of and a temporary victory over despotism. Cythna is the ideal woman—lover, help-mate, friend. As a further challenge to conventionality, Shelley made the lovers, Cythna and Laon, brother and sister; but, finding that he thereby hurt the ·cause he had at heart, and served no good end, he finally excised or altered certain lines and passages. The good cause is erelong overwhelmed, and both the lovers are martyred for the sake of liberty. As they awake from the darkness of death they are greeted by a lovely child-spirit, Cythna's daughter, who guides them in her pearly boat down a great river which flows towards the Temple of the Spirit where sits the "mighty Senate" of the dead. The beautiful first canto is familiar to many who have never found their way through the poem to the twelfth. From "the peak of an aërial promontory," around whose caverned base the vexed surge of ocean for ever breaks, the poet sees "a golden dawn" illumine the world, and speedily (in verse quivering with poetic emotion) he describes a skiey conflict between an eagle and a serpent—emblems of tyranny and free-thought—and how the wounded and nigh-slain serpent succumbs and falls into the waters, but at last finds refuge with a woman "beautiful as morning" (the spirit of nature and love). This lovely phantom takes the poet with her in her magic boat, and as they sail speaks to him of the eternal struggle between good and evil—that having been a typical conflict which they had just witnessed. In due time they reach the Temple of the Spirit, whereat have just arrived two spirits, Laon and Cythna—by whom henceforth, the story is told. There is nothing of the kind in our literature to compare with the magnificent conflict of the eagle and the serpent—a struggle so terrible that from the passionate encounter "a vapour like the sea's suspended spray " is gathered, while far away in the void air the shattered plumes and riven scales float or flash. Anon the snake will triumph and rear, radiant with victory, his " red and burning crest ; " then again the eagle will exert " the strength of his unconquerable wings," and soar from the whirling sea-surge as swiftly as smoke that is suddenly belched forth from a volcano. In " Laon and Cythna " Shelley has owed nothing directly to any poetic predecessor. Its shortcomings— and they are many when looked for critically—are no less his own than its merits. Occasionally he reiterates an echo of his own music, as in that stanza so suggestive of certain lines in " Alastor," the thirty-third of the twelfth canto.

> " Till down that mighty stream, dark, calm, and fleet,
> Between a chasm of cedarn mountains riven,
> Chased by the thronging winds whose viewless feet
> As swift as twinkling beams, had, under Heaven,
> From woods and waves wild sounds and odours driven,
> The boat fled visibly—three nights and days,
> Borne like a cloud through morn, and noon, and even,
> We sailed along the winding watery ways
> Of the vast stream, a long and labyrinthine maze."

At the instance of Ollier, the publisher, Shelley courteously, though reluctantly, made the alterations already referred to ; the copies (a very limited number) which had been issued were called in, and the book was shortly republished (January, 1818) under the title, " The Revolt of Islam "—the name by which to the great majority of people it is known. The original was finished late in September, about three weeks after the birth of his and Mary's second child.

It is uncertain whether or not " Rosalind and Helen " was begun before or after " Laon and Cythna," though it was not finished until the summer of the following year at the Bagni di Lucca, in Northern Italy. Here, as in " Alastor," "The Revolt of Islam," "Prince Athanase," "Epipsychidion," the dominant theme is Love ; but the treatment is less ideal and less epic than in the second of the great poems named. In his choice of metre (mainly the iambic tetrameter) Shelley was plainly influenced by Scott and Byron, and probably also by Coleridge. If there is little that is directly autobiographical in this poem, there is much we can discern to be due to circumstances and experiences within Shelley's ken. In Lionel there is something of himself; Helen and Rosalind have each their shadowy prototypes. Helen and Rosalind have been alienated on account of the latter's connection with Lionel, but at last have become reconciled, and, meeting by the Lake of Como, narrate to each other their diverse experiences. Helen speaks of her lover, describes his imprisonment, release, and death, and tells how their son has inherited his father's qualities, and may one day nobly carry on the work of the redemption

of the world to which Lionel had devoted himself.
Rosalind, on the other hand, had been perforce married
to a tyrannical husband. Her life was wretched, but even
after her husband's death she had not the comfort of her
children; for by his will she was deprived of her little
ones. Finally Rosalind and Helen agree to live together;
the former regains her daughter, who in due time becomes
betrothed to Helen's son. The motive of the poem is probably due to Mary Shelley's interrupted friendship with a
well-loved school-friend named Isabel Baxter, who, on
her marriage to a Mr. Booth, was commanded by her
husband to cease all communication with the Shelleys.
The episode of the children severed by law from their
mother's care; the good wrought by the unlegalized
union of Helen and Lionel; the evil and misery of the
"consecrated" thraldom which bound Rosalind and her
husband—these are easily traceable to real experiences
on the part or within the knowledge of the author.
As a poem, "Rosalind and Helen" is the least successful of Shelley's longer productions. It has some fine
lines, but if it were not for its personal interest it would
be little read, and if it had been the sole work of its author
it would not be read at all. A much more powerful,
interesting, and beautiful production is the unfinished
poem entitled "Prince Athanase," which, although not
published until the issue of the "Posthumous Poems"
in 1824, was written at Marlow shortly after "Laon and
Cythna." Originally entitled "Pandemos and Urania,"
it describes that quest for the ideal Beauty—symbolized
by Venus Urania—which mortals are apt to ignore for
something less spiritual, something more sensuous and

mortal—Pandemos, the earthly Venus. The poem is more akin to "Alastor" than any other; but where in the latter the poet-hero dies ere he can fall to any earthly worship, in the former the hero is betrayed by Pandemos. Shelley left it a fragment, for he came to the conclusion that the psychological analysis was over-refined and even morbid, though he valued the poem too highly to discard it as a non-publishable piece. He himself is Prince Athanase, even as he is the Poet in "Alastor," Laon in "The Revolt of Islam," and Lionel in "Rosalind and Helen." Like his latest great poem, "The Triumph of Life," "Prince Athanase" is written in *terza rima*, a difficult metre, and one not specially appropriate to our language, but which Shelley handles with dexterous ease.[1]

Among the shorter poems written by Shelley at this time may be specially noted the splendid, if technically irregular, sonnet entitled "Ozymandias" and the lyric "To Constantia, Singing." The latter is known to have been addressed to Claire Clairmont, whose voice was of surpassing sweetness. While Shelley cared but slightly for what may be called musician's music, he was keenly susceptible to that thrilling melody, instrumental or vocal, which is the outcome of nature rather than of art. This "Constantia" lyric shows how absolutely music could take possession of his whole being.

Throughout the autumn of 1817 Shelley's health deteriorated, and after one specially severe spasmodic attack

---

[1] A short extract describing Prince Athanase's mentor, Zonoras, was quoted in Chapter ii., pages 33 and 34.

he came to the conclusion that a change to Italy was the
only chance whereby his life might be prolonged. I have
not space wherein to dilate on his intervening correspondence and interviews with Godwin, his meetings with
Leigh Hunt, Keats, Horace Smith, and others. Before
quitting the record of the Marlow period, however, brief
reference must be made to Shelley's prose writings of this
time. Among those of prior date which have not yet been
mentioned is the admirable " Essay on Christianity," a
composition which every thinking person should read.
Succinctly, it may be said to be a reverent recognition
of the character, mission, and teaching of Christ, and
an impassioned reprobation of dogmatic Christianity.
While he loved and revered the Prophet of Nazareth, he
pointed out that so-called Christians worship a figment
of their own creation, and that even among the least
bigoted sectarians Christ, if He were to return to earth
to-day, would be vehemently despised and hated, and,
where possible, persecuted. Throughout, the author
writes with moderation, and with a logical grasp of his
subject which render his conclusions practically irrefu-
table. As Mr. Symonds has well said, " It is certain
that, as Christianity passes beyond its mediæval phase,
and casts aside the husk of outworn dogmas, it will more
and more approximate to Shelley's exposition."

Early in 1817 he published—by the " Hermit of
Marlow "—" A Proposal for Putting Reform to the
Vote "—a tractate characterized by moderation and
understanding. To the inquiry he thus wished to inaugurate he was willing to subscribe £100 from his
slender means. While ardent for reform, he did not

advocate universal suffrage, but urged the adoption of annual Parliaments; while, Republican though he was, he pointed out that the abolition of royalty and aristocracy must be gradual. Of less importance is his second Marlow pamphlet, " An Address to the People on the Death of the Princess Charlotte."

When Shelley left Marlow he must have been sorely missed. He was ever wont to practise as well as preach the Christian ideal. Not only did he give largely of his means to all whom he considered had any public or private claim upon him, and expend much upon the necessitous in his. neighbourhood, but he also devoted many hours weekly to visiting the sick and infirm. At all times his heart went out towards the poor. He would even, on occasion, give needy wayfarers articles of his own apparel. One day he returned home shoeless, having met some weary vagrant whose wants he could not alleviate, having no money with him, and to whom he had given his boots, so that the toil of the journey might be mitigated. It was not his habit to carry money about with him, but this was no bar to his ever ready charity. If he met some one whom he desired to help, he would tear out a leaf from a book or a blank page from a letter and write upon it a succinct cash order to be discharged by Mary on presentation. During part of the stay at Marlow there was great distress among the lace-workers who then congregated in the old river-town, and during his visitations to those in dire need Shelley caught a bad attack of ophthalmia.

When Shelley left Marlow for London, preliminary to the journey to Italy, it was with poor and failing health.

His irregularity in his hours of eating, his inadequate
diet, his prolonged fasts, the fire of his mind for ever
consuming his excitable body, his swift and ardent
emotions, his over-keen susceptibilities, all combined
to increase the frailty of his physical health. It was
with little belief in ultimate recovery, and with but a
dubious hope in any prolonged postponement of the
end, that he made the final arrangements for leaving
England.

Shortly before the travellers left, their two children
were duly christened at St. Giles'-in-the-Fields with the
names of William and Clara Everina. On the same
occasion Miss Clairmont had little Alba baptized by the
name Allegra (Clara Allegra), the father's name being
duly entered in the register as Lord Byron. It had been
decided that Claire was to be of their party. The
Shelleys had not yet lost faith in Byron, and believed
that he would act honourably by the mother of his child
if the twain could be brought together once more.

On the 11th of March, 1818, Shelley saw the English
cliffs fade slowly from his view. He did not surmise
that their familiar aspect would never more attract his
homeward-yearning gaze, nor did Mary dream that when
she should recross these narrow seas it would be in bitter
and lonely sorrow.

CHAPTER VI

THE travellers made direct for Milan, through South-eastern. France and Switzerland. It had been Shelley's great wish to settle somewhere on the shores of Como, that loveliest of Italian lakes, but to his chagrin he could nowhere find suitable accommodation. Visits were then paid to Pisa and Leghorn, where the Shelleys became intimately acquainted with the Gisbornes. Mrs. Gisborne had led an eventful and romantic life, was a beautiful and cultivated woman, and in every way one to attract her new friends. The summer was spent at the Bagni di Lucca, high up among the Tuscan forests. Shelley, still far from robust, felt himself unable for the excitement of prolonged poetical composition, though more than one great idea for future development began to germinate in his ever active mind. "Rosalind and Helen," however, was finished, not at all to Shelley's regret, as he valued it little. The weeks passed delightfully. In the early mornings and in the starlit evenings the young people would ride through the alleys of chestnut and beech, but while others drowsed in the heats of the day, Shelley would steal out and disappear to a loved haunt in the forest, where a

mountain torrent precipitated itself into a basin. In one
of his letters the poet affords a delightful picture of himself in this lovely spot. Beyond the vast screen of
chestnut leaves the sun fiercely flared, but underneath
were currents of cool air and perpetual freshness from
the spray of rushing water; so translucent was the
water in the rocky basin, that the sand and stones at its
bottom trembled as in the light of noonday. "My custom
is to undress and sit on the rocks, reading ' Herodotus,'
until the perspiration has subsided, and then to leap from
the edge of the rock into this fountain. . . . The torrent
is composed, as it were, of a succession of pools and
waterfalls, up which I sometimes amuse myself by climb-
ing when I bathe, and receiving the spray over all my
body whilst I clamber up the moist crags with difficulty."
Ere the great heat of summer had abated, Shelley, however, had accomplished at least one delightful task.
Plato's "Symposium" had been the fountainhead of his
inspiration on the subject of Love, and to introduce Mary
to this charmed world was his aim. To this affectionate
desire we owe his admirable and beautiful, if not very
literal, abridged version of the "Symposium."

Before this, Claire Clairmont—against Shelley's advice
—had, at Byron's demand, sent Allegra to her father at
Venice. As the weeks elapsed, and as strange and painful
rumours came to her ears, her anxiety overbore all other
considerations, and she determined to set out at once to
see Byron. Shelley foresaw probable failure in any case,
and certain failure if Claire went alone, so, with his
usual unselfishness he agreed to accompany her. From
the Bagni di Lucca the two travellers journeyed to

Florence, thence to Padua, and thence by water to Venice, which they reached on the 22nd of August. They were fortunate in at once encountering kind friends in the persons of Mr. Hoppner, the English Consul-General, and his wife, an amiable lady to whose charge Byron had temporarily surrendered Allegra. In the afternoon of the day of their arrival, Shelley went alone to see Byron. The elder poet took his friend's pleadings and remonstrances in good part, though it is clear that Shelley spoke with much restraint, not considering the moment a suitable one for speaking too plainly or requesting overmuch. Allegra's father, then living a life of reckless debauchery, half scornfully agreed that Claire might have her child again if she wished, but dropped a vague hint that if she thus acted she might find herself absolutely and entirely discarded by the father of her child. From this time forth Shelley could no longer esteem or even care for the man whom, with justice, he then and always so much admired as a poet. But he believed that Byron's actions to a great extent belied him; that he lived his dissolute and degraded life out of mere weariness and disgust, and that he had in him all the possibilities of a worthier life.

When the long-anticipated and, doubtless, painful interview was over, Byron took Shelley in his gondola across the lagoons to the wave-washed Lido—the long, narrow, sandy island which acts as a barrier to Venice against the stress of the Adriatic. There the former's horses were in waiting, and, to Shelley's delight, he found himself riding along that magic strand which he afterwards immortalized in song. There was one direct and

practical outcome of this visit. Byron then temporarily
owned a lovely villa, "I Cappuccini," at Este, high up
among the Euganean hills, and a few miles away from
that Arqua where Petrarch spent his latter days and died.
This villa he offered to the Shelleys and their companion,
Miss Clairmont; an offer which was willingly accepted.
Shelley at once wrote to his wife to join him with the
children, and Mary accordingly set forth from the
Baths of Lucca with her little ones. When Este was
reached, the baby Clara was suffering from dysentery,
and in great weakness; the local doctor's services were
worse than useless, and it was determined to go to
Venice for medical help. Shelley had already gone
thither to make arrangements, but he hastened to Padua
to meet Mary and the child. At Fusina the military
guard would fain have prevented the passportless wayfarers from travelling further without official consent, but
Shelley's urgency and the pitiable state of little Clara
overcame their scruples. When Venice was reached in
the hot September afternoon, Shelley sped away to find
the well-known physician, Dr. Aglietti, but about an hour
later the little one died in her mother's arms. The blow
was all the more cruel, as the parents had hoped the child
had passed the worst.

Early in October the Shelleys were again at the villa
in hill-set Este. One splendid poetic idea had been
taking form in the poet's brain—the conception of a
Prometheus Unbound, whose agony, endurance, and
release would typify more than the chief character in the
lost play of Æschylus could have done. The wonderful
melodies, the splendid harmonies, all the music and

magnificence of Shelley's greatest production began to haunt his spirit while the winds of the autumnal equinox swayed the pines and chestnuts on the mountain slopes looking seaward over the Trevisian plain. But brain and pen were also busy on poetic work only less noteworthy. The famous poem "Julian and Maddalo" was mainly written in a summer-house adjacent to the villa, whence a spacious and magnificent view southward could be obtained; and late in October was composed the first draft of the " Lines written among the Euganean Hills." The former poem, apart from its great beauty, has permanent literary interest, in that it affords us portraitures of two great poets. Both are idealized, yet each is recognizable—Byron as Count Maddalo, and Shelley as Julian. In parts the poem is obscure, but, as a whole, it is one of Shelley's most memorable productions. It is composed in the heroic metre, but with a familiarity and ease which charm alike the cultivated and the uncultivated ear. It records a "conversation" between Count Maddalo and Julian, as they ride towards sundown along the wave-washed Lido ; to obtain a finer view of the setting sun they embark in a gondola, and pass the Isle of San Servola, where there is a great mad-house, whence resounds the heavy tolling of the vesper bell.

> " I rode one evening with Count Maddalo
> Upon the bank of land which breaks the flow
> Of Adria towards Venice : a bare strand
> Of hillocks, heaped from ever-shifting sand,
> Matted with thistles and amphibious weeds,
> Such as from earth's embrace the salt ooze breeds,
> Is this ; an uninhabited seaside,
> Which the lone fisher, when his nets are dried,

Abandons; and no other object breaks
The waste, but one dwarf tree and some few stakes
Broken and unrepaired, and the tide makes
A narrow space of level sand thereon,
Where 'twas our wont to ride while day went down.
This ride was my delight.   I love all waste
And solitary places; where we taste
The pleasure of believing what we see
Is boundless, as we wish our souls to be.

※   ※   ※   ※   ✿   ※   ※   ※

From that funereal bark
I leaned, and saw the city, and could mark
How from their many isles, in evening's gleam,
Its temples and its palaces did seem
Like fabrics of enchantment piled to heaven.
I was about to speak, when—' We are even
Now at the point I meant,' said Maddalo,
And bade the gondolieri cease to row.
' Look, Julian, on the west, and listen well
If you hear not a deep and heavy bell.'
I looked, and saw between us and the sun
A building on an island, such a one
As age to age might add, for uses vile,—
A windowless, deformed, and dreary pile;
And on the top an open tower, where hung
A bell, which in the radiance swayed and swung."

Next day Julian calls and sees the lovely and fragile little
daughter of Count Maddalo (Allegra), and then the twain
go again to San Servola, and visit the maniac of whom
Maddalo had spoken to his companion, and whom he had
befriended.   The " Maniac " is another vague likeness of
Shelley, as perceived by himself, "but with respect to time
and place, ideal," to quote from a letter of his own.   The

maniac's soliloquy is partly autobiographical, so far as
Shelley is concerned, and partly ideal, but in portions of
it there is little difficulty in tracing the sources whence
the poet's fancy has taken flight. There is great power
in the description of the mad-house and the unhappy
man whom they go to visit amidst the rain and wind of
a wildly tempestuous day.

In "Julian and Maddalo" occur one often-quoted line
and one famous passage. "Thou paradise of exiles,
Italy !" is now done to death as a quotation, but no use
or misuse can deprive of their pathos and significance
the lines setting forth how some unhappy men

> "Are cradled into poetry by wrong :
> They learn in suffering what they teach in song."

In the very beautiful "Lines written among the
Euganean Hills" (revised and, probably, in part re-
written a few weeks later at Naples) Shelley, for the
first time, uses the seven-syllabled trochaic metre, which
afterwards became a favourite with him and may fairly
be considered as peculiarly suitable to his lyrical genius.
A sombre note is struck at the commencement, and
again at the close. The ideal island home referred
to was more fully dwelt upon later on in the "Epipsychidion."

Before October had passed away with the drifting
leaves it was found advisable for Shelley to seek a
warmer clime, and Naples was finally determined upon.
Before the departure Allegra was (to Claire's passionate
grief) returned to Byron's care, for the unfortunate
mother could not but see that she might wholly ruin

her child's prospects if she went against the wishes of
Allegra's father.   A great elation was in Shelley's heart.
"Julian and Maddalo" and the "Lines written among the
Euganean Hills" were productions of which any poet
might be proud ; but sweet and keen in his ears was the
haunting music of the as yet in great part unwritten
" Prometheus Unbound."   He could not but feel that he
was engaged on a poem which would have no rival in
modern times, nor fail to realize that at last he was about
to give adequate expression to the marvellous music which
had long enchanted his spiritual sense.   When, however,
Naples was reached,[1] a deep melancholy settled upon
him.   All that he wrote through the remaining weeks
of the year was tinged with gloom or poignant sadness.
His apprehensions of impending death, his distraught,
nervous condition—his disappointments, hopes, and fears,
and his recent sorrow—were probably mainly accountable
for this.   But there seems to have been another cause.
Medwin narrates a strange story of a beautiful woman
who had long passionately loved the fragile poet, and
often crossed his path even after she had learned from
Shelley's own lips that his whole heart was bound up in
Mary, and that he could love none other: this fair
woman died in Naples shortly after the man whom
she so loved had reached that southern city.   The
incident preyed upon Shelley's mind, always painfully
susceptible to emotional influences.   In his profound
despondency he composed, among other mournful lyrics,

---

[1] During the brief stay in Rome, *en route*, Shelley wrote his
prose fragment, "A Tale of the Coliseum," besides several delightful letters.

those exquisite stanzas "Written in dejection, near Naples," which every lover of his poetry has read again and again with thrilling sympathy. The pathetic music of the fourth stanza is unequalled in subjective poetry :—

> " Yet now despair itself is mild
> Even as the winds and waters are ;
> I could lie down like a tired child,
> And weep away the life of care
> Which I have borne and yet must bear,
> Till death like sleep might steal on me,
> And I might feel in the warm air
> My cheek grow cold, and hear the sea
> Breathe o'er my dying brain its last monotony."

The first days of December found the Shelley household settled in a charming residence facing the royal gardens and overlooking the sea. Shelley's delight in his environment, his keen pleasure in his excursions to Baiæ, to the summit of Vesuvius, and to the silent city of Pompeii, found immediate expression in letters to friends. The series addressed to Peacock are full of delicate observation, love of all that is rarely beautiful, and an eloquence that is unstudied and the outcome of an essentially poetic mind. Pompeii, as was natural, strongly affected his imagination. In the "Ode to Naples," written many months after his first visit to the ruins of the buried city, he refers thereto :—

> " I stood within the city disinterred ;
> And heard the autumnal leaves, like light footfalls
> Of spirits, passing through the streets ; and heard
> The mountain's slumberous voice at intervals
> Thrill through those leafless halls."

Shelley's health now began to improve, and naturally his despondency decreased, if it did not wholly vanish. With the first days of spring came the desire to fulfil the intention of a few months' residence in Rome; but before leaving the Neapolitan kingdom a journey was made southward to Paestum, amidst its desolate waste. The approach thereto was toilsome, but exceptionally impressive; and Shelley was deeply stirred by the splendour and magnificence of the ruins. The travellers' time was limited, and they could only bring away "as imperfect a conception of these sublime monuments as is the shadow of some half-remembered dream."

On the last day of February (1818) they looked back on the vision of sea and mountain which they had come to love so well, and five days later they entered Rome— where they obtained lodgings on the Corso. By the end of January Shelley had completed the first act of "Prometheus Unbound"—begun a few months earlier, and in great part composed in the villa gardens at Este, among the Euganean hills. Now that he was in Rome, the most magnificent of all the cities in the world, he strove to finish his greatest poem among the ruins of the Baths of Caracalla. There has been no finer delineation of this solitary and inexpressibly beautiful locality than that given by the poet himself in one of his letters to Peacock; nor should any one omit to read Shelley's description of the well-loved haunt, amidst whose waste places he mainly wrote the supreme lyrical drama in our literature. By the beginning of April the poem was concluded, according to its original design. What is now the fourth act was an afterthought, and was written at the close of the same year: this magnificent addition was completed in Florence, and "Prometheus Unbound" was published some eight or nine months later.

As the season advanced it became advisable—for little William's sake, if for nothing else—to remove to a less debilitating climate. Mary was not well, and was anxious. In the autumn she expected the birth of another babe, and she could not but see that her eldest-born was over-delicate. The 6th of June had been decided upon as the date of their departure for Leghorn, but before this day arrived the child was in a dangerous state of fever. The parents, who idolized their little boy, exhausted themselves in nursing. After sixty hours of absolutely sleepless watching, Shelley saw the beloved little face suddenly pale, and the eyes, which every one had noted as of so rare and beautiful a blue, lose their soft light. The calamity almost broke the hearts of father and mother. He for whom they had hoped and dreamt so much was now no more for them than a beloved memory. He was laid beneath the flowers in that lovely Protestant burial-ground at Rome, of which, some months before his bitter loss, Shelley had written to a friend, "it is a green slope near the walls, under the pyramidal tomb of Cestius; and is, I think, the most beautiful and solemn cemetery I ever beheld." Ere long, yet another whom he knew was to be hid away, under the shadow of the same pyramid, from the passionate turmoil of his life—one whom he was to mourn in strains whose endurance shall be measured with that of our language.

CHAPTER VII

A T the Villa Valsovano, near Leghorn, Shelley strove to forget his grief and check his spiritual despondency in the composition of poetry in a direction as yet untried by him. It is to Mary that we owe gratitude for having persuaded her husband that he had underrated his powers as a dramatic poet, and that he should attempt some adequate performance on an impressive theme. Perceiving how his imagination had been affected by the story of Beatrice Cenci, whose supposed portrait in the Palazzo Barberini at Rome had haunted him ever since he had seen it, she suggested that he should attempt a drama on the strange and tragic history of the evil Count Cenci. At that time the real facts thereof were unknown, and what Shelley had to work upon were legends fascinating and terrible, but distorted by romance and added horrors. The theme took entire possession of him; and the sombre, magnificent, repellent, fascinating, and, in modern times, unsurpassed, drama of "The Cenci" was begun and finished at the villa near the busy Tuscan seaport.

It is impossible to quote with any satisfaction from either "The Cenci" or the "Prometheus Unbound"; the spirit and majestic beauty of productions so perfect

cannot be conveyed in brief excerpts — fragments of
fragmentary parts. Both works must be earnestly and
lovingly read, and the second, at any rate, read again
and again.[1]

From Leghorn the Shelleys went to spend the autumn
and winter in Florence, but the cold months proved
harmful to Shelley. It was not, however, until after the
arrival of the new year that a move to Pisa was made.

[1] Nowhere have I encountered a better, while so concise an
estimate of the greater work as that in Mr. William Rossetti's
"Memoir." This I cannot do better than quote :—

"There is, I suppose, no poem comparable, in the fair sense of
that word, to 'Prometheus Unbound.' The immense scale and
boundless scope of the conception ; the marble majesty and extra-
mundane passions of the personages ; the sublimity of ethical
aspiration ; the radiance of ideal and poetic beauty which saturates
every phase of the subject, and almost (as it were) wraps it from
sight at times, and transforms it out of sense into spirit ; the rolling
river of great sound and lyrical rapture ; form a combination not to
be matched elsewhere, and scarcely to encounter competition.
There is another source of greatness in this poem neither to be
foolishly lauded nor (still less) undervalued. It is this :—that
'Prometheus Unbound,' however remote the foundation of its
subject-matter, and unactual its executive treatment, does in reality
express the most modern of conceptions — the utmost reach of
speculation of a mind which burst up all crusts of custom and
prescription like a volcano, and imaged forth a future wherein man
should be indeed the autocrat and renovated renovator of his planet.
This it is, I apprehend, which places 'Prometheus' clearly, instead
of disputably, at the summit of all latter poetry : the fact that it
embodies, in forms of truly ecstatic beauty, the dominant passion
of the dominant intellects of the age, and especially of one of the
extremest and highest among them all, the author himself. It is
the ideal poem of perpetual and triumphant progression—the Atlantis
of Man Emancipated."

One of Shelley's chief delights during his stay in Florence was to walk alone in the Cascine, watching the wind-swayed or drifting leaves "and the rising and falling of the Arno."

This year, wherein the poet's genius attained its loftiest flight, was not to elapse without an ode as supreme in its degree as is "The Cenci" as a dramatic poem, or "Prometheus Unbound" as a lyrical drama. One day, when the autumnal equinox was at its height, Shelley walked rapturously amid the swaying boughs and whirling leaves of the Cascine, watching the tumult of the driving rain-clouds, and hearkening to the triumphant voice of the wind. Autumnal decay and the barrenness of winter may make the world desolate indeed, but beyond lies waiting the spring of another year. It is the ebb and flow, the endless "baffling change," of the great tide of humanity which Shelley sings, as well as the death and advent of drear or regenerative seasons. There is not in our language a lyrical poem more epically grand than this "Ode to the West Wind."

What fire and passion dwell in these lines :—

"If I were a dead leaf thou mightest bear;
 If I were a swift cloud to fly with thee;
 A wave to pant beneath thy power, and share

The impulse of thy strength, only less free
Than thou, O, uncontrollable! If even
I were as in my boyhood, and could be

The comrade of thy wanderings over heaven,
As then, when to outstrip thy skiey speed
Scarce seemed a vision ; I would ne'er have striven

As thus with thee in prayer in my sore need.
Oh! lift me as a wave, a leaf, a cloud!
I fall upon the thorns of life! I bleed!

A heavy weight of hours has chained, and bowed
One too like thee: tameless, and swift, and proud—"

what lyrical rapture and prophetic exaltation in this
culminating stanza—

"Make me thy lyre, even as the forest is:
What if my leaves are falling like its own!
The tumult of thy mighty harmonies

Will take from both a deep, autumnal tone,
Sweet though in sadness. Be thou, spirit fierce,
My spirit! Be thou me, impetuous one!

Drive my dead thoughts over the universe
Like withered leaves to quicken a new birth!
And, by the incantation of this verse,

Scatter, as from an unextinguished hearth
Ashes and sparks, my words among mankind!
Be through my lips to unawakened earth

The trumpet of a prophecy! O wind,
If Winter comes, can Spring be far behind?"

The severe weather which prevailed at Florence in the
last month of 1819 made Shelley anxious to escape to a
climate where his constant suffering would be less, and
where his capacities for work would be stimulated. A
move was accordingly made to Pisa, and in the latter
part of January comfortable lodging was found in the
ancient city. Here the climate and, what was of importance to Shelley owing to the nephritic complaint which

troubled him, the water excellently suited the invalid, whose health began to improve steadily. In Pisa and the neighbourhood he spent the greater part of the life that was left to him. In the city itself the poet's household remained till about mid-June. It was a period of much mental worry. Godwin was in worse monetary straits than ever, and treated his son-in-law in a fashion as importunate as undignified; Mary was distraught by paternal complaints, appeals, and de-nunciations, by her husband's dubious health and melancholic depression, and by the far from welcome continuous presence of Claire Clairmont; while Claire fretted sorely anent Byron's cruel treatment of her, and about her absent Allegra. Their chief pleasure was in intercourse with the Gisbornes. There was for Shelley much need of something to alleviate his troublous state. It was an aggravation of his suffering that both in England and Italy he should be the subject of relentless abuse. A bitter onslaught upon him in *The Quarterly Review*, on the occasion of the review of " The Revolt of Islam," caused him real pain; while the attitude of most of the English with whom he came in contact was to the last degree impertinent and unpleasant. Once he was even grossly attacked. While waiting one day at the Pisan post office he was overheard by a " gentleman," an Englishman in foreign service, inquiring for letters bearing his name. This man was a powerful fellow, so that when with full force he struck Shelley on the chest—calling out as he did so, " What, are you that damned atheist Shelley?"—the latter was felled, stunned, to the ground. To make matters worse, a former servant, Paolo, who

bore a grudge against him, set afloat a scandalous rumour
which it took some time to trace and cause to be publicly
refuted.

By June the summer heats had become severe. The
Gisbornes had left the neighbourhood for a time, and
their house, Casa Ricci, near Leghorn, was placed at
the disposal of their friends, who accordingly moved
thither for a few weeks. With the advent of August it
would be necessary to seek higher land, but until then
Casa Ricci was a pleasant abode. Before he left Pisa
Shelley wrote his famous and lovely little poem "The
Cloud," charged with an impetuosity of music surpassed
by no earlier English lyric. It is a shame to dissever a
stanza or two from so perfect a thing, but the space at
my command is now limited, and extracts—it is hardly
necessary to say—are not for those who already know the
poet's work, but are meant to afford an enticing echo of
exquisite music to those whose ears have not yet been
charmed therewith. Here, then, are the first and last
stanzas of

THE CLOUD.

I bring fresh showers for the thirsting flowers,
    From the seas and the streams ;
I bear light shade for the leaves when laid
    In their noonday dreams.
From my wings are shaken the dews that waken
    The sweet buds every one,
When rocked to rest on their mother's breast,
    As she dances about the sun.
I wield the flail of the lashing hail,
    And whiten the green plains under,

And then again I dissolve it in rain,
And laugh as I pass in thunder.

*   *   *   *   *   *

I am the daughter of earth and water,
And the nursling of the sky ;
I pass through the pores of the ocean and shores ;
I change, but I cannot die.
For after the rain, when with never a stain
The pavilion of heaven is bare,
And the winds and sunbeams with their convex gleams
Build up the blue dome of air,
I silently laugh at my own cenotaph,
And out of the caverns of rain,
Like a child from the womb, like a ghost from the tomb,
I arise and unbuild it again.

It was very shortly after the adjournment to Casa
Ricci that one summer evening, when among the myrtle-
hedges the fire-flies were adventuring their wandering
fires against the sundown-glow, Shelley and Mary were
arrested in their walk by the impassioned song of a skylark. The result was that universally known lyric, of a
music altogether wild and matchless, whereby alone,
even if he had written nothing else, a poet's name
would have been rumoured to "all the days that are
to be." It would be superfluous to quote even a
single stanza of the "Ode to a Skylark." On the first
day of July the poet wrote that charming epistle in
verse, the letter to Maria Gisborne, which so well exem-
plifies the range of his genius. The poet who could write
" Prometheus Unbound," " Epipsychidion," "The Witch
of Atlas," could also write, as inimitable in their own
degree, " Julian and Maddalo " and the " Letter to Maria

Gisborne." There is another celebrated poem, written during the early part of the stay at Pisa, which should be mentioned here, though not published till late in the same year. This is "The Sensitive Plant," said to have been suggested by the numerous flowers which turned the Pisan residence of Mary and himself into a haunt of spring. The same yearning for the ideal beauty which is the mainspring of some of Shelley's finest poems animates this exquisite lyric. It is not, perhaps, well understood of many, but it is ever fervently admired even where the reader, swallow-like, skims but the surface and catches only vague fleeting glimpses of what the shadow-depths withhold.

There is, so far as I remember, no record in biographical literature of three or four years so filled with varied poetic production of the noblest kind as that which any writer upon Shelley has to refer to in the chronicle of the period comprised within 1819–1822. Like his own skylark, he seemed throughout these years to have lived but to give impassioned utterance to "profuse strains of unpremeditated art." That, however, if he sang without stint, he also jealously revised all he wrote is within our knowledge.

The year 1820 was one of national ferment throughout the southern Latin races. In the early months an insurrection broke out in Spain owing to the tyranny under which the people travailed, and the revolutionary cause triumphed at Madrid : in the autumn the Neapolitans rose against the hated and worthless Bourbon dynasty. Throughout Europe a thrill of sympathy united all who worshipped at the shrine of liberty. Naturally these events keenly excited Shelley, and as the outcome of his joy, his hopes, and his fears, he bequeathed to us his "Ode to Liberty" and his "Ode to Naples"—splendid and noteworthy poems, which, moreover—as Mr. Addington Symonds has pointed out—added a new lyric form to English literature.

About four miles from Pisa, among the hills, are the Baths of San Giuliano. Thither in August the Shelleys went to escape the heats of the Tuscan plain. On the 12th, a day of extreme heat, while his wife and Miss Clairmont were at Lucca to see the churches and ramparts, Shelley scaled the heights of Monte San Pellegrino, on the summit of which mountain is a shrine revered of pilgrims. He returned on the morrow, delighted, but greatly fatigued. On the three following days Mary saw her husband arduously employed. When his labour was over, he handed to her that strange, fantastic, fanciful "Witch of Atlas," which to so many readers is as incomprehensible as though written in Hebrew. On his mountain excursion the poet had beheld or fashioned forth a vision. In Professor Dowden's eloquent words, he "beheld for a moment, through the veil in which she hides her loveliness, the form of the great and beneficent enchantress—she whose shadow is the beauty of the world ; whose words, though too fine to be articulate to mortal ear, fill us with a longing for all high truth ; whose presence, though invisible, quickens within us all hope and joy and love." This central idea the poet "encircled with exquisite and inexhaustible arabesques of the fancy." It is not improbable that this poem was the outgrowth of the Homeric "Hymn to Mercury" which

Shelley had freely translated in *ottava rima* before he left Leghorn. There is, at any rate, a literary relationship between them which is clearly perceptible. In it, as in all Shelley's long poems of a non-dramatic character, the animating central idea is that of spiritual beauty : the 'Witch' is kin to Queen Mab and the 'Veiled Maid' of "Alastor." "The Witch of Atlas" is a fascinating intellectual *fantasia*—a production by its very nature meaningless and valueless to some and infinitely charming to others. It is not, however, a great poem in any sense of the word : being not of this mortal world, and being wrought, as it were, of moonbeams and dawn-rays. It is, indeed, like that " subtle veil " which the " Witch " wove for herself :—

> " Which when the lady knew, she took her spindle
> And turned three threads of fleecy mist, and three
> Long lines of light such as the dawn may kindle
> The clouds and waves and mountains with, and she
> As many star-beams, ere their lamps could dwindle
> In the belated moon, wound skilfully ;
> And with these threads a subtle veil she wove—
> A shadow for the splendour of her love."

Mary, jealous for her husband's long-delayed fame— of whose ultimate and even speedy arrival she had no shadow of doubt—was somewhat disappointed with the poem. She saw that it was not of the stuff to win wide greeting for its author, and she was eager that he should produce that which would make general recognition of his genius inevitable. Shelley himself, though well aware hat in his time his audience must be a limited one, found it difficult indeed to bear up against the gross abuse or contemptuous indifference which his poetry met with at the hands of the critics.

It is only in theory that the poet is able to devote himself, year after year, to the art he loves, if he meet not with the slightest encouragement and sympathy from without. If, like Shelley, he be well aware that his productions are of no common order, the discouragement is tenfold greater. In a letter accompanying "The Witch of Atlas"—on its transmission to Mr. Ollier, the London publisher—the author gives vent to a transient doubt "whether I *shall* write more. I could be content either with the Hell or the Paradise of poetry ; but the torments of its Purgatory vex me, without exciting my powers sufficiently to put an end to the vexation." Though at first perhaps a little disconcerted at Mary's criticism, Shelley knew that he had been but giving his genius a holiday. In the charming dedicatory stanzas to his wife he playfully refers to her as being "critic-bitten," but immediately adds—

> " Prithee, for this one time
> Content thee with a visionary rhyme."

Shortly after the composition of "The Witch of Atlas" Shelley wrote his satire, " Œdipus Tyrannus, or Swellfoot the Tyrant," in every way a feeble production. It is no longer read save by literary students, nor did it ever deserve even "a day's possession of the town."

In October the household was disturbed by the partially voluntary, partially involuntary, secession of Claire Clairmont. She was not the most amiable of companions to Mary, and the latter was genuinely glad when their companion left to fulfil an engagement as governess in the house of a Florentine gentleman. Shelley escorted Claire to her new abode, and continued to write to her friendly and consolatory letters, couched in a strain of ardent friendship. To Claire's faults he was quite alive, but he felt a real affection for her, and probably regarded the infidelity of Byron as all the more reason for *his* loyalty.

When Shelley returned to San Giuliano, he brought with him his cousin and former schoolfellow, Captain Thomas Medwin, of the 24th Light Dragoons. The poet was glad of his cousin's companionship, though it was not long ere he discovered that Medwin was far from being the intellectual compeer of Mary or himself. Medwin's account of Shelley's appearance at this time is interesting—

" It was nearly seven years since we had parted, but I should immediately have recognized him in a crowd. . . . His figure was emaciated and somewhat bent ; his hair, still profuse and curling naturally, was partially interspersed with grey ; but his appearance was youthful, and his countenance, whether grave or animated, strikingly intellectual. There was also a freshness and purity in his complexion which he never lost."

October passed rather heavily, owing to the inclement weather. Shelley read much, but wrote little poetry, while Mary was busy upon a new novel dealing with the adventures of Castruccio, Prince of Lucca. The heavy

rains caused the Serchio to increase in volume rapidly.
On the night of the 25th the banks of the river gave
way, and the flood swept across San Giuliano. In the
Casa Prinni the water rose four feet from the ground.
The Shelleys escaped from an upper window in a boat,
and with no little difficulty made their way to neigh-
bouring Pisa, where on the Lung' Arno they found
commodious lodging, though it was not for some ten
days that they recovered the possessions they had perforce had to leave at the Baths.

The ensuing months at Pisa were full of pleasurable
experiences for Shelley and his wife. Agreeable and
varied company made the time pass wonderfully, and a
fresh creative mood came upon the poet. Just at first,
however, there were drawbacks, ill-health not being
the least potent among them.

Among the earliest acquaintanceships made was that
with a certain Francesco Pacchiani, commonly designated
" il Professore," from his official position—most in-
adequately filled—at the University. This clever, but
unscrupulous, and rather shunned than courted, ornament
of Pisan society sought the Shelleys, and was by them
tolerated for a time. He was indirectly of good service,
however, to English literature, for had it not been for him
it is just possible that we might have had no "Hellas," and
probable that we should have had no " Epipsychidion."
On the 1st December Pacchiani introduced to his new
friends Sgricci, a famous *improvisatore*, and also took the
former to call on a lady called Viviani, of whom more
anon.   In her journal for the following day, Mary
writes—after recording her readings in " Œdipus," " Don

Quixote," and Calderon—"Pacchiani and a Greek prince
called, Prince Mavrocordato." This prince was the
patriotic Alexander Mavrocordatos (*Mavrocordato* in
Italy), ere long to become the most eminent statesman
of the Greek Revolution. Of a keenly intellectual bias,
Mavrocordatos was as ardent a student as he was a
patriot. From the very outset of his acquaintance with
the Shelleys a mutual friendship, compact of admiration, sympathy, and liking, arose between the
Greek exile and the English poet. In their literary
hours Shelley would instruct the prince in the poetry
of Milton, or Mavrocordatos would recite the "Aga-
memnon" in a manner which to Shelley's northern
ear seemed anything but charming. An hour or more
daily was devoted by Mary to teaching her new friend
English, which he acquired with remarkable ease, and he
in turn instructed Mrs. Shelley in his country's ancient
language, and read with her the two "Œdipi" and the
"Antigone." With the advent of spring these literary
pleasures came to an end. The spirit of revolution was
alive in the south. The Austrians and Russians determined to suppress the Neapolitan uprising, and in the
end triumphed and re-set on his throne the treacher-
ous coward who had been King of Naples. Early in
March the troops at Turin made a *pronunciamento*, de-
manding a constitution; and a week or so later Genoa
declared herself free. There were wild hopes abroad
that Italy was at length about to shake off her chains,
and take her place among the nations. Few there were
among the enthusiasts who acclaimed the advent of
liberty who foresaw the baffling ebb and flow of the good

cause ere the proclamation of a free and united *Italia*
would be made by a king of all Italy from the heart of
Rome. It was at this time of excitement, hopes, fears,
and wild elation, that Prince Mavrocordatos came round
to the Casa Aulla one Sunday, " gay as a caged eagle
just free," as Mary recorded in her diary, and told his
friends great news about Greece. He had been aware
for many weeks of the effort which was about to be
made, and at last he was able to announce that
his country had declared its freedom.   On Monday,
April 2nd, he called upon the Shelleys *" rayonnant
de joie."* With him he brought the famous proclamation
of the insurgent prince, Hypsilantes.   This prince,
better known abroad as Ypsilanti, had collected an army
of ten thousand Greeks, and had entered Wallachia.
The Morea, Epirus, and Servia were in simultaneous
revolt, and a cry of fury and consternation had gone up
from Stamboul.   Mavrocordatos, of course, was eager to
join his countrymen, and his ardour and excitement were
shared by the Shelleys, especially by the poet, who at
once took up the Greek cause as one of the worthiest
struggles of modern times.   The poetical result was
the lyrical drama entitled " Hellas," the latest work
published by Shelley ere death overtook him, although it
was finished in the autumn of the same year as witnessed
the Greek proclamation of Independence. It was appropriately dedicated to Prince Mavrocordatos, and was
preceded by some remarks which show how ardently the
writer realised the greatness of his subject.   In this
preface occurs Shelley's well-known phrase, "We are all
Greeks."

It is unnecessary to mention all the friends and acquaintances who made up society for the Shelleys in Pisa. Their friends Mr. and Mrs. Williams were those with whom they were most intimate. Both were in every way charming people, cultured, refined, full of sympathy for all that was worthy. The fates of Edward Williams and Shelley were to be indissolubly linked in death, and therefore the former must always be remembered. Rather younger than Shelley, he too had been an Etonian, though unacquainted with his elder schoolmate. After a short experience of the navy, he had entered a dragoon regiment in India, married, sold his commission, and gone to reside with his wife and child at the Lake of Geneva. His friend Medwin persuaded him to journey to Pisa, and as his tastes were literary (as genuine as those of Medwin, while he had nothing of the latter's vanity and commonplaceness of mind), it was an extra inducement to know that he would there meet Shelley. The two families at once became intimate and friendly; indeed, Williams' advent was particularly welcome at a time when the boredom of Medwin's company was becoming almost intolerable. It is to the latter, however, that we owe the narrative of Shelley's intimacy with Emilia Viviani.

In the previous autumn "the professor," Pacchiani, had told the Shelleys about a beautiful and unfortunate young lady of noble birth, whom (as the family confessor —for the versatile chemist was also a priest, though he laughed at his calling) he attended. Count Viviani had two daughters growing to womanhood, when he took unto himself a second wife. The new countess was

jealous of her young rivals, and contrived, under the
false pretence of education, to have them immured in
the Convent of Santa Anna, a dreary and wretched residence for Emilia and her sister.   Emilia, who at the time
of the Shelleys' advent to Pisa had been two years in
this convent, was described by Pacchiani as a girl of
extraordinary beauty of mind and body, and rarely
accomplished.   Her father, desirous to get her off his.
hands without the customary dowry, was anxious to have
her married to a wealthy gentleman who would accept
her beauty as equivalent to hard cash.   Shelley had not
changed much since the days when his boyish heart
suffered anguish at the thought of Mr. Westbrook's
awful tyranny in sending one of his girls to school against
her will.   Here was a more evil case, with an added air of
romance.   Still, more circumspection was now necessary,.
and Mary and Claire Clairmont went one day about the
end of November in company with Pacchiani, and
saw the lovely prisoner.   Both were charmed, though
Mary found certain minor flaws, invisible to her impressionable husband, when some days later, along
with Medwin and Pacchiani, he first met Emilia
Viviani.   Her rich Italian beauty, essentially classic in
type, her enthusiastic nature, lofty aspirations, and im-
pulsive demeanour, entirely fascinated the poet.   Shelley
and his wife thereafter visited the Contessina Viviani as
frequently as practicable; brought her books and flowers,
and gave to her life new interests and delights.   As was.
almost inevitable, Shelley's heart expanded to this new
luminary.   In her physical and spiritual loveliness she
appeared to him as the ideal woman, type of that Ideal

Beauty which had haunted his imagination from his early boyhood. He loved Mary none the less because Emilia Viviani entered into his deepest life, because the influence of this beautiful and unfortunate lady swept him out of himself as if he were but a leaf on a whirling current. His passion (for by no other name could his emotion be described) was purely of the mind and spirit; nor does it appear that Mary resented the Platonic love which she could not but have perceived had arisen. A year later—disillusion! Emilia turned out to be mortal, even to Shelley's rapturous gaze. She married a Signor Biondi, and led him and his luckless mother "a devil of a life." In that aversion from disenchantment, which is natural to us all, it is almost welcome to know that she did not settle down to the deadly common-place which environed her after her marriage. Her great beauty waned, and the malarious air of the Maremma put an end ere long to a brief and unfortunate life. But before her marriage Shelley, inspired by his feelings towards her, and by his impassioned idealization, had composed one of his most memorable poems, that extra-ordinary and absolutely unique production, the "Epipsy-chidion." In the following year he wrote of it to a friend, "I cannot look at [it]; the person whom it celebrates was a cloud instead of a Juno; and poor Ixion starts from the centaur that was the offspring of his own embrace. If you are curious, however, to hear what I am and have been, it will tell you something thereof. It is an idea-lized history of my life and feelings. I think one is always in love with something or other; the error—and I confess it is not easy for spirits cased in flesh and blood to avoid it—consists in seeking in a mortal image the likeness of what is, perhaps, eternal." The meaning of "Epipsychidion" may be given as "a poem on the soul." The poem itself is the rhapsody of an ecstatic spirit upon the theme of ideal love. Plainly inspired by, if not actually based upon, Plato's "Symposium" and Dante's "Vita Nuova," it has manifest points of resemblance to both these testaments of love. In "Emilia" the poet recognizes the long-sought-for union of the Uranian and Pandemic Venus; but even in his lyrical rapture he does not give himself wholly to the new influence. If Emilia be the sun of his soul, Mary is to be the moon— under whose alternate empire he will gladly live. There are few wives, however, who would abdicate the throne of the sun for that of the moon, howsoever charming in theory that of the latter might be. The poem is obscure in many of its allusions, allusions probably to mental rather than to actual experiences. Like the "Vita Nuova," it can only be understood of those who know the secret of spiritual passion. But there can be none who fails to appreciate the exquisite beauty of its verse, the vital poetry which animates it from the first line to the last, the intensity of emotion with which it vibrates. Is it to a woman that these passionate words are uttered?—

> "Seraph of Heaven! too gentle to be human,
> Veiling beneath that radiant form of Woman
> All that is insupportable in thee
> Of light and love and immortality!
> Sweet Benediction in the Eternal Curse!
> Veiled Glory of this lampless Universe!
> Thou Moon beyond the clouds! Thou living Form
> Among the Dead! Thou Star above the Storm!
> Thou Wonder, and thou Beauty, and thou Terror!"

or what love is this which would fain annihilate indivi-
duality, so that spirit in spirit might merge, and in their
supreme height of passion be veritably as one—a love, the
full expression of which is beyond human utterance?—

> " One hope within two wills, one will beneath
> Two overshadowing minds, one life, one death,
> One Heaven, one Hell, one immortality,
> And one annihilation. Woe is me !
> The wingèd words on which my soul would pierce
> Into the height of love's rare Universe,
> Are chains of lead around its flight of fire—
> I pant, I sink, I tremble, I expire ! "

There is not in the whole range of our poetry anything
more beautiful in description than the following lines de-
lineating the Ægean island, the ideal abode, where refuge
is to be had from all the weariness and pain of life, a
" Far Eden of the purple East," set where the ocean hath
forsworn its treacheries, where for ever "the halcyons
brood around the foamless isles."

> " It is an isle under Ionian skies,
> Beautiful as a wreck of Paradise,
>
>   *   *   *   *   *   *
>
> The blue Ægean girds this chosen home,
> With ever-changing sound and light and foam,
> Kissing the sifted sands, and caverns hoar ;
> And all the winds wandering along the shore
> Undulate with the undulating tide :
> There are thick woods where sylvan forms abide ;
> And many a fountain, rivulet, and pond,
> As clear as elemental diamond,
> Or serene morning air ; and far beyond,

The mossy tracks made by the goats and deer
(Which the rough shepherd treads but once a year),
Pierce into glades, caverns, and bowers, and halls
Built round with ivy, which the waterfalls
Illumining, with sound that never fails
Accompany the noonday nightingales ;
And all the place is peopled with sweet airs ;
The light clear element which the isle wears
Is heavy with the scent of lemon-flowers,
Which floats like mist laden with unseen showers,
And falls upon the eyelids like faint sleep ;
And from the moss violets and jonquils peep,
And dart their arrowy odour through the brain,
Till you might faint with that delicious pain.
And every motion, odour, beam, and tone,
With that deep music is in unison ;
Which is the soul within the soul—they seem
Like echoes of an antenatal dream.
It is an isle 'twixt heaven, air, earth, and sea,
Cradled, and hung in clear tranquillity ;
Bright as that wandering Eden, Lucifer,
Washed by the soft blue oceans of young air.
It is a favoured place. Famine or Blight,
Pestilence, War, and Earthquake, never light
Upon its mountain-peaks ; blind vultures, they
Sail onward far upon their fatal way.
The winged storms, chanting their thunder-psalm
To other lands, leave azure chasms of calm
Over this isle, or weep themselves in dew,
From which its fields and woods ever renew
Their green and golden immortality.
And from the sea there rise, and from the sky
There fall, clear exhalations, soft and bright,
Veil after veil, each hiding some delight,
Which sun or moon or zephyr draws aside,
Till the isle's beauty, like a naked bride
Glowing at once with love and loveliness,
Blushes and trembles at its own excess ;
Yet, like a buried lamp, a soul no less

Burns in the heart of this delicious isle,
An atom of the Eternal, whose own smile
Unfolds itself, and may be felt not seen
O'er the grey rocks, blue waves, and forests green,
Filling their bare and void interstices.

It was not long after Shelley's first call upon
Emilia Viviani that he valorously set himself to refute
Peacock's essay on "The Four Ages of Poetry," the
remarks in which against poetry itself had excited
Shelley to "a sacred rage." Peacock had published his
dissertation in "Ollier's Literary Miscellany," and his
antagonist was desirous of a tourney with him in the
same magazine, and with as little delay as practicable.
So when he had finished his admirable "Defence of
Poetry" (which every literary student should read
and master) he sent it to Ollier, who, however, was
unable to use it owing to the stoppage of the magazine. The manuscript consisted of the first of three
parts; the second and third were never written, and the
first was restricted to a survey of the history of poetry,
and a treatise on its elements and principles. As
might be expected, Shelley takes up the loftiest ground.
In reading it, we are not only convinced by its argu-
ments and charmed by its literary power, but also realize
that we are perusing an account of all that moulded the
views of one of the greatest of English poets.

In the spring Shelley, along with one or more friends,
was wont to horrify the Pisans and Livornese by his excursions along the Pisan canal in a frail, flat-bottomed boat.
On the occasion of the trial trip Williams and another
friend were with the poet; suddenly rising and steady-

ing himself by the mast, the former overturned the boat. Shelley, though unable to swim a stroke, behaved with his usual courage and self-possession, and Williams found no difficulty in towing him ashore.

When the summer heats came on with May, a move to the Baths of San Giuliano was determined upon, an additional temptation to this choice lying in the fact that there was a chance of Byron's going thither also. Early in May the Shelleys therefore found themselves at the Baths. Their friends, the Williamses, were at a villa at Pugnano, some four miles distant. Here, day after day, the poet, either alone, or with Mary, or often with Williams, would sail in his boat along the waters of the Serchio, or over the river-like canal which meandered between Pugnano and San Giuliano. The quiet and rest of these days were greatly enjoyed by Shelley who had again grown weary and depressed. Life became a dream, when he could lie in his frail craft drifting along the Serchio's current, watching the clouds trailing their shadows over water and hill, or when in the cool of the evening the boat set towards home adown the picturesque *canale*, with the aziola crying softly through the dusk, and the fireflies, one by one, lighting their tiny lamps among the overhanging myrtles. The poetical outcome of one such water excursion with Williams, one lovely July morning, was " The Boat on the Serchio." Every one who knows must love this short poem, as simple in style as it is beautiful in effect. "Melchior" and "Lionel" respectively represent Williams and the poet. As for Mary, when not sailing with her husband, she was busy reading Homer and the English dramatists, working at her historical novel, "Valperge," or visiting Emilia Viviani or Jane Williams.

It was while at the Baths that Shelley wrote a poem which, artistically regarded, is one of his most perfect achievements, and ranks at the same time as one of the finest elegiac poems in any language.

In February he had heard of Keats' severe illness of the lungs, and of his arrival in Italy. He at once wrote to the young poet, and urged him to come to Pisa. In the previous summer, when Keats' complaint first declared itself, Shelley had sent a similar invitation, which the author of " Endymion," however, could not see his way to accept. And now he was far too unwell to be able to act upon his correspondent's kind and courteous suggestion ; indeed, the shadow of death was already upon him. Shelley did not hear of Keats' death until some weeks after the event, and when he received the news it was with mourning for the loss of one whom he knew to be a great poet, and who had been even more harshly treated than himself. On his first acquaintance with his younger comrade's early poetry, he had not been greatly impressed, considering that more promise than accomplishment was shown. When, however, he came to read " Hyperion " he not only realized the genius therein displayed, but believed that Keats was destined to a higher place in poetry than he himself could ever hope to occupy. There were certain radical differences between the two poets which prevented full recognition on either part. Keats, according to Shelley, dallied too much with the earthly beauty of poetry ; Keats, on the other hand, thought that Shelley was

blinded by the splendour of his vision, and that he forgot
that the poet must also be first and foremost the artist.
It is a fact that though the elder poet recognized in
" Hyperion" one of the finest modern poems, he seemed
indifferent not only to "Lamia " and " The Pot of Basil,"
but to Keats' noblest odes.   As the seer, as the prophet,
as the poet of humanity, Shelley ranks far above Keats ;
as the heart-whole devotee of beauty for beauty's sake,
as the artist before aught else, Keats must be adjudged
the superior.   Comparisons, however, are generally futile.
It is enough for us to know that Shelley is the supreme
singer, the divinest lyric voice, in all our realm of literature, and that since Shakespeare no poet has exceeded
Keats in fulness of poetic utterance.

Very soon after the sad tidings were made known to
him Shelley, enthusiastic for the fame of his dead friend,
and indignant at the gross attacks of the reviewers—
attacks which he naturally enough, though wrongfully,
believed to have been the main cause of the young
poet's breakdown—began an elegy upon the death of his
unfortunate friend.   He chose the Spenserian stanza as
most suitable, and indubitably had in his mind the
" Laments " of Bion and Moschus, and the " Lycidas "
of Milton.   In selecting the name "Adonais " as that by
which to personate Keats, he probably was influenced by
Bion's "Adonis," of which " Adonais " is the more melli-
fluous Doric form.   Curiously enough, this poem on the
death of Keats was of all Shelley's productions that
which its subject would unhesitatingly have pronounced
the author's masterpiece : even the " Prometheus Unbound " could never have satisfied Keats' jealous poetic

sense as adequately as "Adonais"—so rich with the
precious ore of poetry unadulterate. On the whole, the
latter portion of the poem is the finer. It is more interesting, because it is more directly the expression of
Shelley's self, and because it owes less to classic models.
Nowhere, however, is it disfigured by inappropriate
images. In place of mourning fauns and satyrs there are
Splendours and Glooms, wild-voiced Echo silent now
among her mountain hollows, Morning clad in a strange
grief, the Dreams which haunt Adonais dead, Spring
sorrowing for her lover who is no more, Urania herself
weeping by the bier of her beloved—around which throng
the desolate Hours, and, among others, Desires and
Adorations, winged Persuasions and Veiled Destinies,

> " All he had loved, and moulded into thought,
>   From shape, and hue, and odour, and sweet sound."

All readers of "Adonais" must be familiar with its
loveliest passages, those impassioned verses of consolation, in particular, beginning

> " Peace, peace ! he is not dead, he doth not sleep !
>   He hath awakened from the dream of life."

Nor can any literary student fail to see in the "In
Memoriam" of a later poet the influence of the author
of such lines as

> " He is made one with Nature : there is heard
>   His voice in all her music, from the moan
>   Of thunder, to the song of night's sweet bird."

or

> " He is a portion of the loveliness
> Which once he made more lovely."

There are in "Adonais" no stanzas which touch us more than those representing Shelley himself. After describing how others who had loved or admired the dead poet came to pay reverence he recounts his own advent :—

> " Midst others of less note, came one frail Form,
>   A phantom among men, companionless
>   As the last cloud of an expiring storm
>   Whose thunder is its knell.   He, as I guess,
>   Had gazed on Nature's naked loveliness,
>   Actæon-like, and now he fled astray
>   With feeble steps o'er the world's wilderness,
>   And his own thoughts along that rugged way
> Pursued like raging hounds their father and their prey.
>
>   A pard-like Spirit beautiful and swift—
>   A Love in desolation masked—a Power
>   Girt round with weakness; it can scarce uplift
>   The weight of the superincumbent hour.
>   It is a dying lamp, a falling shower,
>   A breaking billow ;—even whilst we speak
>   Is it not broken ?   On the withering flower
>   The killing sun smiles brightly : on a cheek
> The life can burn in blood even while the heart may break.
>
>   His head was bound with pansies overblown,
>   And faded violets, white, and pied, and blue ;
>   And a light spear topped with a cypress cone,
>   Round whose rude shaft dark ivy-tresses grew
>   Yet dripping with the forest's noonday dew,
>   Vibrated, as the ever-beating heart
>   Shook the weak hand that grasped it.   Of that crew
>   He came the last, neglected and apart ;
> A herd-abandoned deer, struck by the hunter's dart."

When Adonais has been received into the mysterious world beyond our ken, the poem grows less exultant and more charged with sorrow and trouble. Finally, in a strange rapture, and in stranger prescience, the poet feels that he also is soon to join those who have gone before :

" I am borne darkly, fearfully afar ;
  Whilst burning through the inmost veil of heaven,
  The soul of Adonais, like a star,
  Beacons from the abode where the Eternal are."

"Adonais" was printed at the Didot press in Pisa, and was sent in type to London, where, however, it was not republished. Seven years after its author's death it was reprinted at Cambridge by a few enthusiastic students, admirers of the little read poets, Keats and Shelley.[1]

It was while engaged upon "Adonais" that Shelley was much perturbed by the piratical republication, by a London bookseller, of his boyhood's poem, "Queen Mab." He wrote at once to a solicitor, instructing him to procure an injunction, but the man Clark defied all prosecutions, and is said to have sold copies by the thousand. The most gross attacks were in consequence made upon its author in various quarters. The "Government prints" especially distinguished themselves by their brutality : as Horace Smith informed Shelley, the diabolical calumnies which they vented were boundless. The result was a sale for "Queen Mab" far exceeding that of all its author's other publications combined.

[1] Among the Shelley Society's publications there is a facsimile reprint of the exceedingly rare Pisa edition of the "Adonais."

Early in August Shelley received a letter from Byron urging him to proceed to Ravenna for a meeting. Thither accordingly Shelley went, and spent some time in company with his friend. He found Byron improved in most respects. Though living with the Countess Guiccioli in an illegal union, he no longer permitted himself any of that indulgence in vice which had threatened to ruin him wholly during his residence in Venice.

In the nights the two poets would discuss literary matters, or the elder would read, to his companion's delight and admiration, the unpublished cantos of " Don Juan." In the late afternoons and evenings they would ride through the sombre alleys of the pine-forest. But about the middle of the month Shelley grew tired of Ravenna (which interested him not at all, save as containing the shrine of Dante), and of its unhealthy climate; and wearied also of the trying life at the Palazzo Guiccioli, and of the lacqueys, ten horses, eight huge dogs, three monkeys, five cats, the eagle, the crow, the falcon, the five peacocks, the two guinea-hens, the Egyptian crane, and the Venetian valet who had stabbed two or three people, the strange company which with Lord Byron and his mistress made up the extraordinary household. Before leaving he paid a visit to Byron and Claire Clairmont's daughter, Allegra, at the Convent of Bagnacavallo, and was much taken with the latter's beauty, vivacity, and promise of mental power.

Before the autumn was far spent he had composed his lyrical drama " Hellas," to which reference has been already made. It was probably finished in October, as the dedication to Prince Ypsilanti bears date November 1st.

Shelley himself did not lay great stress upon this poem, and notwithstanding its great and varied beauty his wisest critics are inclined to endorse his opinion of it to a considerable extent. It is markedly unequal. The original Prologue holds out a promise which is not exactly fulfilled —indeed, Shelley's original conception for his drama would seem to have been on a more epical scale than that which for some reason he allowed to take its place. It is in " Hellas," however, that we have a supreme manifestation of the poet's lyrical genius. The choric chants beginning—

> " Worlds on worlds are rolling ever
>   From creation to decay ; "

> " In the great morning of the world ; "

and—
> " The world's great age begins anew,"

mark Shelley's highest reach in what may be termed the epic treatment of lyrical themes.

In the autumn the Shelleys again settled down at Pisa, sharing the Tre Palazzi on the Lung' Arno with the Williamses, and delighting more than ever in the company of these good friends. Williams was a pleasant companion for the poet, and his wife inspired in Shelley a deep and ardent while a purely friendly affection. Byron, also, lived close by, and altogether Shelley and his wife enjoyed a more homely feeling than it had ever been their lot to experience. Early in 1822, another friend was added to the Pisan society of which they were members. There is no more striking figure among

Shelley's circle of friends than Edward John Trelawny, commonly called Captain Trelawny. He is interesting to us now not only as one of the most entertaining and reliable biographers of Shelley's latter days, but also for his own sake. Eminently a man of action and, in the best sense of the word, a man of the world, Trelawny had sojourned in most parts of the globe, and had studied human nature in all its phases. In person he was singularly striking. That he knew how to write almost as well as he knew how to live, is evident from his interesting semi-autobiographical work "The Adventures of a Younger Son," and from his practically immortal "Records of Byron and Shelley." There could, perhaps, be no more decisive testimony to the beauty of Shelley's life and nature than the witness of this brilliant, shrewd, often cynical, experienced wayfarer upon the earth. Trelawny was impressed by Shelley at the outset, and came to consider him the purest and finest nature, as well as the most intellectual mind, with which he had ever come in contact. In his fascinating "Records," there is nothing more delightful or more memorable than his account of his first encounter with the poet. He had arranged to pass the ensuing winter in hunting, in company with his friends Captains Roberts and Williams, in the Maremma, but wished first to spend some time in Pisa so as to be near Byron and Shelley, the two poets whose writings he so much admired and whom he was anxious to meet. Shelley, especially, it was his wish to become acquainted with, though curiously enough he does not seem to have received from mutual friends any account of the poet's personal

appearance. After a long stop at Genoa, he mentions
that, anxious to see the poet, he left his companion and
drove to Pisa alone.

"I arrived late, and after putting up my horse at the inn and
dining, hastened to the Tre Palazzi, on the Lung' Arno, where
the Shelleys and Williams's lived on different flats under the same
roof, as is the custom on the Continent. The Williams's received
me in their earnest cordial manner; we had a great deal to com-
municate to each other, and were in loud and animated conversation,
when I was rather put out by observing in the passage near the open
door, opposite to where I sat, a pair of glittering eyes steadily fixed
on mine; it was too dark to make out whom they belonged to.
With the acuteness of a woman, Mrs. Williams's eyes followed the
direction of mine, and going to the doorway, she laughingly said,

"'Come in, Shelley, it's only our friend Tre just arrived.'

"Swiftly gliding in, blushing like a girl, a tall thin stripling held
out both his hands; and although I could hardly believe as I looked
at his flushed, feminine, and artless face that it could be the Poet,
I returned his warm pressure. After the ordinary greetings and
courtesies he sat down and listened. I was silent from astonishment:
was it possible this mild-looking beardless boy could be the verit-
able monster at war with all the world?—excommunicated by the
Fathers of the Church, deprived of his civil rights by the fiat of
a grim Lord Chancellor, discarded by every member of his family,
and denounced by the rival sages of our literature as the founder of
a Satanic school? I could not believe it; it must be a hoax. He
was habited like a boy, in a black jacket and trousers, which he
seemed to have outgrown, or his tailor, as is the custom, had most
shamefully stinted him in his 'sizings.' Mrs. Williams saw my
embarrassment, and to relieve me asked Shelley what book he had
in his hand? His face brightened, and he answered briskly:

"'Calderon's "Magico Prodigioso," I am translating some
passages in it.'

"'Oh, read it to us!'

"Shoved off from the shore of common-place incidents that could
not interest him, and fairly launched on a theme that did, he instantly
became oblivious of everything but the book in his hand. The

masterly manner in which he analyzed the genius of the author, his lucid interpretation of the story, and the case with which he translated into our language the most subtle and imaginative passages of the Spanish poet, were marvellous, as was his command of the two languages. After this touch of his quality I no longer doubted his identity; a dead silence ensued; looking up, I asked,

" ' Where is he ? '

" Mrs. Williams said, ' Who? Shelley? Oh, he comes and goes like a spirit, no one knows when or where.' "

Both Byron and Shelley were greatly attracted by Trelawny, and a very sincere friendship at once arose between the two latter. The days passed quietly but pleasantly, without even such extraneous excitement as was caused one day before Trelawny's advent, when news came that a man who had committed sacrilege at Lucca had been sentenced to be burned—a sentence which had so horrified Shelley that he had proposed to Byron a scheme for the forcible release of the condemned wretch, which only fell through on receipt of the news that the galleys had been substituted for the stake.

When not in the pine-forest adjacent to Pisa, Shelley spent most of his time with one or other of his friends, in his boat. Trelawny has told us how the days passed for his friend. "He was up at six or seven, reading Plato, Sophocles, and Spinoza, with the accompaniment of a hunch of dry bread; then he joined Williams in a sail on the Arno, in a flat-bottomed skiff, book in hand, and thence he went to the pine-forest, or some out-of-the-way place. When the birds went to roost he turned home, and talked and read till midnight." Further on, Trelawny narrates how one fine spring morning he went with Mrs. Shelley in search of the errant poet. Having traversed the Cascine for some two or three miles, they dismissed their calèche and wandered through the forest. Crossing a sandy plain they proceeded until the noon-heat fatigued Mary, who sat down in a sheltered spot while her companion roamed off to continue the quest. Finally, when the afternoon shadows were beginning to lengthen, Trelawny encountered an old contadino, of whom he made enquiries.

"L'Inglese malincolico haunts the woods maledetta. I will show you his nest."

" As we advanced, the ground swelled into mounds and hollows. By and by the old fellow pointed with his stick to a hat, books, and loose papers lying about, and then to a deep pool of dark glimmering water, saying, ' Eccolo !' I thought he meant that Shelley was in or under the water. The careless, not to say impatient, way in which the Poet bore his burden of life, caused a vague dread amongst his family and friends that he might loose or cast it away at any moment.

"The strong light streamed through the opening of the trees. One of the pines, undermined by the water, had fallen into it. Under its lee; and nearly hidden, sat the Poet, gazing on the dark mirror beneath, so lost in his bardish reverie that he did not hear my approach. There the trees were stunted and bent, and their crowns were shorn like friars by the sea breezes, excepting a cluster of three, under which Shelley's traps were lying ; these overtopped the rest. To avoid startling the Poet out of his dream, I squatted under the lofty trees, and opened his books. One was a volume of his favourite Greek dramatist, Sophocles,—the same that I found in his pocket after his death—and the other was a volume of Shakspeare."

The poet had been writing that dainty lyric " Ariel to Miranda take," and his disturber tells how he gazed in amazement at the frightful scrawl—" a marsh over-grown with bulrushes, and the blots for wild ducks," as he describes it.

It was about this time—some weeks earlier than the pine-forest episode—that the friends talked over the scheme of a yacht to be jointly owned. The sugges-tion, indeed, was Trelawny's, who little guessed of what ill-omen it was to prove. Shelley was delighted, and might have accepted his friend's practical suggestions as to its build, had he not been overruled by Williams, who was insistent on the adoption of a model made by a naval friend of his. This design was ultimately sent to Trelawny's friend, Captain Roberts, then resident in Genoa, who, after expostulating upon what he considered its untrustworthy features, consented to undertake the superintendence of its building. Before the ill-fated boat left the Genoese dockyard, the Shelleys and Williamses had left Pisa, late in April, for Casa Magni, a house literally on the sea-marge between the village of Lerici and San Terenzo. The house was large though not roomy, and would have been desolate had it not been for the splendid vision of sea, sky, and moun-tainous background, which was visible from its win-dows. But for the verandah the visitors would not have taken it. Provisions had to be fetched from a village some three or four miles distant, and the peasants in the neighbourhood were half-savage. Trelawny describes it as more like a bathing-house than a comfortable residence, and gives a hint as to its prevailing lack of

accommodation, by remarking that the sea was his only
washing-basin. The few weeks that were to ensue before
the terrible catastrophe of early July were amongst the
happiest in Shelley's life. Seasons as pleasant he had
hitherto spent—during the autumn at Great Marlow for
instance, when the boating excursion to the Thames'
source took place; but now he was happier than of
yore in that he had reached a mental standpoint whence
he could adequately survey his past achievements, and
look forward with definite assurance, " if the heaven
above me is calm for the passing moment," to a future
of yet worthier accomplishment.

On the 12th of May, about a fortnight after the
settlement at Casa Magni, the small schooner-built craft
arrived from Genoa. Though fast, strongly built, and
not deficient in beam, she was, as Trelawny remarked,
very crank in a breeze : two tons of iron ballast, moreover, were required to bring her down to her bearings.
On Byron's initiative, though rather against Shelley's
approval, she was christened *Don Juan*. An English
lad named Charles Vivian had accompanied the boat,
and was retained by Shelley to help him and Williams
in its management. Naturally the owners of the *Don
Juan*, whose title they ere long changed to *Ariel*, were
upon the water morning, noon, and night. The mag-
netic fascination of the sea held Shelley in thraldom
at once welcome and irresistible. As a seaman, he was
not a reliable member of the crew. " It was great fun,"
says Trelawny, " to witness Williams teaching the poet
how to steer, and other points of seamanship. As usual,
Shelley had a book in hand, saying he could read and

steer at the same time, as one was mental, the other mechanical. . . . The boy (Vivian) was quick and handy, and used to boats. Williams was not as deficient as I anticipated, but over-anxious, and wanted practice, which alone makes a man prompt in emergency. Shelley was intent on catching images from the ever-changing sea and sky ; he heeded not the boat."

The evenings were generally passed in a manner pleasant to all—conversation, readings from great writers, and music. Sitting on the terrace of Casa Magni, they could see the moonlit waters lip-lapping almost at their feet, and from the woods behind came the soft cry of the aziola, or the dissonant whirr of the night-jar.

As the summer heats advanced one or two incidents occurred, strange at the time, stranger to those who re-membered them a little later. One of these was the appari-tion of Allegra, who, a short time before, had succumbed to the malarious fever which, arising from the marshes of Ravenna, had reached the wretched convent of Bagna-cavallo. On the evening of the 6th of May, Shelley and Williams were walking on the terrace of the villa, when the former suddenly grasped his companion's arm, and seemed violently excited as he stared seaward. "There it is again—there !" he exclaimed, pointing across the moonlit surf. The vision he had seen was that of Allegra, who had risen from the sea, clapping her hands and laughing joyously, and beckoning to him. On another occasion, one of the household dreamed that the poet was dead. Once, later, Shelley was distinctly seen to walk into a little wood near Lerici, when he was indubitably in an opposite direction. One night, every one was aroused by screams proceeding from the sitting room. Shelley was found rigid with the horror of a vision which had just appalled him. A cloaked figure, he said, had come to his bedside and had beckoned him to follow : when they had reached the sitting-room, the figure had withdrawn the cloak from its features, and in them Shelley beheld his own. " Siete soddisfatto," the apparition said, and vanished. The origin of this vision has been supposed to be a drama of Calderon's, which Shelley is understood to have read while at Casa Magni, wherein a somewhat similar episode occurs.

On the 1st of July, Shelley and Williams left in the *Don Juan* for Leghorn, where the former hoped to meet Leigh Hunt and arrange with him and Byron for the publication of the projected newspaper to be called *The Liberal.*

Before he left Shelley was engaged upon the composition of a poem which, fragmentary as it is, ranks among his loftiest achievements. Had " The Triumph of Life " been finished, it would have ranked only second to " Prometheus Unbound." This was the poem for which he had discarded the drama of " Charles I.," begun at Pisa during the winter. The latter is an exceedingly fine composition so far as it goes, and further demonstrates its author's capacity for dramatic poetry; but we cannot wish it had been completed at the cost of " The Triumph of Life." Shelley was the first English poet who successfully used the *terza rima*, and nowhere has he attained the same delicacy and fluency as in his latest poem. The word " Triumph "

was possibly meant to signify a "pageant," rather than a
jubilation.   The vision is, broadly speaking, the triumphal
procession of the powers of life dragging captive the
spirit of Man.   The mighty dead obey the poet's
summons, but from none is there any tidings of good,
or sure prophecy of man's redemption.   We know not
to what triumphant or despairful end the solemn music
would have attained had the poet lived.   The poem
closes abruptly with these words : "Then what is Life?'
I cried "—a sentence, indeed, of profound significance
when we remember—as Mr. Symonds says—"that the
questioner was now about to seek its answer in the halls
of Death."

When Shelley left for Leghorn, he had to leave Mary
behind.   Weak and ailing from a recent miscarriage,
and perhaps depressed by the various ominous incidents
to which I have already referred, she was disturbed by
vague alarms and forebodings.

At Leghorn Shelley met the Hunts and went with
them to Pisa, where they had anything but a cordial
welcome from Byron.   As soon as it was practicable,
he prepared to return : Mary was anxious about him, and
Williams was fretting to be back again.

The painful story has been so often told and is so-
familiar, that it will be best narrated here with the utmost
brevity.   On the afternoon of Monday, the 8th of July,
Shelley and Williams, with the boy Vivian, set sail from
Leghorn.   Trelawny, who was then taking charge of
Byron's yacht the *Bolivar*, was unable to accompany
them.   The glory of the day had changed.   An intense
sultry furnace-glow had replaced the flood of sunlight :

the thunder brooded among the jagged clouds which gathered above the horizon. From the top of the lighthouse Captain Roberts uneasily watched the progress of the *Ariel.* On the *Bolivar,* the Genoese mate remarked to Trelawny, "the devil was brewing mischief." Ere long a sea-fog came up, and the boat was shrouded from view: those who were on shore or in harbour were glad that they were not upon the sea, which had become discoloured and moaned with premonition of storm.

Trelawny had gone to his cabin, but about half-past six was awakened by a sudden tumult. The sea was like lead, and was covered with scum: so sluggish was the water that the heavy thunder-drops spurted from its impenetrable surface, and the wind, passing over, failed to ruffle forth an oily wavelet. At last the tempest came, brief in duration, but fiercely violent. In about twenty minutes the seaward expanse was clear again, but on it was no sign of the *Ariel.* Trelawny was uneasy, but believed she had made Via Reggio by the time the storm had burst.

Three days afterwards Trelawny suspected the truth, and communicated his fears to Byron. Meanwhile Mrs. Shelley and Mrs. Williams waited at Casa Magni in an agony of suspense; hope and despair alternating until the latter wholly prevailed. More days of dreadful anxiety passed, and at last news came to Trelawny that two bodies had been washed ashore. One had been found near Via Reggio, the other—three miles distant— near the Tower of Migliarino, at the Bocca Lericcio. The former proved to be the corpse of Shelley, and the latter, that of Williams. The soilure of the sea had so

disfigured both that recognition was difficult ; the faces
and hands were fleshless, and the bodies pitiably frayed.
Three weeks later the skeleton of the boy Vivian was
washed ashore, but it was not until September that the
Ariel was recovered : the schooner was found to have
been not capsized, but sunk, in from ten to fifteen
fathoms of water, and was injured by a hole in her stern.[1]
When Shelley's body was found, Trelawny noticed that
in one pocket was a volume of Sophocles; and in the
other, a copy of Keats' last volume, doubled back at
" The Eve of St. Agnes," as if the poet had been reading
there at the moment of the catastrophe.

To Trelawny fell the painful duty of breaking the
news to the two waiting wives.   It is needless to dwell
on their agonized grief, or on the days that followed
for them in Pisa, whither their friend had taken them.
It had been arranged that Shelley's remains were to
be buried at Rome, near his little son William and
his friend Keats: Williams's were to be conveyed to
England.   But first it was advisable that the ceremony

---

[1] There is no necessity to go into details concerning the much-
disputed point as to whether the *Ariel's* misadventure was due to
other causes than the fury of wind and sea and mismanagement of
those on board.   It will be sufficient to state here that there can
hardly any longer be a doubt that the boat was intentionally run
into by a small craft manned by men who thought that the *Ariel*
was owned by the rich English " Milord " Byron, who was on
board with a large supply of gold.   The men did not foresee, or had
miscalculated, the fury of the sudden gale.   The *Ariel* sunk, without the treasure the Italians hoped to find; nor was it till long
afterwards that one of the wretched men confessed his share in the
crime.

of cremation should be gone through. Trelawny saw
to all the manifold preparations, and when these were
complete, he summoned Byron and Leigh Hunt, and
proceeded in the *Bolivar* to the spot where Williams
had been washed ashore. No one should omit to read
Trelawny's vivid and picturesque account of what
followed. By the afternoon the funereal pyre had burnt
low, and the friends of the dead had departed.

Next morning, the same party set forth in the same
way for the place where three white wands in the sand
marked Shelley's temporary resting-place. The day was one
of extreme beauty, and Trelawny records how he was more
than ever impressed by the splendour of the scenery—the
sea, now calm and radiant in front, and, behind, the massed
Apennines. In addition to the cremating necessaries,
there were frankincense, wine, salt, and oil, to pour
upon the burning ashes. As Trelawny grimly remarks,
more wine was poured over Shelley's dead body than
the poet had consumed during his life. The wine, and
the oil and salt, made the flames glisten and quiver.
So intense grew the heat from the white-hot iron and
the fires which encompassed it, that the atmosphere
became tremulous and wavy. Higher and higher the
flames arose, now sombre with smoke, now, when with
them the sun's light was interfused, glowing with strange
gold. The corpse had become of a dark indigo colour,
and at last fell open, laying bare the heart—which on a
sudden impulse Trelawny snatched forth, burning his
hand severely as he did so. Slowly the skeleton became
calcined, till almost nothing was left save some few
fragments of bones. And still overhead the funereal

fires rose and waved to and fro : around them wheeled a
curlew, wildly wailing, and heedless of those who would
have driven it away. At last all was over. The ashes
of the dead, having been placed in an iron box, were
conveyed to Rome. Here they were finally buried in a
spot in the Protestant Cemetery, selected and purchased
by Trelawny. In the adjoining burial-ground lay the poet's
son William, and Keats. Around Shelley's grave Trelawny
planted several cypresses and laurels; among whose
branches the thrush now calls at morn, and whence
in the evening the song of the nightingale is heard.
Behind rises the pyramid of Caius Cestius : on one side
is the flowery city of the dead : on the other, immemorial
Rome and leagues of desolate Campagna. On the flat
gravestone, now environed by violets and pansies, is the
following inscription :

PERCY BYSSHE SHELLEY,

COR CORDIUM

Natus iv. Aug. MDCCXCII.

Obiit viii. Jul. MDCCCXXII.

"Nothing of him that doth fade
But doth suffer a sea-change,
Into something rich and strange."

Now that my brief task is at an end, I have but a
further word to say. I have endeavoured to do
little more than recount the narrative of Shelley's life,
devoting here and there a few lines to his most noteworthy productions. It would, naturally, have been

a more agreeable task to have written a critical essay upon his works, his genius, and his rank in and influence upon literature; but for the reasons set forth in the beginning of this monograph, I came to the conclusion that best service could be done by contenting myself with biographical narrative. There is more than enough of criticism—good, bad, and indifferent—upon Shelley's poetry, and further amplification thereof, would, after all, amount to nothing more than the expression of another person's opinion. There is no such individual as a critic whose dicta are invaluable. It is only the sum of the best criticism that is of indubitable value.

So, while what the present writer, or any other Shelleyan critic, might say upon the poetry of Shelley would have little weight with the great mass of his non-critical admirers, there is the sum of all the best criticism of half-a-century to reckon with. What, then, does this declare? More and more assuredly that Shelley is one of the very greatest of English poets, and that as a lyrical poet he is absolutely unrivalled. Posterity will probably rank the "Prometheus Unbound" higher even than we do: as for certain lyrics, would it not be almost an impertinence to attempt to criti-cise productions which belong to the supreme height of art!

He was a new force in literature, and his influence is probably as incalculable as it is apparently illimitable. On the forefront of the time, he was prophet and seer as well as poet. Hence the immense influence he has exercised, and must continue to exercise, upon an ever-growing multitude of people. By these Shelley is revered not only as a great poet, but as a reformer and spiritual guide.

Again I must emphasize the fact—for without doubt among my readers will be many who have not yet made acquaintance, or are but slightly familiar, with the longer poems of Shelley—that this biography will not fulfil its purpose, if it fail to induce towards study and individual criticism of the poet. It is, in a word, but an introduction to the study of Shelley's life and work. If it serve this end, I am content.

Of Shelley himself a last word may here be added. Not for this set of readers nor for that, but for all who love what is loftiest and best in poetry, Shelley must always seem one of the highest-enthroned among the kings of song. It can never be that the avarice of time shall take his name and his music from us. Even as "Adonais," of whom he wrote in deathless strains, he veritably wakes or sleeps with the enduring dead.

FINIS.

INDEX.

Hookham, Mr., publisher of "Queen Mab," 93

Hunt, Leigh, imprisoned, Shelley sends a subscription of £20, for the benefit of, 90 ; at his house Shelley meets Keats, 125

"Hubert Cauvin," a romance by Shelley, 78

"Hymn to Intellectual Beauty," extracts from, 32 ; referred to, 120

I.

Imlay, Fanny, daughter of Mary Wollstonecraft, and step-sister of Mary Godwin, 105 ; she poisons herself, 122

J.

"Julian and Maddalo " described, 141

K.

Keate, Dr., head-master at Eton, 29, 35

Keats, John, Shelley's acquaintance with, 23 ; first meeting with Shelley, 125 ; Keats and Shelley agree each to write a long poem, 127 ; illness and death, 171 ; Shelley's opinion of Keats' poems, 171 ; Shelley's elegy "Adonais," upon, 172 *et seq.*

L.

"Laon and Cythna," *see* "Revolt of Islam "

"Leonora," Shelley's third romance written in conjunction with Hogg, 41

"Letter to Lord Ellenborough," 87

"Letter to Maria Gisborne," 154

"Letters," Shelley's, 144-145

Lind, Dr., 32, 33

"Lines to Mont Blanc," composed in Switzerland, 120

"Lines written among the Euganean Hills," 141, 143

M.

Medwin, Capt. Thomas, description of Shelley, 26 ; collaborates in production of "Nightmare" with Shelley, 34 ; claims a share in composition of "Wandering Jew," 40

Medwin, Mr., lends Shelley £25, and refuses to lend further supplies, 69

Munday and Slatter, Messrs., publishers, 40, 47

N.

"Necessity of Atheism, The," 47

"Nightmare," a romance, 34, 37

O.

"Œdipus Tyrannus : or, Swellfoot the Tyrant," 158

"Ode to a Skylark," 154

"Ode to Liberty," 156

"Ode to Naples," 145, 156

"Ode to the West Wind," 150

Oxford, matriculation at, 36 ; takes up residence at, 38 ; Shelley and Hogg expelled, March 25th, 1811, 48

"Ozymandias," 133

BIBLIOGRAPHY.

BY

JOHN P. ANDERSON

(British Museum).

I. WORKS.

The Poetical [and Prose] Works of Percy Dysshe Shelley, now first given from the author's original editions. With some hitherto inedited pieces. With memoir by Leigh Hunt. (Edited, with notes, by R. H. Shepherd.) Series 1-4. London [1871-] 1875, 8vo.
    The title of Series 3, 4, reads, "The Works of P. B. Shelley." This edition does not contain the whole of Shelley's Prose Works.

The Works of P. B. S. in verse and prose. Edited, with prefaces, notes, and appendices, by Harry Buxton Forman. [With portraits, etchings and facsimiles.] 8 vols. London, 1880 [1876-80], 8vo.
    The poetical works were published in 1876-7, in 4 vols., and the prose works in 1880, in 4 vols. The 8 vols. were issued the same year under the above collective title.

II. POETICAL WORKS.

The Poetical Works of Coleridge, Shelley, and Keats. [With memoir of Shelley by Cyrus Redding.] Paris, 1829, 8vo.

The Works of P. B. S., with his life. 2 vols. London, 1834, 12mo.

The Poetical Works of P. B. S. Edited by Mrs. Shelley. 4 vols. London, 1839, 8vo.

Other editions :—London, 1839, 8vo, engraved title with vignette (printed in double columns); London, 1840, 8vo ; London, 1846, 8vo, in 4 vols.; London, 1847, 8vo, in 3 vols. ; London, 1847, 8vo, in one vol. ; London, 1853, 8vo, 3 vols. ; London, 1853, 12mo, one vol. ; London, 1854, 8vo, one vol. ; Boston [U.S.], 1855, 12mo, in 3 vols. ; London, 1856, 8vo ; London, 1857, 8vo, 3 vols. ; London, 1862, 12mo, in one vol. ; Philadelphia [1884], 8vo, with portraits and illustrations.

The Poetical Works of P. B. S. With notes. A new edition, revised and corrected · by G. Cunningham. Illustrated on steel by G. Standfast. London, 1844, 12mo.

The Poetical Works of P. B. S. Complete in two volumes. Illustrated with portrait, etc. London [1851], 16mo.

The Poetical Works of P. B. S. Edited by Mrs. Shelley, with a memoir by J. Russell Lowell. 2 vols. Boston [U.S.], 1857, 12mo.

The Poetical Works of P. B. S., including various additional pieces from MS. and other sources. The text carefully revised, with notes and a memoir by William Michael Rossetti. 2 vols. London, 1870, 8vo.

The Poetical Works of P. B. S. [Unannotated edition.] Edited, with a critical memoir, by William Michael Rossetti. Illustrated by the Society of Decorative Art. London [1870], 8vo.

The Poetical Works of P. B. S. Reprinted from the early

editions, with memoir, explanatory notes, etc. [Chandos Classics.] London [1874], 8vo.

The Poetical Works of P. B. S. Edited, with an introductory memoir and illustrations, by William B. Scott. London [1874], 8vo.

The Poetical Works of P. B. S. With a memoir by J. R. Lowell. Illustrated. New York, 1875, 8vo.

The Poetical Works of P. B. S. Edited by H. Buxton Forman. 4 vols. London, 1876-77, 8vo.

There were also 25 copies on Whatman's paper, privately printed.

The Complete Poetical Works of P. B. S. The text carefully revised, with notes and a memoir by W. M. Rossetti. 3 vols. London, 1878, 8vo.

The Poetical Works of P. B. S. London [1878], 8vo.

The Poetical Works of P. B. S. (Unannotated edition, edited, with a critical memoir, by William Michael Rossetti.) [Moxon's Popular Poets.] London [1879], 8vo.

The Poetical Works of P. B. S. Edited, with an introductory memoir, by W. B. Scott. [Excelsior Series.] London [1880], 8vo.

The Poetical Works of P. B. S. Edited by H. B. Forman. Reissue, with the notes of M. W. Shelley. 4 vols. London, 1882, 8vo.

The Poetical Works of P. B. S. given from his own editions and other authentic sources, collated with many manuscripts, and with all editions of authority, together with two prefaces and notes, his poetical translations and fragments, and an appendix of Juvenilia. Edited by II. B. Forman. 2 vols. London, 1882, 8vo.

——Second edition, with the notes of Mary W. Shelley. 2 vols. London, 1886, 8vo.

III. SMALLER COLLECTIONS.

Poetical Pieces, containing Prometheus Unmasked, a lyrical drama; with other poems. Hellas, a lyrical drama. The Cenci, a tragedy in five acts. Rosalind and Helen, with other poems. 4 pts. London, 1823, 8vo.

The above is merely a collective title-page prefixed to separate editions of the four "Poetical Pieces" indicated, all of which have distinct title-pages and paginations; their dates being 1820-22-21-19 respectively.

Miscellaneous Poems, by P. B. S. London, 1826, 12mo.

According to the *Metropolitan Quarterly Magazine* for 1826, this collection, published by Benbow, appeared in numbers.

Minor Poems. London, 1846, 24mo.

——Another edition. London, 1859, 18mo.

The Lyrics and Minor Poems of P. B. S. With a prefatory notice, biographical and critical. By Joseph Skipsey. London, 1885, 12mo.

IV. SELECTIONS.

The Beauties of P. B. S., consisting of miscellaneous selections from his poetical works, etc. With a biographical preface. London, 1830, 12mo.

——Second edition. London, 1830, 12mo.

The Beauties of P. B. S. A new edition. London, 1831, 12mo.

——Third edition. London, 1832, 12mo.

The Beauties of P. B. S., etc. [With portrait.] London, 1836, 16mo.

Gems from Shelley illustrated. [Printed in letters of gold.] London [1860], fol.

A Selection from the poems of P. B. S. Edited, with a memoir, by Mathilde Blind. (*Tauchnitz Collection of British Authors.*) Leipzig, 1872 ?, 12mo.

Favorite Poems . . . Illustrated. Boston [Mass.], 1877, 16mo.

Poems from Shelley, selected and arranged [with a preface] by Stopford A. Brooke. London, 1880, 8vo.

Fifty copies were printed on large paper.

Poems selected from P. B. S. With preface by R. Garnett. (*Parchment Series.*) London, 1880, 8vo.

There were also fifty copies printed on large paper.

The Shelley Birthday Book and Calendar. Compiled . . . by J. R. Tutin. London, 1885, 8vo.

V. SINGLE WORKS.

Adonais. An Elegy on the Death of John Keats, author of Endymion, Hyperion, etc. By P. B. S. Pisa, 1821, 4to.

Adonais was also printed in *The Literary Chronicle and Weekly Review*, Dec. 1, 1821, pp. 751-754, six stanzas (19-24) being omitted.

Adonais. An Elegy on the death of John Keats, author of Endymion, Hyperion, etc. By P. B. S. Cambridge, 1829, 8vo.

Adonais. Edited by H. Buxton Forman, with notes and an introduction. London [1877], 8vo.

Printed for private circulation. The number of copies was limited ; *six* being upon vellum, *twenty-five* upon Whatman's hand-made paper, and *fifty* upon ordinary paper. An etching of "Shelley's Grave" by W. B. Scott faces the title-page of the vellum and Whatman paper copies.

Adonais . . . Edited, with a biographical introduction, by Thomas J. Wise. (*Shelley Society's Publications*, 2nd ser., No. 1.) London, 1886, 4to.

Three editions have been published by the Society, with an issue respectively of 300, 250, and 150 copies. There were also 3 copies of the first edition worked upon vellum.

Alastor ; or, the Spirit of Solitude, and other poems. By P. B. S. London, 1816, 8vo.

Alastor; or, the Spirit of Solitude, etc. Edited, with notes, by H. Buxton Forman, and printed for private distribution. [London] 1876, 8vo.

This reprint consisted of 50 copies on ordinary paper, 25 on Whatman's hand-made paper, and 5 on vellum.

Alastor ; or, the Spirit of Solitude, and other poems. By P. B. S. A fac-simile reprint of the original edition first published in 1816. [With a Prefatory Note by Bertram Dobell.] London, 1885, 8vo.

The issue consisted of 4 copies on vellum, 50 on Whatman's hand-made paper, and 350 on "toned paper." 200 copies of the 350 were taken by the Shelley Society, who reprinted page 34, correcting an error in the first edition, and issued the work in their own boards.

Alastor. Edited by Bertram Dobell (*Shelley Society*). London, 1886, 8vo.

300 copies were printed, with 15 on large paper, small 4to, 3 copies on vellum, large 4to, with frontispiece of Shelley's Tomb engraved by Finden.

The Cenci ; a Tragedy, in five acts [and in verse]. By P. B. S. Italy [Leghorn], 1819, 8vo.

——Second edition. London, 1821, 8vo.

Copies of this edition, with the Prometheus, Hellas, and Rosalind and Helen, were issued by Ollier in 1823 under the collective title, "Poetical pieces by the late Percy Bysshe Shelley, containing Prometheus Unmasked, etc."

The Cenci. A Tragedy in five acts, by P. B. S. London, 1827, 12mo.

This is a piratical edition issued by Benbow of High Holborn, and is printed from the second edition.

The Cenci, a Tragedy in five acts, by P. B. S. Given from the poet's own editions, with an introduction by Alfred Forman and H. Buxton Forman, and a prologue by John Todhunter. [*Shelley Society Publications*, 4th ser., No. 3]. London, 1886, 8vo.

The Dæmon of the World, by P. B. S. ; the First Part as published in 1816 with Alastor ; the Second Part deciphered and now first printed from his own manuscript Revision and Interpolations in the newly discovered copy of Queen Mab. Edited by H. Buxton Forman. London, 1876, 16mo.

Printed for private distribution. There were 50 copies printed on fine hand-made "wove" paper, and 2 copies on yellow Dutch hand-made paper.

The Devil's Walk. [— 1812] Broadside.

This broadsheet was published by Shelley in 1812, and was quite unknown until it was reprinted by

Mr. Rossetti in his article, "Shelley in 1812-13," which appeared in *The Fortnightly Review*, Jan. 1, 1871. The only known copy of this broadside is in the Public Record Office.

Epipsychidion. Verses addressed [by P. B. Shelley] to the noble and unfortunate lady, Emilia V——[*i.e.*, Emilia Viviani] now imprisoned in the convent of ——[St. Anne, Pisa.] With an advertisement signed S. [*i.e.*, P. B. Shelley]. London, 1821, 8vo.
It is said only one hundred copies were printed.

Epipsychidion. Verses addressed to the noble and unfortunate lady, Emilia V——, now imprisoned in the convent of ——. Edited [from the original edition of 1821], with notes, by H. B. Forman. [London] 1876, 8vo.
Printed for private distribution. There are two varieties of this reprint. Of the first there were printed 50 copies on plain paper, 25 on Whatman's hand-made paper, and one on vellum ; of the second there were 10 on plain paper, 5 on Whatman's, and 5 on vellum.

Epipsychidion. With an introduction by the Rev. Stopford A. Brooke, and a note by Algernon Charles Swinburne. Edited by Robert Alfred Potts. (*Shelley Society's Publications, Second Series, No. 7.*) London, 1886, 8vo.
300 copies were printed.

Hellas, a lyrical drama, by P. B. S. London, 1822, 8vo.
Copies of the Hellas, with the Prometheus, The Cenci, and Rosalind and Helen, were issued by Ollier in 1823 under the collective title "Poetical pieces by the late Percy Bysshe Shelley, containing Prometheus Unmasked, etc."

Hellas, a lyrical drama. Edited and annotated by H. Buxton Forman. London, 1877, 8vo.
Printed for private circulation : *five* copies on vellum, *twenty-five* on Whatman's hand-made paper, and *fifty* on ordinary paper.

Hellas, a lyrical drama. A reprint of the original edition published in 1822. Edited by Thomas J. Wise. [*Shelley Society Publications*, 2nd ser., No. 5.] London, 1886, 8vo.
Of this edition there were 300 on Dutch hand-made paper, 8vo ; 15 copies on large paper, sm. 4to (with an India paper frontispiece of Shelley's Tomb etched by W. B. Scott), and 3 on vellum large 4to, with the same frontispiece.

Hellas . . . Reprinted from the original edition of 1822. Edited by Thomas J. Wise. (*Shelley Society Publications.*) London, 1886, 8vo.
500 copies were printed on ordinary paper, and 100 on fine paper, with a portrait.

Prologue to Hellas, by P. B. S. With an introductory note by Richard Garnett. Edited and annotated by Thomas J. Wise. London, 1886, 8vo.
Printed for private distribution only. Some copies number pp. 1-36, a *Postscript* having been added to the book during its passage through the press. In all, twenty copies *only* were printed. Both varieties have as frontispiece a lithographed facsimile of Trelawny's frontispiece— viz., a portrait of Shelley from the original picture by Clint.

Laon and Cythna ; or, the Revolution of the Golden City : a vision of the nineteenth century. In the stanza of Spenser. By P. B. S. London, 1818, 8vo.

The Revolt of Islam ; a poem in twelve cantos. London, 1818, 8vo.
This book consists of the same sheets as the preceding, with a different title-page and 20 cancel

leaves; the preface, having the final paragraph cancelled, was on page xxi. Some copies of the *Revolt* bear the date 1817 instead of 1818. The same sheets were again used in Brooks' re-issue of 1829.

The Masque of Anarchy. A poem by P. B. S. Now first published, with a preface by Leigh Hunt. London, 1832, 8vo.

Shelley wrote this poem in 1819 on the occasion of the "Peterloo" affair, and sent it to Leigh Hunt, for publication in *The Examiner*, but it was not issued by him until 1832.

The Masque of Anarchy. To which is added Queen Liberty; Song —To the Men of England. By P. B. S. With a preface by Leigh Hunt. London, 1842, 8vo.

Œdipus Tyrannus; or, Swellfoot the Tyrant. A Tragedy, in two acts. Translated from the original Doric. London, 1820, 8vo.

Shelley wrote this poem in August 1820, and when finished it was transmitted to England, printed and published anonymously, but the Society for the Suppression of Vice threatened to prosecute, and it was withdrawn.

Exceedingly scarce, seven copies only were preserved, six of which are known; one belonging to Mr. Frederick Locker, another in the Dyce Collection at South Kensington, the late Mr. Trelawny had the third, Mr. H. B. Forman the fourth, the fifth is now in Paris, and the sixth lately passed through the hands of a well-known bookseller.

Œdipus Tyrannus. . . Edited by H. Buxton Forman. [London, 1876,] 8vo.

Of this reprint for private distribution there are two varieties, neither of them having a dated special title-page, but both printed in 1876. The number of copies were respectively, fifty on plain paper, twenty-five on Whatman's hand-made paper, one

on vellum, and ten on plain paper, five on Whatman's, and five on vellum.

Original Poetry. By Victor and Cazire. London, 1810, 8vo.

The fact that Shelley had issued a volume in 1810 entitled *Original Poetry*, by Victor and Cazire, was not generally known until Mr. Garnett, who had discovered it in 1859, made it known through *Macmillan's Magazine* in 1860 in an article entitled "Shelley in Pall Mall." Fourteen hundred and eighty copies were printed at Horsham when Shelley was eighteen years of age. These were transferred to Stockdale, the publisher, of Pall Mall, who at once advertised their sale. Advertisements appear in the *Morning Chronicle* of Sept. 18, 1810, the *Morning Post* of Sept. 19, and the *Times* of Oct. 12. A few days after publication Stockdale recognised a poem of M. G. Lewis in the collection, and on communicating the fact to Shelley the book was at once suppressed. Cazire is supposed to have been either his cousin Harriet Grove, or Edward Graham. About a hundred copies got into circulation, but there is at present no copy known to exist. The work was reviewed in the *Poetical Register* for 1810-11, p. 617, and in the *British Critic*, vol. xxxvii., 1811, pp. 408, 409.

Poems and Sonnets. Edited by C. A. Seymour. Philadelphia, 1887, 4to.

Reprinted from the first volume of Professor Dowden's Life of Shelley.

A Poetical Essay on the Existing State of Things. By a Gentleman of the University of Oxford. For assisting to maintain in prison Mr. Peter Finnerty, imprisoned for a libel. London, 1811, 4to.

There is no known copy of this essay. An advertisement relating to it was discovered by Mr. MacCarthy in *The Oxford Herald* for March 9, 1811. It appears in the "List of New Works published in June, July, and August 1811 " in the *British R view* for September 1811. (*Athenæum*, Sep. 3, 1887.)

Posthumous Fragments of Margaret Nicholson [*i.e.*, Percy Bysshe Shelley and Thomas Jefferson Hogg]. Being poems found amongst the papers of that noted female who attempted the life of the king in 1786. Edited by John Fitzvictor. Oxford, 1810, 4to.

Posthumous Fragments of Margaret Nicholson. [Edited by R. H. Shepherd]. London, —— 4to.

This reprint is a smaller quarto than the original, and the paper is thicker and stiffer.

Posthumous Fragments of Margaret Nicholson. Edited by H. Buxton Forman, and printed for private distribution. [London], 1877, 8vo.

This reprint was limited to fifty copies on ordinary paper, twenty-five on Whatman's hand-made paper, and five on vellum.

Posthumous Fragments of Margaret Nicholson. Edited by Thomas J. Wise. (*Shelley Society's Publications*, 2nd Ser., No. 9.) London, 1887, 8vo.

Posthumous Poems of P. B. S. [Edited by Mary W. Shelley.] London, 1824, 8vo.

Prometheus Unbound, a lyrical drama in four acts, with other poems by P. B. S. London, 1820, 8vo.

Ollier in 1823 issued copies of the above, with the Hellas, The Cenci, and Rosalind and Helen, under the collective title-page, "Poetical Pieces, by the late Percy Bysshe Shelley; containing Prometheus Unmasked, etc."

Queen Mab: a Philosophical Poem; with notes. By P. B. S. London, 1813, 8vo.

Privately printed. The copy in the Library of the British Museum has a MS. note, two newspaper cuttings, and a portrait of the author inserted. There were numerous piratical editions of Queen Mab published by Clark, Carlile, etc. Shelley tried to suppress Clark's edition of 1821, but without success, and even as late as 1840 Mr. Moxon was prosecuted for republishing it.

Queen Mab. By P. B. S. London, 1821, 8vo.

Queen Mab; a philosophical poem. [With an editor's preface, signed : " A Pantheist," and with an Ode to the author, signed " R. C. F."] New York, 1821, 12mo.

Queen Mab. By P. B. S. [With notes.] London, 1822, 8vo.

Queen Mab; a philosophical poem ; with notes. By P. B. S. London, 1823, 8vo.

Queen Mab. By P. B. S. [With notes.] London, 1826, 32mo.

Queen Mab. By P. B. S. [With notes.] London, 1829, 8vo.

A fresh reprint of Shelley's edition with the title-page engraved.

Queen Mab; or, The Destiny of Man. A philosophical poem. By P. B. S. Revised edition, free from all the objectionable passages. London, 1830, 12mo.

Queen Mab: with Notes. By P. B. S. Second edition. New York, 1831, 12mo.

Queen Mab. By P. B. S. [With notes.] London, 1832, 24mo.

Queen Mab; with notes. By P. B. S. London, 1833, 24mo.

Queen Mab; with notes. To which is added a brief memoir of the author. London [1840], 8vo.

Queen Mab. By P. B. S. Campe's edition. Nürnberg and New York, n.d., 24mo.

Printed on thin bluish paper.

Queen Mab; with notes. By P. B. S. Fourth edition. New York, 1852, 18mo.

Queen Mab and other poems. London, 1865, 32mo.

Relics of Shelley. Edited by R. Garnett. London, 1862, 8vo.

Rosalind and Helen, a modern eclogue; with other poems. [Lines written on the Euganean Hills, Hymn to Intellectual Beauty, Sonnet "Ozymandias."] By P. B. S. London, 1819, 8vo.
Copies of the above, with the Prometheus, the Hellas and the Cenci, were issued by Ollier in 1823, with the collective title, "Poetical Pieces," etc.

Rosalind and Helen. Edited, with notes, by H. Buxton Forman, and printed for private distribution. [London], 1876, 8vo.
This reprint consisted of 50 copies on ordinary paper, 25 on Whatman's hand-made paper, and one on vellum.

The Wandering Jew, a poem. By P. B. S. Edited by Bertram Dobell (*Shelley Society's Publications, 2nd Ser., No. 12*). London, 1887, 8vo.
A portion of this poem originally appeared in *Fraser's Magazine* for 1831.

VI. PROSE WORKS.

The Prose Works of P. B. S. Edited by H. Buxton Forman. 4 vols. London, 1880, 8vo.
There were also 25 copies on Whatman's paper privately printed.

Essays, Letters from Abroad, Translations, and Fragments. By P. B. S. Edited by Mrs. Shelley. 2 vols. London, 1840, 12mo.

Essays, Letters from Abroad, Translations, and Fragments.

By P. B. S. Edited by Mrs. Shelley. A new edition. London, 1845, 8vo.

Essays, Letters from Abroad, Translations, and Fragments. By P. B. S. Edited by Mrs. Shelley. 2 vols. A new edition. London, 1852, 8vo.

Standard Library, comprising the Indicator and the Companion, by Leigh Hunt. The Poetical Works of Charles Lamb. Tales from Shakespeare, by Charles Lamb. The Poems of William Shakespeare. Essays, Letters from Abroad, etc., by P. B. Shelley. London, 1850, 8vo.

___

An Address to the Irish People [upon Catholic Emancipation and the Repeal of the Union]. Dublin, 1812, 8vo.

An Address to the Irish People. Reprinted from the original edition of 1812. Edited, with an introduction, by Thomas J. Wise. (*Shelley Society's Publications, 2nd Ser., No. 6*). London, 1886, 8vo.
300 copies of this book were printed.

"We pity the Plumage, but forget the Dying Bird." An Address to the People on the Death of the Princess Charlotte. By the Hermit of Marlow [*i.e.*, Percy Bysshe Shelley]. [London, 1843], 8vo.
This is merely a reprint of the original edition, no copy of which is now known to be extant.

Declaration of Rights. Dublin [1812], broadside.
Reprinted by Richard Carlile in *The Republican*, Sept. 24, 1819. Two copies are in the Public Record Office. See Mr. Rossetti's article in *The Fortnightly Review* for Jan. 1871, entitled "Shelley in 1812-13."

History of a Six Weeks' Tour through a part of France, Switzerland, Germany, and Holland; with letters descriptive of a sail round the lake of Geneva, and of the glaciers of Chamouni [By P. B. Shelley and Mary W. Shelley]. London, 1817, 8vo.

Re-issued by J. Brooks in 1829 with a new title-page.

A Letter to Lord Ellenborough, occasioned by the sentence which he passed on Mr. D. I. Eaton as publisher of the Third Part of Paine's Age of Reason. [Barnstaple, 1812], 8vo.

The greater part of the edition of this work was destroyed by the printer, Mr. Syle of Barnstaple, but fifty copies were sent to Mr. Hookham of Bond Street, which were distributed. There is only a single copy known to exist.

Free Speech and Free Press. By P. B. S. A Letter to Lord Ellenborough, occasioned by a sentence passed by him upon Mr. D. I. Eaton for publishing Part Third of Paine's "Age of Reason" about the year 1812.

This is an abridged edition preceding (reprinted from the *Shelley Memorials*) which appeared in New York in 1879 as No. 156 of the "Truth Seeker Tracts." It consists of six leaves without title-page or wrapper, but with the above heading.

Shelley on Blasphemy. Being his Letter to Lord Ellenborough, occasioned by the sentence which he passed on Mr. D. I. Eaton as publisher of the Third Part of Paine's "Age of Reason." London, 1883.

Reproduced as a separate pamphlet with the text as given in Mr. Forman's edition, and consists of a single sheet folded in eight, without wrapper.

A Letter to Lord Ellenborough. A reprint of the original edition published in 1812. Edited by Thomas J. Wise. (*Shelley Society's Publications, Second Series*, No. 10.) London, 1887, 8vo.

Of this book 400 copies were printed.

Letters of P. B. S. [A fabrication by G. Byron?] With an introductory essay by R. Browning. London, 1852, 12mo

The Necessity of Atheism. Worthing [1811], 8vo.

Mr. Buxton Forman states that he only knows of two extant copies, from one of which, the copy in the possession of Sir Percy and Lady Shelley, he reproduced the tract in his edition.

The Necessity of Atheism. A reprint of the original edition produced in 1811. Edited by Thos. J. Wise. (*Shelley Society's Publications, Second Series*, No. 8.) London, 1886, 8vo.

300 copies were printed.

A Proposal for putting Reform to the Vote throughout the Kingdom. By the Hermit of Marlow [Percy Bysshe Shelley]. London, 1817, 8vo.

Notes on Sculptures in Rome and Florence, together with a Lucianic Fragment and a criticism on Peacock's Poem, "Rhododaphne," by P. B. S. Given from manuscript sources by H. Buxton Forman. London, 1879, 8vo.

Printed for private distribution, and the issue was limited to 25 copies on Whatman's hand-made paper, and 50 on ordinary paper.

Proposals for an Association of those Philanthropists who, convinced of the inadequacy of the moral and political state of Ireland to produce benefits which **are** nevertheless attainable, are willing to unite to accomplish its regeneration. Dublin [1812], 8vo.

A Refutation of Deism : in a dialogue. London, 1814, 8vo.

In 1843 extracts from this work appeared in *The Model Republic,* but it was not till 1874 that a copy was recovered and purchased by the Trustees of the British Museum. A second copy is in the possession of Mr. Garnett, and a third belongs to Professor Edward Dowden. The Refutation of Deism was printed in 1815 in the *Theological Inquirer,* a political magazine.

Scintilla Shelleiana. Shelley's Attitude towards Religion, explained and defended by himself. Edited by Arthur Clive [Standish O'Grady]. Dublin, 1875, 8vo.

A reprint of the excerpt as given in *The Model Republic* in 1843.

Review of Hogg's "Memoirs of Prince Alexy Haimatoff," by Percy Bysshe Shelley. Together with an extract from "some early writings of Shelley," by Professor E. Dowden, LL.D. Edited with an introductory note, by Thomas J. Wise. (*Shelley Society's Publications, Second Series, No. 2.*) London, 1886, 8vo.

In 1813 Hogg published anonymously a novel, "Memoirs of Prince Alexy Haimatoff," etc. which was reviewed by Shelley in *The Critical Review,* vol. iv., Dec. 1814, pp. 566-574. The review was reprinted by the Shelley Society (1886), with an extract from Professor Dowden's article (*Contemporary Review,* Sept. 1884). Of this edition, 300 copies were printed on paper, and 3 on vellum. A second edition was issued in the same year, of which 250 copies were printed. In the present year a 3rd edition was published, of which 250 copies were printed on small paper, 10 copies on large paper (small 4to,

with India Proof frontispiece of Field Place, etched by A. Evershed), and 3 on vellum (large 4to).

St. Irvyne ; or, the Rosicrucian : a romance. By a gentleman of the University of Oxford [P. B. Shelley]. London, 1811, 12mo.

Some copies made up from the original sheets, and with a new title-page bear the date 1822. This work was reprinted in *The Romancist and Novelist's Library,* 1840, vol. iii., pp. 113-120.

A Vindication of Natural Diet. Being one of a series of notes to Queen Mab, a philosophical poem. London, 1813, 12mo.

This pamphlet is exceedingly rare, there being only three copies known; one is in the British Museum wanting the fly-leaf, and with the bottom of the title-page and the date torn off; another is in the possession of Mr. H. B. Forman, who reprinted it in his edition of Shelley, and the third belongs to the Hon. J. Leicester Warren. It is said to have appeared as an appendix to an American medical work, the "Manual of Health," by Dr. Turnbull.

A Vindication of Natural Diet. A new edition. London, 1884, 12mo.

A reprint by the Vegetarian Society, with a Preface by Mr. H. S. Salt and Mr. W. E. A. Axon. Two other issues of 200 copies each of this edition were distributed by the Shelley Society to its members (*Publications, Second Series, No. 4*). These consisted of the sheets of the above (1884) edition, rebound in the Society's boards.

Zastrozzi, a Romance. By P. B. S. London, 1810, 12mo.

This work was reprinted in *The Romancist and Novelist's Library,* 1839, pp. 145-156.

VII. LETTERS, Etc.

Select Letters. . . . Edited, with an introduction, by R. Garnett. (*Parchment Series.*) London, 1882, 8vo.

There were also fifty copies printed on large paper.

Essays and Letters by P. B. S. Edited, with introductory note, by Ernest Rhys. (*Camelot Classics.*) London, 1886, 8vo.

VIII. APPENDIX.

BIOGRAPHY, CRITICISM, ETC.

Alger, W. R.—The Solitudes of Nature and of Man, etc. Boston [U.S.], 1867, 8vo.
Shelley, pp. 272-276.

Andrews, Samuel. — Our Great Writers; or, popular chapters on some leading authors. London, 1884, 8vo.
Shelley, pp. 226-251.

Armstrong, Edmund J.—Essays and Sketches of Edmund J. Armstrong. London, 1877, 8vo.
Shelley, pp. 127-175.

Bagehot, Walter.—Estimates of some Englishmen and Scotchmen, etc. London, 1858, 8vo.
Percy Bysshe Shelley, pp. 274-329.

——Literary Studies. Third edition. 2 vols. London, 1884, 8vo.
Percy Bysshe Shelley, vol. I., pp. 75-125.

Balfour, Clara Lucas.—Sketches of English Literature, etc. London, 1852, 8vo.
Shelley, pp. 347-361.

Barton, Bernard.—Verses on the Death of Percy Bysshe Shelley, by Bernard Barton. London, 1822, 8vo.

Belfast, *Earl of.* — Poets and Poetry of the Nineteenth Century. A course of lectures. London, 1852, 8vo.
Shelley, pp. 165-197.

Bennett, D. M.—The World's Sages, Infidels, and Thinkers, etc. New York, 1876, 8vo.
Shelley, pp. 719-725.

Bertolotti, A.—Francesco Cenci e la sua famiglia. Notizie e documenti raccolti par A. B. Firenze, 1877, 8vo.

Biographical Magazine.—Lives of the Illustrious. (The Biographical Magazine.) London, 1852, 8vo.
Percy Bysshe Shelley, vol. I., pp. 105-119.

Blind, Mathilde. — Shelley. A lecture delivered to the Church of Progress, in St. George's Hall, Langham Place, London, W., on Sunday evening, January 9th, 1870, by Miss Mathilde Blind. [London, 1870], 8vo.

——Shelley's View of Nature constrated with Darwin's. London, 1886, 8vo.
Only twenty-five copies of this lecture were printed for private distribution.

Bowyer, Sir George.—A Dissertation on the Statutes of the Cities of Italy; and a Translation of the pleading of Prospero Farinacio in defence of Beatrice Cenci, etc. London, 1838, 8vo.

Brooke, Arthur.—Elegy on the Death of Percy Bysshe Shelley. London, 1822, 8vo.

Brooke, S. A. — The Inaugural Address to the Shelley Society. By the Rev. Stopford A. Brooke. London, 1886, 8vo.
Twenty-five copies on paper and three on vellum were privately printed.

Byron, Lord.—The life, writings, opinions, and times of Lord Byron, etc. 3 vols. London, 1825, 8vo.
References to Shelley.

Caine, T. Hall. — Cobwebs of Criticism, etc. London, 1883, 8vo.
Shelley, pp. 191-231.

Calvert, George H.—Coleridge, Shelley, Goethe. Biographic Æsthetic Studies. Boston [1880], 8vo.

Carr, J. Comyns.—Essays on Art. London, 1879, 8vo.
The Artistic Spirit in Modern English Poetry, pp. 3-34. This essay is almost entirely on Keats, with occasional references to Shelley.

Chambers, Robert. — Cyclopædia of English Literature, etc. 2 vols. Edinburgh, 1844, 8vo.
Percy Bysshe Shelley, vol. ii., pp. 395-402.
——Another Edition. 2 vols. Edinburgh, 1860, 8vo.
Percy Bysshe Shelley, with portrait, vol. ii., pp. 355-363.
——Third edition. 2 vols. London, 1876, 8vo.
Percy Bysshe Shelley, with portrait, vol. ii., pp. 129-136.

Chanter, John Roberts—Sketches of the Literary History of Barnstaple, etc. Barnstaple [1866], 8vo.
Contains references to Shelley's connection with Barnstaple.

Characteristics. — Characteristics of Men of Genius; a series of biographical, historical, and critical essays. 2 vols. London, 1846, 8vo.
There is an article, signed M. M., on Shelley, vol i., pp. 215-243, reprinted from the *Dial.*

Chiarini, G. — Ombre e figure. Saggi critici ; Swinburne, Shelley, Heine, etc. Roma, 1883, 8vo.
Shelley comprises pp. 5-49.

Chorley, Henry F.—The Authors of England. A series of medallion portraits of modern literary characters, etc. London, 1838, 4to.
Percy B. Shelley occupies pp. 56-64.
——New edition, revised. London, 1861, 4to.
Percy Bysshe Shelley, pp. 46-52.

Cotterill, H. B.—An Introduction to the Study of Poetry. London, 1882, 8vo.
Shelley, pp. 298-323.

Courthope, William J. — The Liberal Movement in English Literature. London, 1885, 8vo.
The Revival of Romance : Scott, Byron, Shelley, pp. 111-156.

Craik, George L.—A compendious history of English Literature, etc. 2 vols. London, 1861, 8vo.
Shelley, vol. ii., pp. 498-502.

Creasy, *Sir* Edward.—Memoirs of Eminent Etonians. A new edition. London, 1876, 8vo.
Percy Bysshe Shelley, pp. 596-613.

Cunningham, George Godfrey.— The English Nation ; a history of England, with lives of Englishmen. 5 vols. Edinburgh [1863-68], 4to.
Percy Bysshe Shelley, with portrait, vol. v., pp. 528-535.

Dark Blue.—The Dark Blue for 1871. London, 1871, 8vo.
Contains a poem by William M. Rossetti, entitled "Shelley's Heart," on p. 35.

Darmesteter, James. — Essais de Littérature Anglaise. Paris, 1883, 8vo.
Shelley, pp. 199-225. A review of *Select Letters of Percy Bysshe Shelley, edited by Richard Garnett,* 1882.

Dawson, W. J. — Quest and Vision : essays in life and literature. London, 1886, 8vo.
Shelley, pp. 1-44.

Dennis, John.—Heroes of Literature. English Poets. London, 1883, 8vo.
Percy Bysshe Shelley, pp. 373-387.

De Quincey, Thomas. De Quincey's Works. 16 vols. Edinburgh, 1862-71, 12mo.
Percy Bysshe Shelley, vol. v., pp. 1-29.

De Vere, Aubrey.—The poetical works of Aubrey De Vere. London, 1884, 8vo.
Lines composed near Shelley's house at Lerici, on All Souls' Day, 1856, vol. iii., pp. 357-362.

D. vey, J.—A Comparative Estimate of Modern English Poetry. London, 1873, 8vo.
Alexandrine Poets. Shelley, pp. 239-262.

Diguet, Charles.—Béatrice Cenci. Paris, n.d., 8vo.

Dowden, Edward.—The Life of Percy Bysshe Shelley. [Illustrated.] 2 vols. London, 1886, 8vo.

Druskowitz, H.—Percy Bysshe Shelley. Von H. Druskowitz. Berlin, 1884, 8vo.

Edgcumbe, Richard. — Edward Trelawny, a biographical sketch, by Richard Edgcumbe. Plymouth, 1882, 8vo.
Contains matter relating to Shelley.

Encyclopædia Britannica.—Encyclopædia Britannica. Eighth edition. Edinburgh, 1860, 4to.
Shelley, by G. McDonald, vol. xx., pp. 100-104.

——Ninth edition. Edinburgh, 1880, 4to.
Shelley, by W. M. Rossetti, vol. xxi., pp. 789-794.

English Writers. — Essays on English Writers. By the author of "The Gentle Life." London, 1869, 8vo.
Shelley, Keats, etc., pp. 338-349.

Farrar, Adam Storey.—A critical history of Freethought in reference to the Christian Religion. Eight lectures preached before the University of Oxford, etc. London, 1862, 8vo.
The scepticism in the poetry of Byron and Shelley, pp. 285-291.

Forgues, E. D. — Originaux et beaux esprits de l' Angleterre contemporaine. 2 Tom. Paris, 1860, 8vo.
Percy Bysshe Shelley, Tom. ii., pp. 139-186.

Forman, Alfred.—Sonnets. London, 1886, 4to.
Contains two sonnets to Shelley, pp. 47-48.

Forman, H. Buxton.—The Shelley Library; an essay in bibliography, by H. Buxton Forman. I., Shelley's books, pamphlets, and broadsides ; posthumous separate issues ; and posthumous books wholly or mainly by him. London, 1886, 8vo.

——The Vicissitudes of Shelley's Queen Mab. London, 1887, 8vo.
Privately printed.

——The Hermit of Marlow: a chapter in the History of Reform. London, 1887, 8vo.
Privately printed.

——Shelley, Peterloo, the Mask of Anarchy: A chapter in the History of Reform. London, 1887, 8vo.
Privately printed.

Fraser's Magazine. — Fraser's Magazine, vol. 56, for 1857. London, 1857, 8vo.
Contains a poem by Aubrey de Vere entitled "Lines composed near Shelley's House at Lerici."

——London, 1870, 8vo.
"Responsio Shelleiana" (six verses), by J. J. M., vol. i., N.S., p. 657.

Fuller, aft. Ossoli, S. M. — Life Without and Life Within ; or, reviews, narratives, etc. Boston [U.S.], 1874, 8vo.
Shelley's poems, pp. 149-152.

Gilfillan, George.— A Gallery of Literary Portraits. Edinburgh, 1845, 8vo.
Percy Bysshe Shelley, with portrait, pp. 71-105.

Griswold, Rufus W.—The Poets and Poetry of England in the Nineteenth Century. New York, 1875, 8vo.
Percy Bysshe Shelley, with portrait, pp. 270-285.

Gronow, Captain.—Reminiscences of Captain Gronow. London, 1862, 8vo.
Shelley, pp. 212-215.

——Celebrities of London and Paris, etc. London, 1865, 8vo.
"Shelley's Fight at Eton," pp. 99-101.

Hazlitt, William. — Johnson's Lives of the British Poets, completed by W. H. 4 vols. London, 1854, 8vo.
Shelley, illustrated, vol. iv., pp. 281-285.

Hillard, George Stillman. — Six Months in Italy. 2 vols. London, 1853, 8vo.
Shelley, vol ii., pp. 333 338.

Hoffmann, Frederick A.—Poetry, its origin, nature, and history, etc. London, 1884, 8vo.
Shelley, vol. i., pp. 466-483.

Hogg, Thomas Jefferson. — The Life of Percy Bysshe Shelley. Vols. 1, 2. London, 1858, 8vo.
No more published.

Houston, Mrs. M. C.—A Woman's Memories of World-known Men. 2 vols. London, 1883, 8vo.
The Shelley Family, vol. i., pp. 98-108.

Howitt, William.— Homes and Haunts of the most eminent British Poets. 2 vols. London, 1847, 8vo
Shelley, vol. i., pp. 436-466.

—— Third edition. London, 1857, 8vo.
Shelley, pp. 301-321.

Hunt, J. H. L. — Foliage ; or, poems original and translated. London, 1818, 8vo.
Sonnet to Percy Shelley on the degrading notions of Deity, p. cxxii.

Hunt, J. H. L.—Lord Byron and some of his contemporaries. London, 1828, 4to.

——Imagination and Fancy; or, selections from the English Poets. London, 1844, 12mo.
Shelley, born 1792, died 1822, pp. 293-311.

——The Autobiography of Leigh Hunt. 3 vols. London, 1850, 8vo.
Shelley in England, vol. ii., pp. 179-200; Letters of Shelley, pp. 307-322.

Hutton, Richard Holt.— Essays Theological and Literary. Second edition. London, 1877, 8vo.
Shelley's poetical mysticism, vol. ii., pp. 118-152.

Jeaffreson, John Cordy. — The Real Shelley. New views of the poet's life. 2 vols. London, 1885, 8vo.

——The Real Lord Byron. 2 vols. London, 1883, 8vo.
References to Shelley.

Johnson, Charles F. — Three Americans and three Englishmen. Lectures read before the students of Trinity College, Hartford. New York, 1886, 8vo.
Shelley, pp 83-131.

Kent, W. Charles.— Dreamland, with other poems. London, 1862, 8vo.
Shelley at Marlow (20 verses), pp. 85-90.

Kingsley, Charles.—The Works of Charles Kingsley. London, 1880, 8vo.
Thoughts on Shelley and Byron, vol. xx., pp. 35-55.

Kinsley, William W.—Views on Vexed Questions. Philadelphia, 1881, 8vo.
Shelley, pp. 255-302.

L. J., *i.e.*, J. Leadbetter.— A
Pilgrimage to the Shrines of
Buckinghamshire. London
[1861], 8vo.
Shelley : Great Marlowe, pp. 113-
118.

Lang, Andrew.—Letters to Dead
Authors. London, 1886, 8vo.
To Percy Bysshe Shelley, pp.
173-183.

——Lines on the Inaugural Meeting of the Shelley Society.
London, 1886, 8vo.
35 copies on paper and 3 on vellum
were printed for private distribution. The *Lines* were written by
Andrew Lang, edited and annotated
by T. J. Wise.

Langford, John Alfred.—Shelley ;
the Death of St. Polycarp, and
other poems. Loudou, 1860,
8vo.
The poem on Shelley comprises
pp. 3-57.

MacCarthy, Denis Florence. —
Shelley's Early Life, from original sources. With incidents,
letters, and writings, now first
published or collected, etc.
London [1872], 8vo.

Macdonald, George.—Orts. London, 1882, 8vo.
Shelley, pp. 264-281.

——The Imagination, and other
Essays. Boston [1883], 8vo.
Shelley, pp. 264-281.

Maginn, William.— Miscellanies :
Prose and Verse. Edited by
R. W. Montagu. 2 vols. Lou-
don, 1885, 8vo.
Remarks on Shelley's Adonais, vol.
ii., pp. 300-311.

Mario, Jessie White. — Sepolcri
Inglesi in Roma. (Estratto
dalla *Nuova Antologia*, 15
Maggio, 1879.) Roma, 1879,
8vo.
On Keats and Shelley.

Mason, Edward T. — Personal
Traits of British Authors.
Byron, Shelley, etc. Edited by

E. T. Mason. With portraits.
2 vols. New York, 1885, 8vo.
Shelley occupies pp. 75-140 of
vol. i.

Masson, David. — Wordsworth,
Shelley, Keats, and other
Essays. London, 1874, 8vo.

Medwin, Thomas.—The Shelley
Papers. Memoir of Percy
Bysshe Shelley. By T. Medwin,
and original poems and papers,
by P. B. S., now first collected.
London, 1833, 12mo.
The Shelley Papers were republished from the *Athenæum*, in
which they appeared in 1832-3.

——The Life of Percy Bysshe
Shelley. 2 vols. London, 1847,
12mo.

Middleton, Charles S.—Shelley
and his Writings. 2 vols. London, 1858, 8vo.

Mitford, Mary Russell.—Recollections of a Literary Life, etc.
3 vols. London, 1852, 8vo.
Shelley and Keats, vol. ii., pp.
183-192.

Moir, D. M. — Sketches of the
poetical literature of the past
half-century. London, 1851,
8vo.
Shelley, pp. 221-229.

Montgomery, Rev. Robert.—Oxford : with biographical notes,
etc. Sixth edition. London,
1843, 8vo.
Shelley is noticed in the "Biographical Summary," pp. 166-174.

Moore, Helen.—Mary Wollstonecraft Shelley. Philadelphia,
1886, 8vo.
Chap. ii. Percy Bysshe Shelley,
pp. 51-59 ; chap. iii., Union with
Shelley, pp. 60-71 ; chap. iv., Life in
England, pp. 72-95 ; chap. v., Italy,
pp. 96-143 ; chap. vi., Shelley's
Death, pp. 144-243.

Moore, Thomas. — Letters and
Journals of Lord Byron, etc.
2 vols. London, 1830, 4to.
References to Shelley.

Moore, Thomas. — Memoirs, Journal, and Correspondence. 8 vols. London, 1853-56, 8vo.
References to P. B. S

National Instructor.— The National Instructor. London,1850, 8vo.
Vol. i., pp. 305-307," The Maniac," a Tale from Shelley's Poem, Julian and Maddalo.

Noel, *Hon.* Roden B. W.—Essays on Poetry and Poets. London, 1886, 8vo.
Shelley, pp. 114-131.

Notes and Queries.—General Index to Notes and Queries. 5 Series. London, 1876-80, 8vo.
Numerous references to Shelley.

Oliphant, Mrs. — The Literary History of England, etc. 3 vols. London, 1882, 8vo.
Percy Bysshe Shelley, vol. iii., pp. 44-70 and 95-124.

Parkes, Bessie Rayner.—Gabriel. London, 1856, 8vo.

Paton, Joseph Noel.—Compositions from Shelley's "Prometheus Unbound." [London, 1844], fol.
There is also a smaller edition in oblong 4to.

Paul, Charles Kegan.—William Godwin : his friends and contemporaries. 2 vols. London, 1876, 8vo.

Peacock, Thomas Love. — The Works of Thomas Love Peacock. 3 vols. London, 1875, 8vo.
Memoirs of Percy Bysshe Shelley, part 1,vol. iii., pp. 385-413 ; reprinted from *Fraser's Magazine,* June 1858 ; Part 2, pp. 413-443 ; reprinted from *Fraser's Magazine,* January 1860 ; Supplementary Notice, pp. 443-449 ; reprinted from *Fraser's Magazine,* March, 1862 ; Unpublished Letters of Percy Bysshe Shelley, reprinted from *Fraser's Magazine,* March, 1860, pp. 449-479

Philobiblon Society.—Miscellanies of the Philobiblon Society. London, 1857-8, 4to.
Vol. iv.—Contemporaneous Narrative of the Trial and Execution of the Cenci.

Poe, Edgar Allan.—The Works of E. A. Poe. Edited by John H. Ingram. 4 vols. Edinburgh, 1874-5, 8vo.
Shelley and his imitators, vol. iv., pp. 86, 87.

Portrait Gallery.—The Eton Portrait Gallery, consisting of short memoirs of the more eminent Eton men. London, 1876, 8vo.
Percy Bysshe Shelley, pp. 530-534.

Preston, S. E.—Notes on the first performance of Shelley's Cenci. London, 1886, 8vo.
Privately printed.

Rabbe, Félix.—Shelley : sa vie et ses œuvres. Paris, 1887, 8vo.

Republican. — The Republican. Vols.1-14. London,1819-26, 8vo.
Contains numerous references to Shelley.

Richardson, David L.—Literary Chit-Chat, etc. Calcutta, 1848, 8vo.
Shelley, Keats, and Coleridge, pp. 271-281.

Rossetti, William Michael.— Memoir of Shelley. [London, 1870], 8vo.
The "Memoir of Shelley," by W. M. Rossetti, belonging to the e ition of Shelley's Poetical Works, published by Moxon & Co , in 1870.

——Lives of Famous Poets. London [1885], 8vo.
Percy Bysshe Shelley, pp. 300-328.

——A Memoir of Shelley (with a fresh preface, a portrait of Shelley, and an engraving of his Tomb). [*Shelley Society's Publications,* 4th Series, No. 2]. London, 1886, 8vo.
Of this edition 250 copies were printed. A second and corrected edition (of 250 copies) appeared in

the same year. To this edition were added a table of contents, and a full Index.

Rossetti, William Michael.— Shelley's Prometheus Unbound. A Study of its Meaning and Personages. By W. M. Rossetti. London, 1886, 8vo.
Twenty-five copies on paper and three on vellum were privately printed.

S., M. S.—Shelley's Beatrice Cenci and her first interpreter. London, 1886, 8vo.
Privately printed. Signed M. S. S.

Salt, H. S.—A Shelley Primer. (*Shelley Society Publications, Series* 4.) London, 1887, 8vo.

Sarrazin, Gabriel.—Poètes Modernes de l'Angleterre. Walter Savage Landor, Percy Bysshe Shelley, etc. Paris, 1885, 8vo.
Shelley comprises pp. 65-127.

Scherr, Dr. J.—A History of English Literature. Translated from the German. London, 1882, 8vo.
Shelley, pp. 244-254.

Scott, R. Pickett.—The place of Shelley among the English Poets of his time. Cambridge, 1878, 8vo.

Shairp, John Campbell.—Aspects of Poetry, being lectures delivered at Oxford. Oxford, 1881, 8vo.
Shelley as a lyric poet, pp. 227-255.

Shelley, Percy Bysshe.—Shelley's Genius, with a sketch of his Life. London, 1840, 32mo.

——A brief Sketch of the Life of P. B. S. (taken from an edition of his poetical works, published at Paris in 1829, etc.). London, 1854, 12mo.

Shelley Percy Bysshe.—Shelley Memorials, from authentic sources. Edited by Lady Shelley. To which is added an Essay on Christianity, by P. B. S., now first printed. London, 1859, 8vo.

——Second edition. London, 1859, 8vo.

——Third edition. London, 1875, 8vo.

——Memoir of P. B. S., etc. London, 1886, 8vo.
Of this edition 500 copies were printed.

——Shelley Pedigree. From the records of the College of Arms. [With portrait. Edited by H. Buxton Forman.] London, 1880, 4to.
100 copies privately printed; 50 for England and 50 for America.

——Reply to the anti-matrimonial hypothesis and supposed atheism of P. B. S., as laid down in Queen Mab. London, 1821, 8vo.

——The Cenci, five act tragedy, by P. B. S. Extracts from reviews of the first performance, 7th May 1886. With preface by Sidney E. Preston. London, 1886, 8vo.
Thirty-five copies were privately printed.

Shelley Society.—Note-book of the Shelley Society. Edited by the Honorary Secretaries. London, 1887, etc., 8vo.

Silcoates Album.—The Silcoates Album : or original contributions in prose and verse, composed for the Bazaar to be held in Wakefield, July 1, 1840. London, 1840, 12mo.
Contains an Essay on Shelley, pp. 69-93, by T. B. H.

Sketches.—Pen and Ink Sketches of Poets, Preachers, and Politicians. [By John Dix, otherwise John D. Ross.] London, 1846, 8vo.
Personal notices of Shelley and Hazlitt, pp. 140-154.

Smith, George Barnett.—Shelley, a Critical Biography. Edinburgh, 1877, 8vo.

Sotheran, Charles.—Percy Bysshe Shelley as a Philosopher and Reformer; with a portrait of Shelley and a view of his tomb. New York, 1876, 8vo.

Southey, Robert.—The Life and Correspondence of R. S. 6 vols. London, 1849, 8vo.
References to P. B. S.

——The Correspondence of Robert Southey with Caroline Bowles. To which are added, Correspondence with Shelley, and Southey's Dreams. Dublin, 1881, 8vo.

Stoddard, Richard Henry.—Anecdote Biography of Percy Bysshe Shelley. Edited by R. H. Stoddard. (Sans-Souci Series.) New York, 1877, 12mo.

Swinburne, Algernon C.—Essays and Studies. London, 1875, 8vo.
Notes on the Text of Shelley [1869], pp. 184-237.

Symonds, John Addington.—Shelley, by John Addington Symonds. [English Men of Letters.] London, 1878, 8vo.

Talfourd, T. N.—Speech for the Defendant, in the prosecution of The Queen v. Moxon for the publication of Shelley's works, etc. London, 1841, 8vo.

Thomson, James.—Shelley, a poem: with other writings relating to Shelley, by the late James Thomson ("B. V."), etc. London, 1884, 8vo.
Printed for private circulation. 160 copies on toned paper and 30 on Whatman's hand-made paper.

Todhunter, John.—A Study of Shelley. London, 1880, 8vo.

——Notes on Shelley's Triumph of Life. London, 1887, 8vo.
Privately printed.

Trelawny, Edward John.—Recollections of the last days of Shelley and Byron. London, 1858, 8vo.

——Another edition. Boston [U.S.], 1858, 8vo.

——Second edition. Boston, 1859, 8vo.

——Records of Shelley, Byron, and the Author. 2 vols. London, 1878, 8vo.

Tuckerman, Henry T.—Thoughts on the Poets. London [1852], 12mo.
Shelley, pp. 101-115.

Ward, Thomas H.—The English Poets, etc. London, 1883, 8vo.
Percy Bysshe Shelley, by Frederick W. H. Myers, vol. iv., pp. 318-416.

Welsh, Alfred H.—Development of English Literature and Language. 2 vols. Chicago, 1882, 8vo.
Shelley, vol. ii., pp. 283-293.

Whipple, Edwin P.—Essays and Reviews. Third edition. 2 vols. Boston, 1856, 8vo.
Percy Bysshe Shelley, vol. i., pp. 308-318.

White, Mr.—The Calumnies of the "Athenæum" Journal exposed. Mr. White's Letter to Mr. Murray, on the study of Byron, Shelley, and Keats' MSS. London, 1852, 8vo.

——Second Edition. London, 1852, 8vo.

VII.—SONGS, ETC., SET TO MUSIC.

Songs and Etchings. Seven poems by Ben Jonson, T. Hood, P. B. Shelley, etc. Set to music by Thomas Anderton, and illustrated with nine etchings by R. S. Chattock. London [1871], 4to.
Contains "To a Skylark," by Percy B. Shelley.

La Chanteuse ; a series of vocal music. Poetry by S. T. Coleridge and P. B. Shelley. Music by M. Cobham. London, 1849, fol.

Vocal illustrations of Shelley. Music by J. W. Davison. London, 1845, fol.

Seven Songs. The words by Shelley and Burns. Music by J. Gledhill. London, 1878, fol.

Six songs for voice and piano. Words by Longfellow, J. McDermott, Sheridan, and Shelley. Music by T. H. McDermott. London, 1854, fol.

Scenes from Shelley's "Prometheus Unbound." Set to music by C. H. H. Parry. London, 1881, 8vo.

Hellas: a lyrical drama by P. B. S. The choruses set to music by William Christian Selle. (*Shelley Society's Publications, Extra Series, No. 1.*) London, 1886, 8vo.

"Arethusa arose from her couch of snows," by Dolores (Elizabeth Dickson), 1861.

"Behold, spring sweeps over the world" (*Revolt of Islam*), by Dolores, 1862.

"The Cloud," by G. A. Osborne, 1867 ; B. Farebrother, 1869 ; A. Whitley, 1877.

"The cold earth slept below," by H. L. Moysey, 1872.

"The colour from the flow'r is gone," by G. B. Arnold, 1859 ; A. Piatti, 1867 ; E. H. Thorne. 1876.

"The dirge of time" (from "Prometheus Unbound"), by Dolores, 1861.

"Echoes, we listen !" (from "Prometheus Unbound") by Dolores, 1861.

"The flower that smiles," by J. Lodge, 1839 ; A. S. Mounsey (four-part song), 1855 ; C. W. von Gluck (*Pilgrimme auf Mecca*), 1857 ; G. B. Arnold, 1880.

"The fountains mingle with the river," by E. F. Fitzwilliam, 1855 ; J. R. W. Harding, 1859 ; H. Glover, 1861 ; C. K. Salaman, 1866 ; C. F. Gounod, 1871.

"Good-night," by G. J. O. Allman, 1845 : A. J. Kappey, 1859 ; A. Sartoris (duet), 1860 ; G. A. Osborne, 1861 ; W. J. Westbrook, 1866 : C. F. Gounod, 1871 ; H. L. Moysey, 1872.

"Hark ! whence that rushing sound" (from "Queen Mab"), by J. Barnett, 1837.

"Hymn of Pan," by Sir Percy F. Shelley, 1864.

"I arise from dreams of thee," by J. Barnett, 1837 ; H. Lenox, 1844 ; H. Glover, 1854 ; A. Bennett, 1854 ; C. Reinhardt, 1856 ; J. C. Beuthin, 1855 ; J. P. Hullah, 1859 ; Mrs. R. Arkwright, 1866 ; C. K. Salaman, 1866 ; W. Rea, 1868 ; A. J. Sutton, 1870 ; F. A. Marshall, 1877 ; H. Perkins. 1880 ; W. H. Grattan, 1880.

" I fear thy kisses, gentle maiden," by J. W. Davison, 1876 ; L. S. Benson. 1879.

"I pant for the music which is divine," by Dolores, 1861 ; C. M. Ingleby, 1867.

"I sift the snow on the mountains below" (*The Cloud*), by A. Whitley, 1877.

"Like the ghost of a friend long dead," by E M. Lawrence (four-part song), 1879.

"Music when soft voices die," by W. H. Collcott, 1847 ; J. MacEwan, 1850 ; C. A. Dance, 1861 ; N. Bradshaw, 1869 ; C. H. H. Parry, 1873.

"My faint spirit," by J. Bennett, 1837 ; Dolores, 1863 ; K. Loder, 1854 ; Sir A. S. Sullivan, 1866 ; J. Mount (W. M. Hutchinson), 1878.

"My soul is an enchanted boat" (from "Prometheus Unbound"), by Dolores, 1859 ; F. Mori, 1865.

"No change, no pause" (from "Prometheus Unbound"), by J. Barnett, 1837.

"One word is too often profaned," by J. Bennett, 1837 ; Dolores, 1863.

"Oh ! there are spirits in the air," by W. S. Pratten, 1848.

"Orphan hours, the year is dead," by G. B. Arnold, 1859.

"Out of the day and the night," by M. Hine, 1867.

"Queen of my heart," by M. Schroeter, 1879. This was not written by Shelley.

"Rarely, rarely comest thou," by J. Barnett, 1837; Dolores, 1861; J. P. Hullah, 1868.

"The rivulet wanton and wild," by Dolores, 1865.

"Rough wind that moanest loud," by W. H. Grattan, 1852; J. W. Davison, 1860.

"Shelley's Lament," by G. F. Flowers, 1867.

"The Skylark," by Dolores, 1861.

"Song of Beatrice Cenci," by C. A. Ranken, 1876.

"Swifter far than summer's flight," by W. S. Pratten, 1848; G. Linley, 1852; J. T. Harris, 1855; C. G. Verrinder, 1866; E. W. Hamilton, 1870; J. W. Davison, 1876; H. Aidé, 1877.

"Swiftly walk over the western wave," by W. S. Pratten, 1848; E. H. L. Sloper, 1850; P. David (quartett), 1866.

"Tell me, thou star," by J. Lodge, 1844; W. H. Grattan, 1852; O. Wintle, 1871; Helene Müller, 1875; J. L. Hatton, 1879.

"To the Moon," by Helene Müller, 1875.

"When morning came it shone" (from *The Revolt of Islam*), by Dolores, 1864.

"When the lamp is shattered," by J. Barnett, 1860; F. Hecht (trio), 1876.

"Where art thou, beloved," by Dolores, 1863; C. J. Duchemin, 1874.

"A widow bird sat mourning for her love," by Sir G. A. Macfarren, 1867; H. C. Banister, 1870; L. N. Parker, 1874; F. C. Atkinson, 1876.

MAGAZINE ARTICLES.

Shelley, Percy Bysshe. Honeycomb, Aug. 12, 1820, pp. 65-71.—Stockdale's Budget for 1826-7. — Tait's Edinburgh Magazine, vol. 2, 1832, pp

Shelley, Percy Bysshe.

92-103 and 331-342. — Oxford University Magazine, vol. 1, 1834, pp. 1-15.—Hesperion, by O. Curry, vol. 2, 1839, pp. 440-447.—Southern Literary Messenger, by Mrs. Seba Smith, vol. 6, 1840, pp. 717-720, 826-828.—Canadian Monthly, by W. Townsend, vol. 14, p. 673, etc. —Southern Literary Messenger, by H. T. Tuckerman, vol. 6, 1840, pp. 393-397 ; vol. 7, 1841, pp. 28, 29,—Western, by B. P. Druro, vol. 7, p. 215, etc.— Westminster Review, by G. H. Lewes, vol. 35, 1841, pp. 303-344.—Dial, by M. M. vol. 1, 1841, pp. 470-493. — Eclectic Review, vol. 107, p. 319, etc.— Prospective Review, vol. 5, 1849, pp. 58-85.—National Review, vol. 3, 1856, pp. 342-379.— Knickerbocker, by E. N. V., vol. 49, 1857, pp. 219-224. — New Quarterly Review, vol. 7, 1858, pp. 166-174. — Westminster Review, vol. 13, N.S., 1858, pp. 97-131.—British Quarterly Review, vol. 30, 1859, pp. 360-391. — Quarterly Review, vol. 110, 1861, pp. 289-328 ; same article, Littell's Living Age, 3rd series, vol. 15, 1861, pp. 443-465.—Atlantic Monthly, by Thornton Hunt, vol. 11, 1863, pp. 184-204.—Temple Bar, by J. M., vol. 24, 1868, pp. 457-472. —Lippincott's Magazine, by Helen Pierson, vol. 5, 1870, pp. 318-322. — Victoria Magazine, by E. Roscoe, vol. 16, 1870, pp. 52-65.—Blackwood's Magazine, vol. 111, 1872, pp. 415-440 ; same article, Littell's Living Age, vol. 113, 1872, pp. 387-405 ; Eclectic Magazine, vol.

Shelley, Percy Bysshe.

16, N.S., 1872, pp. 17-37.— Contemporary Review, vol. 30, 1877, pp. 336-347.—La Revue Politique et Littéraire, by Léo Quesnel, 1877, pp. 320-326.— Temple Bar, by R. C. Seaton, vol. 61, 1881, pp. 218-240. ——Adonais. Blackwood's Edinburgh Magazine, vol. 10, 1821, pp. 696-700. ——Alastor. Blackwood's Edinburgh Magazine, vol. 6, 1819, pp. 148-154. ——and Byron. Censor, 1829, pp. 38-41 and 49-51.—Fraser's Magazine, by Charles Kingsley, vol. 48, 1853, pp. 568-576 ; same article, Eclectic Magazine, vol. 31, 1854, pp. 82-89.—Westminster Review, vol. 13, N.S., 1858, pp. 350-369.— Temple Bar, vol, 34, 1872, pp. 30-49.— Southern Magazine, by W. A. Cocke, vol. 11, p. 496. ——Byron et la poésie Anglaise. Revue des Deux Mondes, by E. de Guerle, Tom. 19, seconde période, 1859, pp. 69-88. ——Byron and Wordsworth. Temple Bar, vol. 40, 1874, pp. 478-494. ——and Byron, Last Days of. Chambers's Journal, May 1858, pp. 276-278. ——and Christianity. Tait's Edinburgh Magazine, by T. De Quincey, second series, vol. 13, 1846, pp. 23-29. ——and Cowper. Hogg's Instructor, vol. 4, N.S., 1850, pp. 257-259. ——and Dialect Schools in English Literature. Lakeside, by E. Phelps, vol. 8, p. 331, etc. ——and Godwin. Cornhill, by Leslie Stephen, vol. 39, 1879,

Shelley, Percy Bysshe.

pp. 281-302 ; same article, Littell's Living Age, 5th series, vol. 26, pp. 67-80, and Appleton's Journal, vol. 6, N.S., 1879, pp. 344-356.

——*and his recent biographers.* North British Review, vol. 34, 1861, pp. 33-64.

——*and his Tomb.* Temple Bar, by M. B., vol. 16, 1866, pp. 450-454.

——*and his Writings.* Chambers's Journal, vol. 9, 1858, pp. 148-151.

——*and Keats.* To-Day, 1883, pp. 188-206, etc.

——*and Poetry.* Our Corner, by John Robertson, vol. 4, 1884, pp. 212-218, 269-275, 339-350.

——*and the Letters of Poets.* Westminster Review, vol. 1, N.S., 1852, pp. 502-511.

——*and Tennyson.* Democratic Review, vol. 28, N.S., 1851, pp. 49-54.

——*and Vegetarianism.* Book-Lore, No. 17, 1886, pp. 121-132.

——*as a Lyric Poet.* Fraser's Magazine, by J. C. Shairp, vol. 20, N.S., 1879, pp. 38-53.

——*as a Poet.* St. James's Magazine, by Thomas Bayne, vol. 34, 1878, pp. 1111-1118.

——*as a Teacher.* Temple Bar, by H. S. Salt, vol. 66, 1882, pp. 365-377.

——*at Oxford.* New Monthly Magazine, by T. J. Hogg, vol. 34, 1832, pp. 90-96 and 343-352 ; vol. 35, pp. 65-73 and 505-513.

——*Bibliomania in* 1879. Fraser's Magazine, by Shirley, July 1879, pp. 71-88.

Shelley, Percy Bysshe.

——*Birthplace of, Notes on.* Macmillan's Magazine, by W. H. White, vol. 39, pp. 461-465.

——*Cenci.* American Bibliopolist, by J. H. Dixon, vol. 7, p. 165, etc.; London Magazine, vol. 1, 1820, pp. 546-555.—Monthly Review, vol. 94, 1821, pp. 161-168.—Literary Gazette, April, 1820, pp. 209, 210.—New Monthly Magazine, vol. 13; 1820, pp. 550-553.

——*Character of.* Atlantic Monthly, by W. Dowe, vol. 6, 1860, pp. 59-66.—Fortnightly Review, by John Verschoyle, Dec. 1886, pp. 766-775.— Quarterly Review, vol. 164, 1887, pp. 285-321.

——*Chatter about.* Macmillan's Magazine, by H. D. Traill, July, 1887, pp. 174-181.

——*Declaration of Rights.* Brighton Magazine, 1822, pp. 541-544.

——*Dowden's Life of.* Saturday Review, Dec. 18, 1886.— Atlantic Monthly, April 1887, pp. 559-567. — Quarterly Review, vol. 164, 1887, pp. 285-321.—Illustrations, Jan. 1887, pp. 117-119. — Nation, Feb. 1887, pp. 146, 147.

——*Drowning of.* Fraser's Magazine, by R. H. Horne, vol. 2, N.S., 1870. pp. 618-625.

——*Early Years of.* Cornhill Magazine, vol. 31, 1875, pp. 184-206. — Fraser's Magazine, vol. 23, 1841, pp. 700-710.

——*Early History of, Some passages in.* Lippincott's Magazine, by J. Searle, vol. 12, 1873, pp. 113-116.

——*Epipsychidion.* Gossip, June 23, 1821, pp. 129-135.—Black-

Shelley, Percy Bysshe.

wood's Edinburgh Magazine,
1822, vol. 11, pp. 237, 238.
——*Essays, Letters from Abroad.*
Athenæum, Dec. 1839, pp.
939-942, and 982-985.
——*Expulsion from Oxford,
History of.* New Monthly
Magazine, by T. J. Hogg, vol.
38, 1833, pp. 17-29.
——*Forman's Edition of.* London
Quarterly Review, vol. 48, 1877,
pp. 376-403.—Academy, Sept.
23, 1882.
——*Gossip about.* New Monthly
Magazine, vol. 81, 1847, pp.
235-240 and 288-294.
——*Hermit of Marlow.* Gentleman's Magazine, by H. Buxton
Forman, May 1887, pp. 483-
497.
——*His Friends and Critics.*
Westminster Review, vol. 119,
1883, pp. 1-54.
——*Hogg's Life of.* New Monthly
Magazine, vol. 113, 1858, pp.
337-343.—Living Age, vol. 57,
1858, pp. 1008-1012, reprinted
from the Spectator.
——*House of, at Erenzo.* Athenæum, by Alfred Austin, April
29, 1882.
—— *The Improvvisatore Sgricci in
relation to.*—Gentleman's Magazine, by H. Buxton Forman,
vol. 246, 1880, pp. 115-123.
——*in* 1812-13. Fortnightly Review, by W. M. Rossetti, vol.
9, N.S., 1871, pp. 67-85.
——*in Pall Mall.* Macmillan's
Magazine, by Richard Garnett,
vol. 2, 1860, pp. 100-110.
——*Last Days of.* Fortnightly
Review, by Richard Garnett,
vol. 23, N.S., 1878, pp. 850-866.
——*Letters of, edited by Browning.*
Tait's Edinburgh Magazine, vol.

Shelley, Percy Bysshe.

19, second series, p. 252.—
Littell's Living Age, vol. 33,
1852, pp. 45, 46; reprinted from
the Examiner.—New Monthly
Magazine, vol. 94, 1852, pp.
357-360. — Athenæum, 1852,
pp. 214, 278, 279, 301, 325, 326,
355, 381, 431. — Westminster
Review, vol. 1, N.S., 1852, pp.
502-511. — Gentleman's Magazine, vol. 37, N.S., 1852, pp.
378, 379. — Literary Gazette,
1852, pp. 173-175, 205, 230, 239,
254, 279, 280.
——*Life and Character of.* Dublin University Magazine, vol.
67, 1866, pp. 292-309; same
article, Littell's Living Age,
vol. 1, fourth series, pp.
135-149.
——*Life and Poetry of.* Macmillan's Magazine, by D.
Masson, vol. 2, 1860, pp. 338-
350.—Temple Bar, vol. 3, 1861,
pp. 538-551.
——*Life near Spezzia, his Death
and Burials.* Macmillan's
Magazine, by H. B. Forman,
vol. 42, pp. 43-58.
——*Life and Writings.* Quarterly Review, vol. 21, 1819, pp.
460-471; vol. 26, 1821, pp.
168-180.—Museum of Foreign
Literature.—vol. 5, p. 458, etc.—
Eclectic Review, vol. 23, N.S.,
pp. 149-171.—Edinburgh Review, by W. Hazlitt, vol. 40,
1824, pp. 494-514.—Edinburgh
Review, vol. 69, 1839, pp. 503-
527.—Democratic Review, vol.
13, N.S., pp. 603-623.—British
and Foreign Review, vol. 10,
1840, pp. 98-127.—Tait's Edinburgh Magazine, by T. De
Quincey, vol. 12, 2nd series,
1845, pp. 760, 761, and vol. 13,

Shelley, Percy Bysshe.

1846, pp. 23-29 ; same article, Eclectic Magazine, vol. 7, 1846, pp. 233-236 and 520-529.— North British Review, vol. 8, 1847-48, pp. 218-257 ; same article, Littell's Living Age, vol. 16, 1848, pp. 49-66, and Eclectic Magazine, vol. 13, 1848, pp. 1-23.—Saturday Review, vol. 5, 1858, pp. 215-217. —Dublin University Magazine, by W. M. Rossetti, vol. 1, N.S., 1878, pp. 138-155 and 262-277.

——*MacCarthy's Early Life of.* London Quarterly Review, April 1873, pp. 239-241.

——*Masque of Anarchy.* Monthly Review, vol. 3, N.S., 1832, pp. 580-585. — Athenæum, 1832, pp. 704-706.

—— ——"*Peterloo*" *and the Masque of Anarchy.* Gentleman's Magazine, by H. Buxton Forman, March 1887, pp. 235-252.

——*Medwin's Life of.* Eclectic Review, vol. 23, N.S., pp. 149-171.—Westminster Review, vol. 48, 1848, pp. 568-577.—New Monthly Magazine, vol. 81, 1847, pp. 295-296.—Revue des Deux Mondes, by E. D. Forgues, Tom. 21, série 5, 1848, pp. 250-277.—Saturday Review, 1858, pp. 215-217.—London and Paris Observer, vol. 23, 1847, pp. 445-447 (from the American Magazine), and pp. 644-647 (from the Athenæum).

——*Memoirs of.* Athenæum, 1832, pp. 472, 488, 502, 522, 535, 554. — Fraser's Magazine, by T. L. Peacock, vol. 57, 1858, pp. 643-659 ; vol. 61, pp. 92-109 ; vol. 65, pp. 343-346.

Shelley, Percy Bysshe.

——*Memorials of.* Littell's Living Age, vol. 63, pp. 43-46 ; reprinted from the Literary Gazette.—New Monthly Magazine, vol. 113, 1858, pp. 91-95.— Athenæum, July 1859, pp. 139-141.

——*Metaphysics of.* Dark Blue, by A. Cordery, vol. 3, 1872, pp 478-488.

——*Necessity of Atheism.* Brighton Magazine, 1822, pp. 540-544.

——*Note on.* Progress, by James Thompson, vol. 3, 1884, pp. 113-117.

——*Notes on the Text of.* Fortnightly Review, by A. C. Swinburne, vol. 5, N.S., pp. 539-561.

——*Original Poetry. By Victor and Cazire.* Poetical Register for 1810-11, p. 617.—British Critic, vol. 37, 1811, pp. 408, 409.

——*Pedigree of.* The Antiquary, vol. 3, 1881, pp. 53-55, 141.

——*Philosophical Element in.* Journal of Speculative Philosophy, by G. S. Bower, vol. 14, pp. 421-454.

——*Philosophical View of Reform.* Fortnightly Review, by Edward Dowden, November 1886, pp. 543-562.

——*Le Poète Panthéiste de l'Angleterre.* Revue des Deux Mondes, by Edouard Schuré, Tom. 19, 1877, pp. 537-569.

——*Poetic Character of.* Metropolitan Quarterly Magazine, by D. C. (probably Derwent Coleridge), vol. 2, 1826, pp. 191-203.

Shelley, Percy Bysshe.

——*Poetical Mysticism of.* National Review, vol. 16, 1863, pp. 62-87.

——*Poetical Works.* Edinburgh Review, vol 69, 1839, pp. 503-527; vol. 90, 1849, pp. 419-424; vol. 133, 1871, pp. 426-459, by Professor T. S. Baynes. —Fraser's Magazine, vol. 17, 1838, pp. 653-676. — London Quarterly Review, vol. 38, 1872, pp. 124-149.—Westminster Review, vol. 38, N.S., 1870, pp. 75-97. — North British Review, vol. 53, 1870, pp. 30-58; same article, Littell's Living Age, vol. 108, pp. 3-18. —Tait's Edinburgh Magazine, vol. 8, N.S., 1841, pp. 681-685.— Canadian Monthly, by F. Louise Morse, vol. 12, 1878, pp. 247-257.—Boston Quarterly Review, by H. S. P., vol. 4, 1841, pp. 393-436. — Tait's Edinburgh Magazine, vol. 7, N.S., 1840, pp. 56-59.—Athenæum, Dec. 1839, pp. 939-942.

——*Poetry of.* British Quarterly Review, by Roden Noel, vol. 82, 1885, pp. 277-287.

——*Politician, Atheist, Philanthropist.* — Cornhill Magazine, vol. 31, 1875, pp. 345-365.

——*Posthumous Poems.* Literary Magnet, vol. 2, 1824, pp. 342-344.—Edinburgh Review, vol. 40, 1824, pp. 494-514.—Quarterly Review, vol. 34, 1826, pp. 148-153.

Prometheus Unbound. Monthly Review, vol. 94, 1821, pp. 168-173.—Southern Literary Messenger, vol. 8, 1842 pp. 194-197. — Gentleman's Magazine, by A. Clive, vol. 12, N.S.,

Shelley, Percy Bysshe.

1874, pp. 421-437. — Blackwood's Edinburgh Magazine, vol. 7, 1820, pp. 679-687.— Gentleman's Magazine, Feb. 1848, pp. 150-152.—Quarterly Review, vol. 26, 1821, pp. 168-180.—Literary Gazette, Sept. 1820, pp. 580-582.—Month, by T. Slater, vol. 31, 3rd series, 1884, pp. 181-193, 383-395.

——*Prometheus of, and of Æschylus.* Manchester Quarterly, by the Rev. W. A. O'Conor, vol. 1, 1882, pp. 29-45.

—— *Prose Works.* Edinburgh Review, July 1886, pp. 42-72.

——*Queen Mab and Prometheus Unbound.* Dublin University Magazine, vol. 89, 1877, pp. 773-779. — Literary Gazette, May 1821, pp. 305-308.

——*Relics of Shelley (Mr. Garnett's).* Weldon's Register, by William White, 1863, pp. 429-432.— Athenæum, July 1862, pp. 10-12.

——*Religion of.* Nation, vol. 28, 1879, pp. 30, 31.

——*Revolt of Islam.* Quarterly Review, vol. 21, 1819, pp. 460-471.—Monthly Review, vol. 88, 1819, pp. 323-324. — Blackwood's Edinburgh Magazine, vol. 4, 1819, pp. 475-482.

——*Rosalind and Helen.* Blackwood's Edinburgh Magazine, vol. 5, 1819, pp. 268-274.— Monthly Review, Oct. 1819, pp. 207-209.

——*St. Irvyne; or, the Rosicrucian.* British Critic, vol. 37, 1811, pp. 70, 71.

——*Scott, Byron.* National Review, by W. J. Courthope, vol. 5, 1885, pp. 220-237.

Shelley, Percy Bysshe.

——*Select Letters of, by Mr. Gar-nett.* Nation, vol. 37, 1883, pp. 100, 101.—Academy, by William Minto, Dec. 16, 1882. —Saturday Review, Dec. 30, 1882.

——*Some Thoughts on.* Macmillan's Magazine, by S. A. Brooke, vol. 42, 1880, pp. 124-135 ; same article, Appleton's Journal, vol. 24, p. 119, etc., and Eclectic Magazine, vol. 95, 1880, pp. 217-227.

——*Soul of.* Western, by R. A. Holland, vol. 2, N.S., 1876, pp. 129-161.

——*Stanzas on.* Macmillan's Magazine, by Frederic W. H. Myers, vol. 41, 1880, pp. 391, 392.

——*Symonds on.* Nation, vol. 27, 1878, pp. 401, 402.— Athenæum, Nov. 2, 1878, p. 553.

——*Talfourd's Speech for Publisher of.* Monthly Review, vol. 2, N. S., 1841, pp. 545-552.

——*Thoughts on.* Fraser's Magazine, vol. 48, 1853, pp. 568-576.

Shelley, Percy Bysshe.

——*Todhunter's Study of.* Pall Mall Gazette, Aug. 21, 1880.

——*Trelawny's Recollections of.* Littell's Living Age, vol. 57, 1858, pp. 580-591 ; reprinted from the Westminster Review.— Saturday Review, Feb. 27, 1858, pp. 215-217.

——*Unpublished Letters of.* Fraser's Magazine, by T. L. Peacock, vol. 61, 1860, pp. 301-319, and 738.

——*Wandering Jew.* Fraser's Magazine, vol. 3, 1831, pp. 529*-536, Introduction ; pp. 666-677, Poem.

——*Was he Consistent?* Penn Monthly, by W. W. Kinsley, vol 7, pp. 444 and 513.

——*Works of.* Monthly Review, vol. 1, N.S., 1840, pp. 125-130. —National Magazine, vol. 1, 1830, pp. 285-300.

——*Worship of.* Illustrations, by Alfred Emery, Feb. 1887, pp. 158, 159.

——*Zastrozzi.* Critical Review, 3rd ser., vol. 21, 1810, pp. 329-331.

IX.—CHRONOLOGICAL LIST OF WORKS.

Zastrozzi, a romance . .	1810
Original Poetry. By Victor and Cazire . . .	1810
Posthumous Fragments of Margaret Nicholson .	1810
St. Irvyne ; or, the Rosicrucian	1811
Poetical Essay on the Existing State of Things.	1811
The Necessity of Atheism .	1811
An Address to the Irish People	1812
Proposals for an Association	1812
Declaration of Rights .	1812
Letter to Lord Ellenborough . . .	1812
The Devil's Walk . .	1812
Queen Mab . . .	1813
Vindication of Natural Diet	1813
A Refutation of Deism .	1814
Alastor	1816
Proposal for Putting Reform to the Vote throughout the Kingdom	1817

History of a Six Weeks' Tour through a part of France	1817
An Address to the People on the Death of Princess Charlotte . . .	1817
Laon and Cythna (The Revolt of Islam) . .	1818
Rosalind and Helen . .	1819
The Cenci . . .	1819
Prometheus Unbound .	1820
Œdipus Tyrannus . .	1820
Epipsychidion . . .	1821
Adonais	1821
Hellas	1822

Posthumous Poems . .	1824
The Masque of Anarchy .	1832
Essays, Letters from Abroad, etc. . . .	1840
Essay on Christianity (In *Shelley Memorials*) .	1859

For the bibliography of the early editions of Shelley, the Compiler has found Mr. Buxton Forman's valuable " Shelley Library " of the greatest service.

www.ingramcontent.com/pod-product-compliance
Lightning Source LLC
Chambersburg PA
CBHW030115030726
47498CB00007B/2396